HANGMAN'S ROOT

A CHINA BAYLES MYSTERY

SUSAN WITTIG ALBERT

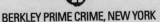

BERKLEY PRIME CRIME, NEW YORK

This is a work of fiction. Names, characters, places, and incidents either
are the product of the author's imagination or are used fictitiously.
Any resemblance to actual events or persons, living or dead, is entirely
coincidental.

HANGMAN'S ROOT

A Berkley Prime Crime Book / published by arrangement with
Charles Scribner's Sons, an imprint of Macmillan Publishing Company

PRINTING HISTORY
Charles Scribner's Sons edition published 1994
Berkley Prime Crime edition / August 1995

The Penguin Putnam Inc. World Wide Web site address is
http://www.penguinputnam.com

ISBN: 0-425-14898-X

Berkley Prime Crime Books are published
by The Berkley Publishing Group,
a member of Penguin Putnam Inc.,
375 Hudson Street, New York, New York 10014.
The name BERKLEY PRIME CRIME and the BERKLEY PRIME CRIME
design are trademarks belonging to Berkley Publishing Corporation.

PRINTED IN THE UNITED STATES OF AMERICA

10 9 8 7 6

Acknowledgments

My grateful thanks go to Claudia Cabiness for her contributions to this book, and to all the wonderful herbalists who have supported this series: most especially Gwen Barclay, Marge Clark, Rosemary Gladstar, Portia Meares, Paulette Oliver, Jeanne Rose, Dixie Stephen, and Susun Weed. I also want to thank the Anderson Mill Animal Clinic and the Texas Veterinary Medical Center of Texas A&M University for help with the research for this book; and to People for the Ethical Treatment of Animals, many thanks. Above all, of course, to my husband, Bill Albert, for many patient hours of invaluable help.

Author's Note

This novel is set in the imaginary Texas town of Pecan Springs, which includes such fictitious elements as the campus of Central Texas State University. Readers familiar with the central Texas hill country should not confuse Pecan Springs and its inhabitants with such real towns as San Marcos, New Braunfels, Wimberley, or Fredericksburg, or CTSU with any local university. The author has created the fictional characters and events of this book for the reader's pleasure, and intends no connection to real people or happenings.

CHAPTER 1

"Why do I let myself get roped into these things?" I was almost shouting over the carnival din. "It must be a personality defect."

McQuaid grinned. "The snakes are probably thinking the same thing." He turned to a burly Texan whose vest, suspenders, and boots were all made of rattlesnake skins. "That'll be three bucks."

"Snakes can't think," the Texan said. "They got no brain."

His companion sported a red gimme cap turned backward. "Got no feet, neither," Red Hat said, forking over three ratty ones. "I don't trust nothin' with no feet."

The two men broke into raucous laughter as they left the ticket booth and headed for the bleachers in the arena. A couple hundred people were already there, drinking beer and eating hot dogs while they gawked at the buzzing, writhing tangle of rattlers in the twelve-by-twelve glass-walled enclosure in the center. It was the annual Heart of Texas Booster Club Rattlesnake Sacking Championship, a day of fun and frolic for everybody—except the rattlers.

Rattlesnake sacking, a sport indigenous to Texas, is played by a sacker, a catcher, and a dozen live rattlesnakes, all confined in a glass-sided pen. The snakes are dumped out of a burlap bag onto the floor. The sacker snares a snake with a metal hook, pins its head, grabs it barehanded, and pitches it back into the burlap bag, which is held by the catcher. After three rounds of this circular exercise, the team that has sacked its rattlesnakes fastest is declared the winner. Five-second penalties are assessed for failure to pin properly and for scooping. Getting bitten tacks on ten seconds. A deposit of seventy-five dollars is required for ambulance service.

"Three-seven point three-nine seconds!" the announcer bellowed into the mike. "Hey, folks, don'cha know that's real dangerous work out there? Let's show these guys how much we 'preciate 'em!" Earsplitting whistles, rebel yells, and foot stamping showed that the crowd in the bleachers appreciated the guys a whole bunch. It wasn't an opinion I shared.

"Tell me again why we're giving up a perfectly good weekend morning to do this," I growled to McQuaid. "I forget."

McQuaid peeled another ticket off the roll and handed it to a short, plump woman wearing a blue T-shirt emblazoned with a rattler coiled over a red outline of Texas and the words "Hill Country Snake Handlers." I wondered whether she was a snake handler herself or whether she was married to one. Either way, did her life insurance company know about the hobby?

"I don't know how come *you're* doing it, China," McQuaid replied, "but I'm doing it to raise money for a dialysis machine." He gave me a superior look. "You don't have to hang out here on my account."

I definitely did not want to hang out here. It is true that snakes are not my favorite creatures. I go out of my way to avoid them, and I fervently hope they will return the favor. But feelings aside, it seems to me that there's something bar-

baric about a pair of men slinging snakes into a burlap bag while spectators whoop themselves into a frenzy, rooting for somebody's luck to run out so the loser will have to forfeit the ambulance deposit.

But it's the snakes who are out of luck. There they are, peacefully sunning themselves on a warm rock after a cold winter, when a rattlesnake hunter shows up. Next thing they know, they've got a starring role in the sacking olympics. But fame is fleeting, and they take their curtain calls at the snake factory in Waco. For four bucks a pound, live weight, the skins are turned into belts, boots, hatbands, and billfolds; the rattles and heads and skeletons into keyrings and jewelry; and the meat into gourmet goodies. Even the insides are good for something. Powdered, the gall bladder brings three thousand dollars an ounce in the Orient, where it's prized as an aphrodisiac. After only a couple of rounds of snake sacking, I was already on the side of the animal rights protesters who were marching up and down in the parking lot, carrying signs that said things like "No Fun for the Snakes," "It's Not Cool to Be Cruel," and "A Voice for the Voiceless." I agreed. It was time to speak up for the snakes or leave.

On the other hand, my reason for being here was still here—tall, dark, and not quite handsome in jeans and a blue denim workshirt with the sleeves rolled up. His name is Mike McQuaid.

I met McQuaid five or six years back, when he was with Houston Homicide and I was a defense attorney in a firm that defended big-time clients who were not always as pure as the driven snow. Four years ago, I got fed up. I cashed out my retirement, stepped out of the fast lane, and found myself in Pecan Springs, a small, quiet town located halfway between Austin and San Antonio, on the rim of the Texas hill country. I bought an herb shop in a century-old stone building with living quarters in the back, met my neighbors and made some friends, and settled down to discover whether there's any truth to the rumor that a high-powered career isn't the only ticket to a life of success and happiness.

A year or so later, McQuaid showed up. He'd traded his badge for a Ph.D. and his Homicide assignment for a teaching job in the criminal justice department at Central Texas State University, on the north side of Pecan Springs. It didn't take long to figure out that our relationship was something larger than simple friendship. But we've kept it casual—or I have. Until McQuaid, I'd never had a commitment longer than three months, and a wedding ring was the farthest thing from my mind. While other women were watching the biological clock, I was ticking off the career advancements.

McQuaid leaned one hip against the counter and popped the top on a cold Lone Star. "If you want to go to Dottie's, for pete's sake, go," he said. Dottie Riddle had asked me to come over that afternoon to see her new cattery. Some people rescue old cars. Others rescue beached dolphins and whales. Dottie rescues stray cats. Her new cat hotel houses over a hundred animals, and there's a waiting list. I don't share Dottie's passion for cat collecting, but that doesn't keep me from liking her.

I looked at McQuaid. "You won't mind if I leave?"

"Hell, no." McQuaid pulled at his beer. "What I mind is your standing around like the SPCA taking names."

"It's that obvious, huh?"

"You've been glaring at every person who buys a ticket."

"So let her glare," Barry Hibler said, stepping into the ticket booth. "Stick a sign in her hand and put her out in the parking lot. We need all the protesters we can get."

I stared. In pink-and-yellow-striped shirt and purple golf pants, Barry looked like a cheerleader for the Rainbow Co-alition, rather than president of the local Boosters and a prominent real estate broker. "You *want* those protesters out there?"

"When it comes to publicity, those crazies are worth their weight in rattlesnakes." Barry opened the cash drawer and put in a bundle of ones. "You got any idea how hard I work to make sure they're here every year?"

McQuaid laughed. "So you're the one."

"Durn tootin'," Barry said. He pulled out a ten and two twenties and stuck them in his pocket. "Six weeks ahead, I call around and find out who's in charge of the snake lovers this year. I give them the date and tell them that the TV crew will be here." He slammed the cash drawer. "Then I call the TV stations and tell them that the snakers and the anti-snakers will be toe-to-toe in the parking lot. Last year some guy put on a black skeleton suit painted with Day-Glo bones and carried a kid's toy pistol. His sign said, 'Save a Rattlesnake—Kill a Booster.' " He grinned broadly. "Boy, don't you know that got attention? We made the six o'clock news in both Austin *and* San Antonio. Made the *Houston Post*, too. My cousin sent me the clipping." He sighed regretfully. "Too bad Day-Glo didn't show up this year. We mighta made it to *Nightline*."

McQuaid gave me an arched eyebrow. "How about it, Bayles? We can probably scare up some Day-Glo paint."

Barry looked eager. "Hey, yeah, China. We could make you a 'Free the Snakes' sign. That always gets a laugh."

I declined hastily, said my goodbyes, and left McQuaid trading snake jokes with Barry. Out in the parking lot, a dozen animal rights people were marching in a tight circle, carrying signs and chanting. I recognized Janine Nolan and Dan Matthews from the Pecan Springs Humane Society, but the other demonstrators looked like college students. One of them, a tall redhead, came toward me. Her hair was cut short on the sides with a little braided tail in back, and she had large hazel eyes. She looked vaguely familiar.

"We represent PETA," she said. "People for the Ethical Treatment of Animals." She didn't have to tell me. She was wearing a button the size of a saucer. "We hope you'll ask the Boosters to stop sponsoring the mistreatment of rattlesnakes." She held out a leaflet. "And please call the TV stations in Austin and San Antonio and tell them they should be here, covering our protest."

She looked like a nice girl. I didn't have the heart to tell her that PETA's presence in the parking lot was adding coins to the Boosters' coffers. I stuck the leaflet in my shoulder bag, climbed into my old blue Datsun, and drove off, reflecting that our ability to persecute other species is exceeded only by our ability to victimize our own.

If I had anything to do with it, I had just attended my last rattlesnake sacking championship.

CHAPTER 2

On the way out to Dottie's, I swung by Thyme and Seasons. My friend Laurel Wiley comes in to take care of things every now and then so I can take a break. She was there today. So were a half dozen customers, browsing the shelves and meandering through the herb beds out front.

"How's it going?" I asked. I suspect that I have the same guilty feeling when I leave my shop to somebody else that a mom has when she drops her toddler off at day care.

"Great," Laurel said. Her full name is Laurel Walkingwater Wiley. She's half Navajo and has a deep interest in southwestern herbs and ethnobotany. "Too great, actually," she added, flipping her loose dark hair over her shoulder. "Things are pretty calm right now. But a few minutes ago the place was so crowded that people could hardly move. Oh, yes," she added, "I sold out of that new cookbook about four minutes before Constance Letterman came in asking for it. Got any more?"

Thyme and Seasons is small, and there's no room to store stock. The cookbook was stashed in my living quarters behind the shop, with the boxes of books, bags of bulk herbs and seasoning mixtures, and too many other things I couldn't make room for up front. "I'll get a couple of copies for you," I said. "What else are we out of?"

Laurel gave me the list. "Have you thought of building on?" she asked, then laughed. "Cancel that." She knew as well as I did that the lot was too narrow for an addition.

I guess there are cycles to everything. When I was practicing law, my biggest problem was not having enough time. For a couple of years after I opened the shop, I didn't have enough money—not *nearly* enough. Now I have the money to buy a little time, but it's space I'm short on.

My building has two retail shops in the front. Thyme and Seasons is one. Ruby Wilcox's Crystal Cave—Pecan Springs' only New Age shop—is the other. At Thyme and Seasons, every square inch is functional. Bundles of dried herbs hang from the ceiling, along with ropes of garlic and peppers, onion braids, and wreaths. Bulk herbs and herb products—handmade soaps, natural cosmetics, bags of potpourri, vials of oils, gleaming bottles of herbal vinegars, fragrant teas—pack the wooden shelves. Dried tansy and yarrow, celosia and goldenrod, sweet annie and salvia and love-in-a-mist fill baskets and corners. A book rack occupies one wall. The front yard is an herbal patchwork of fragrant beds and paths, and wooden racks of potted herbs line the front of the building. There's not another nook or cranny for anything else, although there are lots of things I'd like to add to my inventory.

I'd been aware for the past several months that Thyme and Seasons has a space problem. As far as I could see, there was only one possible solution: Evict Ruby Wilcox and expand Thyme and Seasons into her space. But that's out. Ruby is my best friend, and the Cave is what she does for a living. I'm not about to throw her out. But what could I do for space? I asked myself as I filled Laurel's list out of the boxes behind the sofa. What *can* I do?

But today was Sunday, not a day for beating my head against the current intractable problem. I had squandered the morning at the rattlesnake rodeo, but the afternoon was free to spend with Dottie—most of it, anyway.

"I'll be back about a half hour before closing time," I told Laurel, stacking the replacement stock behind the counter. She turned away from the register to flash me a quick grin. I left, feeling good about having plenty of customers and bad about not having enough space for them.

Driving north from town, out the narrow Falls Creek blacktop toward Dottie's, I relaxed, forgot about the shop, and congratulated myself on having the good sense to abandon the asphalt deserts of Houston for the hill country. The woods were splashed with masses of purple redbuds and laced with creamy branches of Mexican plum and rough-leaf dogwood. The afternoon sky was watercolor blue, and the still-bare branches of pecans and elms were penciled in sharp lines against it. But the early March rains had turned the roadside grass spring green and edged it with frills of wild carrot and the flat, silvery rosettes that would blossom into bluebonnets in another week. Spring would be here in a matter of days, accompanied by Monarch butterflies from Mexico, skimming through the trees on the south wind, and sandhill cranes from the coast, flying high, riding one thermal to the next, heading north.

The land from which all this beauty arises was once the warm shallows of a rich Cretaceous sea, brimming with fish and mollusks, with families of dinosaurs wandering its muddy shoreline. So much life, so many species, some transformed in the relentless, rhythmic march of evolution, others swept away in the natural innocence of a random cosmic catastrophy. I couldn't help thinking as I drove past the huge cement plant on the far side of town that the catastrophes created by our species are not so innocent.

The houses in the Falls Creek subdivision, where Dottie lives, are built far back and far apart. When I turned off onto San Gabriel, all I could see were mailboxes on either side of the road. The houses themselves were screened by trees. And when I finally parked on Sycamore in front of Dottie's mailbox, I could barely see the outline of the house behind clumps of yaupon holly and cedar—a long, low brown-shingled ranch, part of which Dottie had built herself. When I stepped onto the porch, I woke a clutch of dozing cats. Samantha, Dottie's favorite black cat, got up to greet me with an amiable sniff. With Dottie, favorite is relative. She has hundreds of favorites.

Dottie Riddle teaches at CTSU, where she's the only woman in the biology department. But when Dottie's name is mentioned, people don't think of her profession, they think of her passion: cats. Black cats, white cats, cats without tails, cats with fleas, mama cats with baby cats, any cats who need a home. For the past five or six years, Dottie has rescued as many cats as she could entice, trap, or trick into the cage she always carries in her Blazer, along with bags of cat food, feeding dishes, a net, and leather gloves. Until recently, she kept the animals in the house and in a small wire pen behind the garage until she could find homes for them. But there's a limit to the number of people in Pecan Springs who are willing to adopt a cat, and the extras keep adding up. When Dottie's mother died and left her some money, she built a spiffy new cattery, doing most of the work herself.

I've known Dottie for a couple of years now, and I like her, but her obsession is a great enigma to me, a mysterious center I've never quite been able to plumb. Here she is—an intelligent, educated, liberated, and otherwise reasonable woman who lets stray animals dictate the terms of her life. I don't get it.

But Ruby does. She told me the other day that Dottie's passion is just another version of the heart-to-heart connection that brings people alive. "Dottie's animals make her human," she said. "So stop trying to figure it out. Just appreciate it."

So today, I was here to appreciate Dottie's all-new, world-class Cat Holiday Hilton, with all the amenities of a luxury feline resort. In honor of the occasion, I had brought pink champagne and lemon basil teacakes for the humans and a dozen catnip mice for the cats.

Dottie answered my knock in a gray sweatshirt and paint-stained jeans, with tendrils of graying hair escaping under a red bandana. Dottie is big boned and muscular, with the look of a woman who isn't afraid to put her muscle to work. When she shifted the orange tabby she was holding from her right arm to her left and took my hand, the strength of her grip was impressive.

"Glad you could come, China." Her voice was raspy from the cigarettes she smokes too much of the time. Her colleagues in the biology department, to a man, consider her strident and abrasive. But her students admire and respect her, even though she believes in calling an F an F. They've voted her Best Science Teacher of the Year for so many years running that it's gotten to be an embarrassment to the rest of the faculty.

I held up the champagne and the catnip. "Party time."

Dottie's face is long and narrow, and her intense eyes signal an impatient, combative disposition. It's hard to tell because her normal expression is somewhere between a frown and a scowl, but it looked like she had something on her mind. She hefted the cat, which had just one ear. "Let me shoot Ariella and we'll see if we can find any clean glasses."

Ariella (the name, I understand, means "Lioness of God") did not appear to object to being shot. Dottie sat down with the cat on her lap and deftly injected something under a fold of shoulder skin. Ariella jumped off her lap and padded purposefully in the direction of the kitchen.

"Insulin," Dottie said, brandishing the empty syringe. "Ariella's diabetic."

"Isn't that pretty expensive?" I asked.

Dottie stood up. "Yeah. But she's a good friend. And a brave one. She lost that ear defending her last litter against a dog. Anyway, if I weren't spending the money on her, I'd be spending it on one of the others." She coughed. "Or on cigarettes."

"I could say I told you so." For Christmas last year, Ruby and I went in together on a present for Dottie: the Surgeon General's warning rendered in needlepoint and framed in black. Dottie hung it over the toilet.

She grinned. "If you did, I'd tell you to mind your own damn business."

"That's why I didn't say it."

I followed Dottie into the kitchen, threading my way through the lineup of feeding dishes for the dozen or so cats she calls her "live-in lovers." Maybe she's a little on the nutty side. But then, aren't we all a little nutty about something? It might as well be cats.

A few minutes later, laden with glasses, champagne, and teacakes, we went into the back yard, where Dottie pushed a calico off a picnic table to make room for the food.

"I want to ask you a question," she said. I saw the look again. Something was definitely bothering her. "But let's take the tour first."

We started out in the new room she had built behind the garage, which served as treatment center and isolation room. It contained a stainless-steel sink, enameled table, and a large storage cabinet. There were several cages in the room. In one, a gray tabby was nursing a litter of five kittens on a bed of clean newspaper.

"I picked these up yesterday behind the freshman dorm."

Dottie's voice was hard. "Students get tired of their cats and dump them, particularly at the end of the semester." She poked a finger into the cage and the tabby licked it. "I isolate the new strays in this room until I'm sure they're not contagious. Then I give them their shots and move them to the cattery."

"Who's your vet?" I asked.

"Joanna Wagner, on Limekiln Road." Dottie unlocked the cabinet and opened it to show me its neat, fully stocked shelves. "She keeps me supplied with free drug samples and sells me medication at cost. She used to handle the euthanizing, but I do that myself now. I hate it, but it has to be done."

Behind the treatment room was Dottie's cat hotel. She had built it out of wooden posts and wire fencing, a six-foot-high, tin-roofed cage on a cement slab that extended the width of the yard and half its depth. It contained dozens of deluxe plywood sleeping cubicles, a feeding center with offerings to appeal to the pickiest kitty, a sand latrine modestly situated behind a privacy hedge, and a playland that rivaled Fiesta Texas. And of course there were cats. Cats playing, cats eating, cats grooming themselves and each other, cats napping. While some were still obviously recuperating from the trauma of life on the lam, most looked sleek, serene, and self-congratulatory, having finally been admitted to cat heaven. When we opened the gate and went inside, they acknowledged Dottie with nonchalant affection but ignored me. I was only a tourist.

But they were a little less nonchalant when I tossed out the catnip mice. After a moment's hesitant sniffing, there was a mad scramble followed by a general free-for-all, as the cats batted the catnip mice, rubbed their faces against them, and rolled over on them in a frenzy of kitty euphoria.

"I've always been curious about catnip," Dottie said, watching the melee. "What makes cats go crazy over it?"

"It's genetic, actually," I replied. "Nearly all cats are attracted to the volatile oils in the bruised leaves, even the big cats—lions, tigers. But only about two thirds have the gene that makes them go bananas.''

"Maybe I should grow some catnip," she said. "Trouble is, the house cats will tear it up.''

"They will if you set out plants," I said. "But they'll probably ignore it if you grow it from seed. I'll give you some.''

Dottie bent over to adjust a watering fountain. "Is it good for anything besides getting cats high?''

"You might try brewing a tea of the leaves if you want to relax before bedtime, or if you have a cough or an upset stomach. And once upon a time people chewed it to relieve toothache." I grinned. "Keep the root away from your enemies, though.''

"Oh, yeah?" Dottie's laugh was not altogether pleasant. "What would happen if I slipped it into the departmental coffee pot? Mass poisoning?''

I shook my head. "Not exactly. According to folklore, you'd get people royally pissed. The root was said to turn even the mildest person into a mad dog, so back in the seventeenth century the hangman would brew a cup of tea from the root before he went out to do his deadly deed. That's how it came to be called hangman's root.''

Dottie made a sound deep in her throat. "The guys in my department don't need hangman's root. They're mad dogs without it." I didn't think she was joking.

I stepped out of the way of a dainty-looking white cat bent on body-slamming a catnip mouse. "Just out of curiosity, how many cats do you think you've rescued over the years?''

"Not enough." Dottie picked up a tattered black kitten and cuddled it against her face. "Did you know that just one pair of fertile cats and their offspring can produce over seventy thousand kittens in six years?''

I goggled. "Seventy thousand!''

"Yeah. Nature is incredibly fecund." She held up the kitten with a grin. "Hey, wouldn't this little guy make a nice herb shop kitty?"

"Thanks," I said hastily. "I have all the pets I can handle." One, that is. He's an arrogant Siamese who permits me to share his home on the condition that I provide lightly cooked chicken livers, chopped, on Monday, Wednesday, and Friday. His former patron named him Pudding. When he came to live with me, he became Cat. After Ruby complained that the name was too low class for His High-and-Mightiness, I renamed him Khat.

"Pets?" Dottie sounded irritated. "Come on, China. Cats are companions, not pets." She put the kitten down in front of a bowl of food and opened the gate for me. "No offense," she added, "but the word is anthropocentric, as well. Actually, we're *their* companions."

I felt chastised, but I knew that Dottie was right. Khat's cosmology is very simple: God is a cat, the devil is a dog, and humans are handy to have around because we have opposing thumbs and money to buy chicken livers.

Dottie closed the gate behind us. "Nice as this new cattery is," she remarked as we went back to the picnic table, "it's not nearly big enough. It only houses a hundred and fifty. There's a little money left in Mother's estate and I'm using it to buy the vacant lot next door. In fact, I've already made an offer on it. But there isn't enough money for construction and operating expenses, so I'm starting a cat rescue foundation— the Ariella Foundation."

Ariella, Lioness of God, champion of homeless cats. I had to smile. "It fits," I said, pouring champagne. "To the Ariella Foundation." We lifted our glasses and I took a sip, glancing over the fence, where I could see a house on the other side of the vacant lot. "What about the neighbors? How are you zoned?"

Dottie put her glass down and took a cigarette out of a pack on the table. "Falls Creek isn't incorporated, and there are no deed restrictions that would keep me from building or expanding." She lit a cigarette like a man, the match bent out of a paper matchbook, sheltered against the slight breeze with her cupped hand. "But that brings me to my question."

"A neighbor?" I guessed.

She leaned on her elbows and exhaled a cloud of blue smoke. "Yeah. Miles Harwick. Over there." She nodded in the direction of the house I had seen. "He's also got the office across the hall from mine in the biology department. I don't know which is worse."

"Harwick. Isn't he the one who's been in the news lately?" For the past couple of weeks, the *Pecan Springs Enterprise* had been full of stories about some professor's animal research. There had also been a piece in the *Austin American-Statesman*, and a segment on the Channel 7 news.

"Somebody leaked the protocol of his latest experiment." Dottie's mouth was sour. "Next week he's planning to hang a hundred guinea pigs in a traction device that will suspend their hind quarters off the ground. After ninety days he'll slaughter them and measure the reduction in bone density. The results are supposed to prove something about the effects of weightlessness."

I frowned. "If I were a guinea pig, I'd rather have a different career. But if Harwick is learning something that's crucial to—"

"He isn't." Dottie exhaled sharply. "I'm not opposed to necessary, well-designed animal research, but this isn't it. What's more, I don't think our department ought to be doing animal research. The faculty was hired to teach students, not get famous doing exotic studies. That's why I'm against the animal lab."

I chuckled. "Castle's Castle?" I'd read about it in the paper.

Frank Castle was the chairman of the biology department and the champion of the proposed science complex, which included a state-of-the-art animal lab that would cost a couple of million dollars—a big investment for a small college. A year ago, the administration decided to raze the old Noah Science Building—familiarly known as Noah's Ark—and start construction on its replacement. The Pecan Springs Humane Society immediately began to raise questions and the project was put on hold.

Dottie nodded. "Yeah. Castle's Castle. The Sierra Club and the Humane Society have joined forces against it. The greenies say the complex will have a negative impact on the environment, and the Humane Society people argue that it will only encourage unnecessary experimentation, like this absurd study of Harwick's."

"What's wrong with the experiment? Other than the fact that it involves animals."

"It's stupid, that's what's wrong with it." Dottie was contemptuous. "The basic assumption is flawed. What can you learn about weightlessness in a gravity environment? Anyway, NASA's already done a number of long-term studies of astronauts. So the experiment is not only flawed, it's unnecessary. No reputable, caring scientist sacrifices animals to produce data that are of no use. I've already filed a complaint with CULAC."

"CULAC?" Universities are as bad as the government when it comes to coining acronyms.

"The Care and Use of Laboratory Animals Committee." She snorted. "A bunch of good old boys with rubber stamps— the 'You-approve-my-protocol-and-I'll-approve-yours' Club." She took a heavy drag on her cigarette. "They're studying my complaint. At least that's what they say. But that's so much bullshit. In the end, they'll come down on Harwick's side. Old boys hang together."

I studied Dottie. Annoyance, frustration, anger—it was all written on her face. I wondered if there wasn't something else behind this whole thing. "If the experiment is all the things you say, why is Harwick doing it?"

Her tone was dry. "If you're thinking it has anything to do with science, forget it. Castle made a new rule that everybody has to go after at least one grant every year. The ones who get outside money will also get the goodies—promotion, salary increases, a course or two off. The ones who don't, won't. And Castle and Harwick are buddies, of course. Castle will see that Harwick gets all the goodies he wants."

I had met Frank Castle several months ago at a faculty and staff reception at the home of Dr. Patterson, the chairman of the criminal justice department, who also happens to be McQuaid's boss. Castle is a handsome man, and well dressed, which struck me as slightly odd. Most of the scientists I know don't much care about their appearance. Castle seems to care. In fact, I had the impression that, in general, appearance means a great deal to him, which is probably why he's pushing his faculty to get grants. The chairman whose department brings in the most outside money is the BMOC with the administration.

Dottie poured herself another glass of champagne. "You know, China, it's funny how people who make noises about Harwick and Castle get shafted. We get the extra committee assignments, more student advising, heavier class load, less travel money." She slugged the champagne as if it were Gatorade. "No, it isn't funny. It's sick. The whole damn department is dysfunctional."

I poured her another glass. "Have you thought of finding a new job? Women biologists are probably in demand these days."

"Actually, what I've been thinking about is hanging Harwick out to dry. Seeing that the bastard gets what he deserves.'' Dottie stabbed out her cigarette. ''That's what I want to talk to you about, China. I need some legal advice.''

I sighed and reached for a teacake. Once a lawyer, always a lawyer. Unfortunately, people ask about things I don't know anything about—tax law, for instance, or property law. I had to hire a lawyer when I sold some commercial property I inherited from my father, although I could have given you chapter and verse on the Penal Code and the Code of Criminal Procedure.

But not anymore. It's been a few years since I lived the part, and I've been trying to forget my lines. My reasons for walking out were valid—and good. I was frazzled and weary, tired of never having time for anything but work, sick of living on the margin of life. I was afraid that as long as I thought of myself solely as a lawyer I'd never know who else I was. I'd given up believing that our legal system actually worked to serve justice. But worst of all, I'd given up believing that there was a difference between right and wrong. I'd bought into the notion that it was okay to advocate any position, right or wrong, good or bad. That *every* defendant, innocent or guilty, deserved the best defense that could be bought. After a while I began to feel like a hired gun, working for anybody who could pay. I could have gone into a different firm, or a different kind of law, but I was sick of the life as well. I've never been sorry I quit.

''What kind of legal advice?'' I asked.

But Dottie wasn't listening. A gray cat had jumped up on her lap and was purring loudly. Picking up the cat, she stood and walked around the fence. She bent over to examine a spot behind the latrine area where a board had come loose.

''So that's how you got out,'' she said to the cat, annoyed. She pushed it through the fence. ''Get in there and behave yourself, you hear?'' Holding the board with one hand, she turned to me. ''China, would you mind getting the hammer and some nails out of the shed?''

On the shelf in the shed I found a paper bag of shiny spikes and the largest carpenter's hammer I had ever seen. The handle was as long as my forearm, and the head seemed half again as heavy as the one I owned. I carried it outside.

"Thanks," Dottie said. She took several of the large nails from the bag and stuck them in her mouth. With her left hand, she held the board in place and positioned the nail. I noticed the strength and thickness of her wrist. It had taken plenty of hammering to create a wrist like that. "About that legal matter," she said. With her right hand, she hit the nail dead on four times, sharp blows and terse words coming together. "Harwick's—sending me—hate—mail." One last blow. "Anonymously."

Why wasn't I surprised? "If it's anonymous, how do you know he's sending it?"

She propped the hammer against the fence and straightened up. "Because he's a dimwit. He uses the department's computer printer. One of the guide pins on our laser printer has worn a groove in the platen. It leaves a ridge down the left margin of the paper. His letters have the ridge."

"Why couldn't somebody else in the department be using the printer?"

Her laugh was harsh. "The printer doesn't do envelopes without a lot of fiddling, so he addresses them by hand. He must *really* be a knucklehead if he thinks I can't recognize that lousy handwriting after all these years of serving on committees with him."

I leaned against the post. "What do the letters say?"

"That if I don't stop opposing the lab I'll wake up one morning and find my cats dead. All of them." She looked bleakly into the cattery, where the animals were still making amorous fools of themselves over the catnip mice. "It wouldn't be hard for him to do it, either. He could put poison in their food or water. There's no way I can stop him, short of sitting out here day and night with a gun." She looked at me. "I was hoping you could help. What can I do?"

I put on my lawyerly face. "First you prove that he wrote the letters. Then you take the letters to the sheriff. But it'd be a better case if he threatened *you*, not just the cats. Has he done that?"

She pushed her mouth in and out, considering. "Not yet." She looked at me. "What if he actually comes over here and does something to the cats?"

"That's a different ballgame. Criminal mischief. Trespassing. Not to mention cruelty to animals, which can get expensive, if it's multiple counts. It's a Class A misdemeanor, two thousand dollars and one year for every—"

Behind me, the yard gate slammed open with a bang. When Dottie spoke, her teeth were clenched over her words. "What's on your mind, Harwick?"

I turned around. Miles Harwick was a short, slight man with a beaky nose and thinning hair artfully arranged to camouflage the gap between his receding hairline and his eyebrows. They were the bushiest eyebrows I had ever seen. His smugness pulled him to his tiptoes, roosterlike. Even so, he was a head shorter than Dottie, and his arms and wrists were as slender as a boy's. He made a noise that just missed being a crow.

"You can say goodbye to that orange cat of yours, Riddle. I caught it trespassing on my property a few minutes ago and—"

"Orange cat?" Dottie's raspy voice hiked up a notch.

"You know. Scrawny, one ear." The tip of Harwick's nose pulled down to his thin upper lip when he talked, and his eyes glinted under those eyebrows. There was something about him that suggested a frustrated libido, channeled into an immature and spiteful pettiness, like a little boy who banged his head on the floor when he couldn't get what he wanted. "It was in my yard, destroying the catnip plants I just—"

"Ariella!" The word was a roar. "You lured Ariella into your yard!"

The eyebrows were righteous. "Damn thing was tearing up my herbs. Deserved to be trapped." The eyebrows became fierce. "What's more, Riddle, I intend to trap every single cat that strays onto my property, so you'd better—"

"You turn Ariella loose this minute, Harwick!" Dottie said, her tone ferocious. "This minute, do you hear? She's diabetic. She has to have insulin every day."

"Not on your life, Riddle. The Adams County animal control officer loaned me the trap. She told me I have the legal right to trap and dispose of every stray that comes on my property."

I didn't see Dottie pick up the hammer. But I saw her brandishing it, the sinews of her wrists like iron struts, and I instinctively stepped in front of her. Harwick retreated while he tried to decide what to say next. I hoped it wasn't the wrong thing. If it was, Dottie might lose whatever self-control was keeping her from braining him. The possible charges against her ran through my mind: threat of serious bodily injury, aggravated assault with a deadly weapon, second-degree murder.

I turned my back on Harwick and grabbed Dottie's arms, wrestling them down. It took all my strength. "We'll get Ariella," I said. "But this isn't the way. Believe me, Dottie. You're not going to make the world any better by—"

"By bashing his bald skull?" Dottie struggled to pull free. "You bet I'll make the world better!"

I tightened my grasp on Dottie's wrists. I tended to agree with her, but now was not the time to say so. I gave Harwick my nastiest glare. "If you've got an ounce of brain you'll release that animal on the double. You're facing at least two criminal charges, and I can probably think of others."

The tip of his nose quivered. "Criminal charges?"

"Theft, since you've already admitted to knowing that Dr. Riddle is the cat's owner. And if you deprive the cat of medical attention, you'll face a cruelty charge."

The eyebrows were unrepentant. "You can't scare me with your threats."

"Then go home and wait for the sheriff," I said. "And while you're waiting, you treat that cat like she was your next of kin."

The nose went up and down while Harwick assessed his options. With one last glance at Dottie's hammer, he slipped through the gate. Safely on the other side, he gathered courage, like a little kid with one foot on the sidewalk, the other in his family's front yard. He raised his voice, taunting. "You'd better make damn sure your cats stay out of my yard, Riddle. Next time, I won't bother to tell you. I'll just get rid of them."

"Go to hell!" Dottie yelled after him, and threw the hammer. It missed his head by inches and shattered the garage window. Harwick turned tail and ran.

"Sonofabitch," I muttered, almost as angry as Dottie as I was at Harwick. People who sling hammers at other people, regardless of the provocation, are liable to find themselves in jail.

Dottie dropped down onto the picnic bench. "I *have* to get Ariella back!" she said desperately. "Maybe I could—"

"Dottie," I warned. "Don't even think it." I wasn't sure I could trust her to stay away from Harwick. But it was getting late and I had to get to the store before closing.

"Look," I said. "On the way back to town I'll stop and ask the sheriff to talk to Harwick." Sheriff Blackwell—Blackie—had gone to school at Sam Houston State with McQuaid, and the two were fishing buddies. Also, I'd given Blackie a hand in solving a difficult matter a few months before, and he still owed me one. I could probably persuade him to take a personal interest in the matter.

Dottie jumped up. "Then get going!" she gritted. "Send Blackwell out here as quick as you can—before I *kill* that filthy bastard!"

Things never quite turn out the way you'd like. When I got to the Adams County sheriff's office, I learned that Blackie had taken his son's Boy Scout troop to Lost Maples State Park on a weekend campout. According to the deputy, a dour, heavyset man in a wrinkled uniform, the sheriff wouldn't be in the office until the next morning. The deputy wasn't overly enthusiastic about sending somebody out to Falls Creek to mediate a dispute over a trapped cat, even a diabetic cat. When I got to the shop, I had to phone Dottie and tell her to hang on until first thing in the morning, when I was *positive* the sheriff would order Ariella's release.

There was a long silence on the other end of the line. "I see," Dottie said. Her voice was flat. "Thanks anyway, China."

Her tone bothered me. "Dottie, I hope you're not considering anything . . ."

"Rash?" She barked an ascerbic laugh. "You mean, like killing the son of a bitch? Don't worry, China. Whatever I do, I can't afford to get arrested. Not when I'm the sole support of a hundred and fifty-seven cats."

But as I hung up the phone I had the disquieting sense that Dottie had something up her sleeve. And it wasn't catnip.

CHAPTER 3

The next morning, I learned what Dottie had in mind. I had biked to Blackie's office at the crack of dawn and found him behind his desk. I explained the circumstances of Ariella's imprisonment and mentioned, parenthetically, Dottie's suspicion that Harwick was sending her poison pen letters. He agreed, a little grumpily, to drive to Falls Creek and check things out. Then I went for an hour's bike ride, which is my version of jogging. Back home, winded but virtuous, I fed Khat, brewed a pot of spearmint tea, and sat down at the kitchen table to brood on the intractable problem I'd avoided the day before—how to expand something that's already as big as it can get.

Fortunately, the space problem does not extend into my living quarters, which are more than ample and quite lovely. The kitchen is roomy, with limestone walls, a wide-planked wood floor, and a high pine ceiling supported by cypress beams. There are three other rooms behind the shop, also quite large: a living room, a bedroom with bath, and a workroom where I do herb crafting—a very messy operation that litters the floor with dried plant materials and bits of twiggy. There's also a second-floor loft, accessible by a ladder through my bedroom, and a remodeled stone stable at the back of the lot that serves as a guest cottage. The loft handles storage and the cottage doubles as a classroom, although it's not large enough to put up the work tables for herb-craft classes.

No, I told myself as I poured a cup of fragrant tea, my living quarters are quite ample. The problem's in the shop, where there simply isn't another spare inch. And while I was taking inventory, I might as well admit that the shop wasn't my only space problem. The herb gardens around the building are almost lilliputian. Seven people roaming the paths constitute a crowd, ten a herd, twelve a vast migration. Yesterday evening I noticed that my favorite rosemary had been trampled, and several pots of calendula were knocked over. You can't expect people to stay on the paths if there isn't any *room* on the paths.

I shifted in my chair. This was one knotty problem that no amount of brooding was likely to unravel, so I might as well think about something else, such as the hundred or so things I need to do on the one day a week the shop is closed. The hummingbird feeders ought to be filled and hung, because the first contingent of black-chins would be arriving from Guadalajara, ravenous after their long commute. The sage should be trimmed. The artemisia needed thinning (*where* was I going to put the thinned plants?), and I needed to take a sharp spade to the costmary and horehound, both of which are determined to take over the place. Horehound blooms early here. The bees flock to its white flowers, which dry into gray knots that look nice in wreaths. Costmary leaves make a nice herb tea and are delicately fragrant in potpourri and sachets. My grandmother tucked them between the pages of her Bible to mark her place and keep out paper-eating bugs. Both herbs are worth having, if you have the stuff to be stern with them.

But instead of rising immediately to the challenge of the

herb garden, I poured another cup of tea and reached for the phone. The night before, I had dreamed about Dottie and Miles Harwick, one of those absurd chase dreams my psyche dredges up out of my unconscious every now and then. Dottie, astride a ferocious, lion-sized Ariella, was chasing a terrified Harwick around the neighborhood, cracking a whip over his head with a loud "Take that, you flea-brain!"

It was a comic dream, but the real situation was serious enough. Dottie definitely had it in for Miles Harwick, who for his part seemed to get a charge out of provoking her. She was wildly passionate in her defense of cats and emotionally unpredictable: Witness the hammer-slinging incident. I wanted to check in on her and reassure myself that she had not gotten up in the night and bludgeoned Harwick in his bed.

The phone rang as I reached for it. It was Blackie, calling from his car. Blackie sounds the way he looks: square shoulders, jutting jaw, regulation haircut, regulation posture. He's a dry, by-the-book man, but he also has both the intelligence and the wisdom (the two aren't always the same thing) to know when to put the book aside. Right now, his voice was metallic.

"I wanted to let you know that your friend took matters into her own hands sometime last night."

Uh-oh. My insides went cold. My dreams are almost never hooked to actual events, but there's a first time for everything. "What did she do?"

"A little breaking and entering. With a bolt cutter." He chuckled wryly. "Of course, she denies it."

I relaxed a little. Bolt-cutting, while legally impermissible, is more acceptable than head-bashing. "If she denies it," my lawyer-self challenged, "how do you know she did it?"

Funny how I slip into that adversarial stance every time a cop and I discuss anything more significant than the drought or the Dallas Cowboys. For a decade and a half I took one side of the law, the police took the other. They got the crook, I got the crook off. It's a habit I haven't been able to break.

"How do I know?" He made an exasperated noise. "China, who else but that fruitcake would cut the padlock on Harwick's garage, snip the trigger rod on the trap, and leave without taking anything but a cat?"

A reasonable question. Too bad I couldn't think of a reasonable answer. "What *does* she say?" I countered cautiously.

Another exasperated noise. "She says the cat came home by herself early this morning. Very convenient, huh?"

"Convenient for Ariella," I replied. I was glad he couldn't see me smile. "What did you do?"

"I lectured Harwick on theft and cruelty to animals and impounded the damaged trap. I got nothing out of him when I mentioned the letters. Then I went next door and lectured your friend on trespass, destruction of county property, and assault with a deadly weapon." There was a moment's accusing silence. "You didn't tell me about the hammer."

I cleared my throat. "That's because she missed."

"Damn good thing she did. That woman's got the arm of a blacksmith, and he's kind of a wimp. As far as the letters are concerned, I'd say the hammer makes it about even." There was a hint of a grin in his voice, and I breathed a little easier. "If I were you," he added, "I'd tell her to cool it. The county's out forty bucks for that trap she disabled."

"I'll see that the county gets its money," I said, "but I'm not sure it'll do any good to tell her to back off on Harwick. Especially if she gets another letter threatening her cats."

"Sounds like you've got a zoo on your hands," he said, and rang off.

Well, that was that. Dottie might have broken a law or two, but not fatally. With Ariella safely at home, the worst was over. I dialed Dottie's number but there was no answer. She'd probably already gone to the university. Or maybe she was out looking for a twenty-four-hour security guard. I put down the phone. Anyway, she was an adult woman, responsible for her actions. I wasn't going to give her a hard time about liberating Ariella, and I couldn't ride herd on her or her animals. Blackie's remark to the contrary, it wasn't *my* zoo. In the meantime, there was the garden.

I went out to the storage shed behind the kitchen to look for the spade. But before I could locate it in the messy clutter of tools, garden equipment, and empty pots that fills the storage shed and overflows into the area around it, I was attacked.

"Gotcha!" McQuaid said with lustful enthusiasm, and fastened his arms around me from behind like a grizzly bear grabbing an unsuspecting camper. His elbow shoved a bag of sulphur granules off the shelf. My foot hooked a hoe, which fell over with a crash and took the hedge clippers with it. There's not enough room in the shed for heavy breathing, let alone a wrestling match.

"Hey!" I caught a box of plant stakes. "Watch it!" Then, as he kissed the back of my neck, under my hair, I stopped squirming, turned around in his arms, and joined in. I'm always surprised at the way McQuaid can arouse me after three years, going on four, of pleasant intimacy. But it was my day off and I had things planned, so after a few minutes I pulled away from what could have turned into something more than an incredibly sexy good-morning kiss.

"Want to help me go after the costmary?" I asked seductively. "I'm sure I can find another spade."

He shook his head. Sex having been postponed, he, too, had something planned—breakfast. He lifted a small white bag. "Lemon custard. How about coffee?"

I put the spade back. "You sure know how to put the screws on," I said. I stay away from sugar, and I cut back on fats where I can. But wave one of the Doughnut Queen's lemon custard doughnuts at me, and I'm tempted. Offer me two and I'm done for.

McQuaid sat down at the kitchen table while I got a bag of coffee beans out of the freezer. He's big—six feet, one-ninety plus—and his presence always seems to organize the space around him. It's not just size that does it, either. He has the commanding presence you'd expect in an ex-cop who is also an ex-UT quarterback. It's in his nature to know what he wants, what it will cost, and how to go for it. He got his nose broken going for extra yardage against A&M on Thanksgiving Day. He got the jagged scar across his forehead going for a druggie with a knife in the parking lot behind the Astrodome. Someday he will leave CTSU, which is pretty small potatoes where criminal justice is concerned, and go after a full professorship in some topflight CJ program. He'll get it, too. He's got the street experience, the academic credentials, and the ambition.

"I thought you had class on Monday morning." I measured Irish Cream decaf into the coffee grinder and flipped the switch.

"Spring break," he said, over the racket.

"Already?" I glanced at the calendar, surprised. "How time flies. Last I looked, the semester had just started." I dumped the ground coffee into the coffee maker, added water, and flipped it on.

"Yeah, spring break." He pushed a boyish shock of dark hair out of his face. McQuaid is thirty-six to my forty-four, a fact that I mostly manage to forget. "Time flies, all right. Two years, in the blink of an eye."

"Beg pardon?" I asked, thinking I had missed something. I got out two plates and opened the bag. Enough jelly doughnuts for an orgy. I put two on McQuaid's plate, one on mine, and stashed the fourth in the cupboard behind the canned soup. No point in bingeing. I'd save it for an emergency.

"My lease has expired," McQuaid said. "Mr. McCreary's nephew is getting divorced and needs a house. He gave us sixty days' notice." Mr. McCreary owns the small fifties bungalow occupied by McQuaid, his eleven-year-old son Brian, and an irascible basset named Howard Cosell, together with McQuaid's gun collection, Brian's Star Trek memorabilia, and numerous rats, spiders, and snakes on temporary loan from Brian's friends.

"Oh." A one-syllable response. Keeping my back to McQuaid, I found two mugs.

"Yeah." He got up from the table, put a hand on my shoulder, and turned me around. "Time to fish or cut bait, China."

I had admitted to McQuaid over a year ago that what I felt for him was love, mixed with good friendship and healthy lust, in approximately equal proportions. The trouble is that McQuaid's teaching stint at CTSU is only temporary. Thyme and Seasons, on the other hand, is definitely permanent. If McQuaid and I got married, I would inevitably have to face the time when he'd want to leave Pecan Springs and I wouldn't. Such a fundamental difference of opinion did not presage a calm and harmonious marriage.

Living together didn't seem like an answer, either. Brian is a bright and amiable child, and I am actually quite fond of him, although I'm not sure about living in sin with an eleven-year-old kibitzer. But there's Howard Cosell, whom I've grown to dislike almost as much as his namesake, and lizards and spiders et al. That may seem like a minor pain, but minor pains can speedily mutate, in the aggregate, into a jumbo-size agony. Moving in with McQuaid meant that two adults, one dog-hating Khat, one Khat-hating dog, and a kid would try to cram themselves and their likes and dislikes into the same space. Heaven forfend.

I took a deep breath. "Do we have to talk about this now?"

"Yes," McQuaid said quietly and firmly. "I realize that

your mother drank, your father was a workaholic, and your family was dysfunctional. But it's time you outgrew that shit.''

"This has nothing to do with my family," I said, feeling besieged. (Actually, it did, but that was beside the point.) "I *like* living alone. I like leaving the bathroom door open when I pee. I like knowing that when I put something down, it'll still be there when I come back. I like things neat and un-cluttered and—''

"Sanitized," McQuaid said. "Controlled.''

I frowned. "Now listen here—''

"No, *you* listen, Bayles." His slate-blue eyes were steely. "I've let you dictate the terms of this relationship for the last three years. It's my turn. I'm not saying we have to get married. But I am saying that I have to get a new place, and that I love you enough to want to live with you." He gave me a dark look. "Although I have to admit that the reason for this madness eludes me at the moment.''

I took a deep breath. The enemy was advancing on my walls. "Love and living together aren't—''

"Shut up," he said. "I know the drawbacks—Brian, the dog, the cat, your business, my work. There's two of every-thing, including egos and refrigerators. But we can handle it. Anyway, if we got a place together, it would solve the space problem you've been bitching about lately.''

I frowned. "How do you figure that?''

"Simple," he said, "Take down the wall between the shop and your bedroom and living room." He looked at me, chal-lenging. "The shop's twenty by twenty. Open up the wall and you double it. And you could use the kitchen for your classes. That'd work, wouldn't it?''

"It . . . might," I said. Actually, taking down the wall was a very good idea. I supposed I hadn't thought of it because I'd have to find somewhere else to sleep. And because I'd been fixated on a solution I *couldn't* accept: evicting Ruby.

"Admit it," he said. "I'm right about the space. Move in with me and double your space."

Surrounded, I fell back to my final defensive position. "Even if I grant you that, there's still the dog and the cat. And the career. The last I heard, you'd sent your vita to NYU. What'll you do if they come through with an offer?"

His face became still. "They did. Yesterday."

"Then what's all this talk about getting a place?"

"If you'll move in with me, I'll stay here."

I stared at him. "You'd turn down . . . NYU?" The brass ring, the Big Apple, fame, fortune?

He grinned crookedly, as if he were acknowledging a major character flaw. "Yeah. Crazy, huh?"

It was one of those awful fork-in-the-road moments. What I wanted was what I had, what I was used to. My shop, my privacy, my life. What I also wanted was McQuaid, and in some corner of my being, a life together. The road I'd taken up to now included both. But not any longer. A turning point. A critical juncture. Fish or cut bait. It was as simple as that, and I was scared.

His grin quit. "Well?"

I looked away, my heart slamming against my ribs. "What if we can't find a place?" Pecan Springs is a small town. Rentals of the kind we'd be looking for aren't that easy to come by.

He didn't miss a beat. "New Braunfels and San Marcos aren't that far. Anyway, it's getting close to the end of the semester. This is the best time to look."

"I've got a business to run. I can't just take a month off to look for somewhere to live."

"I've got spring break," he said. "I can screen places, then we can go see the ones that look like they might work."

There was a silence. I made one final, last-ditch effort. "The dog," I said. "I could live with you. I might be able to live with Brian. But Howard Cosell—''

His face was firm. ''Me, the kid, the dog—we're all part of the deal. If Brian and I can put up with your disagreeable cat, you can live with Howard Cosell.'' He put his hands on my shoulders. ''What've you got to lose, China?'' He was making a joke of it, his voice light. But his eyes were urgent.

What have I got to lose? Nothing but my independence, my privacy, my sanity! I opened my mouth to say no. No, finally, and for all.

''Well,'' I heard myself say, ''if you really think we can find a place big enough to—''

His mouth silenced me. After a moment he said, tenderly, against my hair, ''I'll start with the paper. And I'll give Barry Kibler a call and see what he's got listed.''

We went back to the table and sat down. I got back up and poured the coffee. Then I got up again to get the second jelly doughnut from behind the canned soup.

This was an emergency.

After McQuaid left, I began my attack on the plants, keeping my hands busy and my head disconnected from my heart. Being rational has always been much easier for me than being emotional. Maybe, way back there, it began with keeping my feelings out of the reach of my invasive mother, or with wanting to identify my girl self with the power and potency of my lawyer father, whose remoteness made him even more godlike. Or maybe it was fifteen years of being a lawyer myself. The law has a tendency to reward those who practice with hard-edged, hardheaded logic and penalizes those who let their emotions leak. Whatever it is, I usually deal with emotionally charged issues by locking my feelings into a mental safe and dropping the combination in the john, so to speak. So I concentrated on the horehound and costmary and ignored my anxieties.

In the afternoon McQuaid called to say he was taking Brian to San Antonio to spend spring break with his mother. McQuaid and Sally have been divorced for nearly five years. She suffered some psychological problems and was hospitalized for a while. She and McQuaid were granted joint custody of Brian, but the boy chooses to be with his father, and she seems content to have it this way.

On Monday nights Ruby and I usually go across the street to have dinner with Maggie Garrett at her restaurant, the Magnolia Kitchen. But Ruby was visiting her sister Ramona in Dallas and wouldn't be back until the next day, so Maggie and I shared a light meal of cauliflower soup seasoned with mint marigold (a wonderful substitute for the tarragon that doesn't do well in Texas), jicama and garbanzo salad, and Maggie's famous flowerpot herb bread. In a former incarnation, Maggie was Sister Margaret Mary, head cook at the convent about twenty miles west of town. She has the unmistakeable aura of an ex-nun, open face bare of makeup, direct eyes, and a gentle kindness that rises like an artesian spring out of the bottomless well of her spirit. I enjoyed Maggie's dinner and was grateful when she didn't ask any personal questions.

After I got home, I sat for a long while in the living room, picturing what the place would look like with the wall opened up—although when it actually came to it, I wasn't sure it was a good thing. Tearing down walls always seems so sort of conclusive.

At last, having managed for fourteen hours to keep my head and my heart from getting together, I went to bed.

At nine on Tuesday morning, I unlocked Thyme and Seasons and went through my usual opening ritual: retrieving the cash drawer from its hiding place, sweeping, moving the plant racks outdoors, setting out snacks for customers—this morning, sage cheese crisps and iced spiced tea. I usually enjoy the ordinariness of the activity, which is a little like setting the table for friends.

This morning, though, I kept wondering about that wall. I tried not to think of McQuaid, who was probably out looking for a house large enough to shelter us comfortably, something on the order of the Astrodome. I frowned. Was I translating one of life's most significant decisions into square feet simply because I didn't want to think of its other implications? Were the space and that damn wall metaphors for something else? I made myself stop thinking altogether and went out to do the watering.

At ten I went through the connecting door to open the Crystal Cave for Ruby, who'd be back from Dallas sometime before noon. The prisms hanging in the window splashed showers of rainbows across the wall, and the air, as always, was scented with Ruby's favorite incense. The shelves were loaded with New Age toys designed, as Ruby puts it, "to enhance the subtle energies of your inner journey."

Not my inner journey, thank you. I am dearly fond of Ruby and I would defend to the death (well, almost) her right to sell what she pleases. But sacred candles, astrology, statues of the goddess, and medicine bundles are not really my thing. Ruby tells me I am too left-brained. I tell her that I am continually amazed that she can actually make a living in Pecan Springs by selling tabletop Zen gardens and subliminal tapes that regress the listener through seventeen past lives without being arrested by Bubba Harris, Pecan Springs's chief of philistines.

There was a tape in the player under the counter. I turned it on and the silence was broken by the eerie sounds of whales caroling to one another through unfathomable depths. I had just turned to go back to Thyme and Seasons when the front door opened. A young woman stood, diffident and irresolute, in the doorway. Her triangular face was familiar but I couldn't place it.

"Are you open?" she asked.

"Just," I said, turning down the volume on the whales. I added, encouragingly, "Make yourself at home. If you have any questions, I'll be next door." In the herb shop, many people are browsers, not buyers, at least the first time they come in. Making a sale usually comes second to educating them about herbs. It's the same in Ruby's business, although if this customer wanted to know about pyramid power or the difference between one tarot deck and another, she'd have to wait until Ruby got back.

But the young woman—early twenties, tall, with freckles and red hair cut short on the sides, with a little tail in back— was neither a browser nor a shopper. She walked hesitantly to the counter and stood there, a wary look in her hazel eyes and a mix of apprehension and determination in her expression, as if she were torn between standing her ground and getting the hell out of there.

An odd one, I thought. She held one hand awkwardly behind her, and alarm bells jangled in my head. Ruby's shop was broken into once, but neither she nor I have ever been held up. There's a first time for everything, though. Then I saw the PETA button on the young woman's striped blouse, and I remembered.

"Weren't you handing out leaflets at the rattlesnake sacking championship this weekend?" My question held relief, mixed with guilt for being unreasonably suspicious of her. Somebody who stuck up for rattlesnakes seemed unlikely to stick up the Crystal Cave.

She bit her lip. "Yes," she said. Her freckles were like flecks of copper paint against her pale cheeks, and there was a faint tic at the corner of her eye. Whatever her errand, it was definitely making her edgy. Her glance slid off to one side, then down. Then, as if the act took all her courage, she looked straight at me, meeting my questioning glance.

"My name is Amy . . . Roth," she said, concentrating on my face. The corners of her mouth quivered. "And you are . . ." She swallowed hard, twice.

She was wanting me to introduce myself, I thought. She was probably proselytizing for PETA, and nervous about making cold calls. Well, it wouldn't hurt me to make a donation. After what I'd seen on Sunday, I could certainly find a few bucks to save the snakes. I extended my hand to put her at her ease. "I'm—"

She ignored my hand. "I know who you are." Her voice was thick and she swallowed again. Suddenly, surprisingly, her eyes filled with tears. "You're my mother."

CHAPTER 4

I stared at the girl. Her *mother*? The notion was so absurd that I had to suppress the urge to giggle. But that would have been unforgivable. Amy Roth was dead serious.

"I'm sorry," I said. I dropped my hand. "There's been a mistake."

"Yes." She blinked the tears away fast, pretending they weren't there. Her voice held a childhood's worth of bitterness. "*Your* mistake. Twenty-five years ago last month."

I shook my head. "People get confused about paternity all the time, Amy, but maternity is a different matter. If I had been your mother, I couldn't forget that I—"

"Please," she said wearily. "I didn't come to listen to your excuses. I have a perfectly decent adoptive mother and father who worked hard to give me a good start in life, after you walked out on me. All I want from you is a simple acknowledgment that I exist and—"

The back door banged open. The woman who sailed in was remarkable in ankle-length black skirt, loose green tee that said "My Other Body's in the Shop," and black flats that kept her height to six feet. Her orange hair was frizzed around a green felt beret that sported a cockade of peacock feathers and her peacock feather earrings could have doubled as feather dusters. Ruby Wilcox, my best friend and tenant, in her working clothes. I looked at Ruby and back at Amy, and suddenly I knew why Amy had seemed familiar the first time I saw her.

I straightened up. "Amy, my name is China Bayles. And this is Ruby Wilcox." I turned to Ruby. Over the past three years of being friends, we had often shared our life histories. Obviously, one of us had left something out. "Ruby, this is Amy Roth."

Amy's glance teetered from one of us to the other, finally landing on Ruby. "Uh, hi," she said.

"Hello." Ruby stepped briskly around the counter, her flats making little tap-taps on the floor. "Were you looking for something special?"

"In a manner of speaking," I said.

Amy looked back at me, coloring. "I'm sorry."

"That's quite all right." I smiled. "But you did startle me. I was beginning to wonder whether I'd misplaced nine months of my life."

Ruby frowned. "Excuse me?"

"I think," I remarked diplomatically, "that the two of you have something to discuss. Alone."

It was a good thing business was slow that morning. About an hour after Amy's dramatic appearance, Ruby came through the connecting door. Her face was red and splotchy and the mascara had run in sooty rivulets down her cheeks. Without a word, I handed her a glass of spiced tea and a plate of sage cheese crisps and made her sit down on the stool behind the counter.

"Bad, huh?" I asked.

"Awful." She blew her nose into her paper napkin. "It took

her two years and every cent she could scrape together to get
the court records unsealed and find out who I was. Honestly,
China, I never thought the birth could be traced.'' She thought
for a minute, then shook her head. ''But I didn't have any
other choice. I just did what I had to do and put it out of my
mind. If I'd thought about it—if I'd thought about *her*, I'd
have gone crazy.''

I leaned against the counter, imagining Ruby as she must
have been back then, a scared kid—younger even than Amy—
with no choices. ''Do you want to tell me?''

Ruby nibbled on a crisp. ''I had her before I married
Wade,'' she said. Ruby would have been in college by that
time. She and Wade had a daughter, Shannon, now a junior
at the University of Texas, in Austin. They've been divorced
for four years.

''Why did you give her up?''

''What else could I do?'' Ruby's head was bowed, her voice
heavily scored with twenty-five-year-old guilt. ''All I had was
a part-time job with the phone company, and *Roe v. Wade*
hadn't happened yet. Her father was killed in Vietnam the
same week I found out I was pregnant. Mom took over after
that.''

''Oh,'' I said. I could imagine that. Ruby's mom still took
over, every chance she got.

''Yeah. She sent me to a home for unwed mothers up in
Dallas. I never even saw the baby. A couple of years later,
Wade came along. The next thing I knew, we were engaged.''
She laughed sardonically. ''Mom and Dad thought he hung
the moon. He sang in the choir.''

I took her hand. ''I'm sorry,'' I said. ''God, what a shock
it must have been.''

''It was so long ago,'' Ruby said despairingly. ''I never
thought I'd have to face it. I thought it was over.''

"It *is* over. You gave her birth. Somebody else mothered her."

She lifted anguished eyes. "Over!" she exclaimed. "Now that I see her, I know it will never be over. If only I hadn't let Mom tell me what to do! If only I'd kept her! If only—"

I held up my hand, stemming the tide. "Ruby," I said quietly, "then is then. Now is now. What does Amy want from you?"

Ruby hesitated, not quite ready to relinquish her "if onlys." "Now? Well, she's a graduate student in journalism at CTSU and she works in the pet store at the Pecan Springs Mall. She was very definite about not wanting money. She wants recognition. She wants to be part of the family."

I hesitated. "Are you sure about the family bit? I got the idea that she only wants to be acknowledged." *Only?* Isn't having our existence acknowledged the most important thing there is? Isn't that what we all want, deep down?

"That's what she *said*," Ruby replied. "But she didn't come just to hear me say 'Hi, kid, sure, I'm your mom. Now beat it.' You don't spend two years digging up your mother—"

I smothered a laugh. Ruby's metaphors sometimes get away from her.

Ruby frowned. "I mean it, China. She said she dreamed about finding me for years and years. It was all she thought about. It's not fair to just sort of leave her hanging. Well, is it?"

"I don't know," I said. "I'm no expert on mothers and daughters." In my oldest memories of Leatha, my mother, she's getting blitzed while she waits for my father to come home from the office. After a while she stops waiting and just gets blitzed. Dad died ten years ago, she joined AA and got therapy, and now she's marrying again. But while I'm glad that Leatha is pulling herself together, her recovery doesn't mean much to me. I still feel a deep-down vacant place where the mother part ought to be. I hoped that Amy's adoptive mother had filled that vacancy for her.

Ruby closed her eyes, sighing heavily. "I'll have to tell Shannon."

"Why are you making such a big deal about it?" I asked. "It's none of Shannon's business. It's not like the three of you are going to be living together." When I said that, I remembered I had something important of my own to tell Ruby. Amy's birth announcement had driven it out of my head.

Ruby's eyes popped open. "But Shannon's got a sister! She has to *know*."

"A half-sister," I said. "Really, Ruby, I think it would be a mistake to make a big deal out of this. Let Amy take the lead in this family thing. Wait and see what she's comfortable with."

But Ruby wasn't listening. Where matters of the heart are concerned, her only gait is a flat-out gallop. "I'll have to tell Mother, too," she said. "I wonder how she'll take the news."

"Speaking of news," I said, and told her.

"You're moving in with McQuaid!" She pummeled my arm, shrieking. "China! That's great! That's terrific! I'm so thrilled! We'll have to get everybody together and have a big housewarming party!"

"Not so fast." I pulled my arm back. "I said, *maybe*. Anyway, first we've got to find a house."

"You're looking?"

I nodded. "He is, anyway. He's on spring break."

"Well, then." She was satisfied. "When you move in, *then* we'll have the housewarming." She grinned. "We can't let your Inner Child miss a chance for a party." Ruby started working on her Inner Child last winter, after she and her former boyfriend Andrew Drake broke up. Lately, she's been working on mine. I wondered when she'd start on Amy's.

"Well, at least it'll relieve the space problem," I said practically. "If I'm not living in the back, I can take down the wall and—"

"Is that all you can say?" Ruby was aghast. "Where's the romance in your soul, China? Where's the *love*?"

"Yeah, well, people can love one another and still make a mess of things, you know. Love isn't the magic wand that transforms all life's problems." The phone rang and I reached for it, but Ruby put her hand on mine.

"China," she said, very seriously, "did anybody ever tell you that you have a big issue around intimacy?"

CHAPTER 5

The rest of Tuesday was ordinary, thank God. Since spring was practically here, sales of herb plants were brisk, along with gardening how-to books. The Library Guild bought over a hundred dollars' worth of materials for a potpourri party, and RuthAnn Lansdown, representing the Pecan Springs Garden Club, stopped in to ask if I would give a talk on edible blossoms at the April meeting. I wrote an ad for my spring herb classes and phoned it in to the *Enterprise*, reordered books and essential oils, and tried not to think about McQuaid's house hunt. At about seven he came over to tell me he hadn't had any luck yet, and stayed for a mushroom omelet and an old Robert Redford movie on television. Because Robert Redford always makes me feel sexy, and because Brian was still in San Antonio with his mother, McQuaid stayed all night.

If the day had been ordinary, the night was extraordinary. "Does it strike you," McQuaid said, retrieving the blanket from the floor, "that sex gets better all the time?"

I yawned. "I guess so," I murmured, half asleep.

"Good." He gave me a friendly pat on the rump. "I'd hate for us to find sex boring on the eve of our moving in together."

He climbed under the blanket, pulled me up against him spoon style, and fell asleep almost immediately. But his remark had jolted me awake. I lay there for a long time, alternating between wondering what it would be like to sleep with McQuaid every night, worrying what Brian would think of our sleeping together, and wishing that McQuaid's landlord would say it had all been a terrible mistake and that of course they could renew the lease.

Wednesday was like Tuesday, only more so. McQuaid went night-fishing at Canyon Lake with a buddy from the Pecan Springs PD, so I got more sleep. On Thursday morning, I woke up early, did some garden work, and settled down to another day in the shop. McQuaid called just before lunch to tell me he'd turned up a couple of possible houses and to ask whether he could pick me up at seven that evening for a look. I had just put the phone down when Dottie called. Her voice was tense and even grittier than usual.

"I got another letter," she said without preamble. "Can you come?"

"Come where?"

"My office. And while you're here, there are a couple of other things you ought to see."

"I thought this was spring break."

Dottie's laugh was short, abrasive. "The students get the break. I get to grade papers. Noah's Ark, first floor, two doors down from the chairman's office. Come in by the quad entrance—I want you to see what's going on in front of the building."

"What is it?"

"Just come."

"Let me check with Ruby," I said. I wasn't sure what I

could do about the letters, but I had to admit to being curious about them, and about whatever was happening on the quad.

I put the phone down and went to the connecting door. Ruby was arranging an artful display of crystal balls. "Can you mind the shop for an hour?" I asked.

"Sure," Ruby said. She turned around, holding a crystal ball. "I've decided to have a family get-together tomorrow night. Can you come?"

I looked at her suspiciously. "Don't tell me. Let me guess. You're bringing Amy out of the closet."

Ruby tossed her head. "Mother will be there, and Shannon, and Ramona was coming down from Dallas for the weekend anyway. My mother, my sister, and my *two* daughters. But *you* don't have to come."

I hedged. "I didn't say I didn't want to."

"Good." She rubbed the ball with her sleeve. "You can come early and help with the food. We're going to have a sit-down dinner. That way, we can all get to know one another. Get to know Amy, that is."

"Ruby," I said, "why don't you look in that crystal ball and ask whether this is a good idea? Maybe Amy doesn't want you to know her."

Ruby was indignant. "Of course she does. Why else would she go to all the trouble of finding me?"

"I won't be gone long," I said, and went back to tell Dottie I was on my way.

Central Texas State University started out around the turn of the century as a teachers' college. Its major growth spurt happened when the baby boomers got old enough to pay tuition. Now it's growing again, up from twelve to thirteen thousand students in the last year. The sprawling Spanish-style campus is made up of pink and yellow brick buildings roofed in red tile and located on the north side of Pecan Springs, a dozen blocks from my shop. To get there, you go west on Crockett to the square, hang a right, and go north on Anderson until it dead-ends at a glass kiosk on a cement island, where a uniformed guard checks to see that your parking sticker is valid and you're not wanted for any major crimes, such as failing to pay your last sixteen parking tickets. If you are, they hold you for ransom until you fork over what you owe.

I have no sticker, but today it didn't matter. The kiosk was closed in recognition of the fact that all the paying customers had gone to the beach. I breezed through, made my usual right at the top of the hill and then down and across Pecan River, which flows, cool and green and lovely, through the middle of the campus. I found a spot in the almost-empty parking lot behind the pink-brick behavioral sciences building where McQuaid has his office. McQuaid's blue Ford pickup was parked in the lot. I made a mental note to drop in and see him when Dottie and I were finished, and headed for the Noah Science Building, which is located between the Behavioral Sciences Center and the river.

Noah's Ark is the building that's slated to come down so that Castle's Castle can go up. It's one of the original campus buildings, named for Mildred Noah, a popular science teacher of the 1920s. Although the Ark is unquestionably inadequate, a lot of people feel nostalgic about it. Its high-ceilinged, wooden-floored classrooms remind them of a time (long ago and far away, like a fairy tale) when teachers thought it was important to talk to students and students thought teachers had something to say. Others are worried that the sprawling, modernistic complex that's proposed for the site will have a negative effect on the river's fragile ecosystem. Backed into a corner by the preservationists, the environmentalists, and the Humane Society, the CTSU regents had put the Castle on indefinite hold. There was no telling when, or even if, they'd approve the new complex.

Following Dottie's instructions to come in through the quad entrance, I walked around the building. The long, narrow quad was not nearly as deserted as the parking lot. A sizeable crowd was gathered in front of Noah's Ark under a large banner proclaiming "People for the Ethical Treatment of Animals." Most of the demonstrators carried signs, and several wore animal costumes. I saw an orange Garfield, a couple of gray Snoopys, and one unfortunate white rodent, hung up by the hindquarters in a wooden A-frame. On the frame was a sign that read "Hang Harwick Instead" and another that said "Don't Cast Me in Your Experiment!"

Amy Roth, holding a megaphone and wearing her PETA button, stood on the steps of Noah's Ark. She was not the diffident, hesitating young woman who had come into Ruby's shop on Tuesday morning in search of her mother. She looked sure of herself, authoritative, in command, like an antiwar activist from the sixties. I realized that she must be the PETA organizer.

I came up the steps. "Hi, Amy," I said.

She handed me a clipboard with a petition on it. At the top of the petition was handwritten, in large red letters, STOP SENSELESS MURDERS! "Your signature on this petition can help us keep Dr. Harwick from killing helpless—" She recognized me and broke off. "Oh, hi," she said, in a smaller voice.

I was relieved when she didn't apologize for thinking I was her mother. I glanced at the demonstrators, who were starting to chant on a cue from a kid wearing a "Save the Whales" T-shirt. "Isn't it kind of a waste to hold a rally during spring break? You don't have an audience."

"Are you kidding?" Amy pointed at a TV cameraman I hadn't seen. "The local ABC affiliate is here to cover the regents' meeting. We figured it'd be the best day to demonstrate, so we got a permit."

I had to grin. "Sounds like you play all the angles."

"Animals can't talk," she said fiercely. "Somebody's got to tell their side of the story. Somebody's got to say that animals aren't simply 'resources' to be used up and disposed of. They're living individuals. They deserve respect."

I looked at the rodent hanging helplessly in the A-frame. "You're protesting Harwick's experiment?"

She nodded shortly. "That, and the science complex." She waved at a "Preserve the Ark and Save Our Animal Friends" sign. "We've joined the conservationists and the Humane Society in their effort to keep the university from tearing down Noah's Ark. Do you know about that?"

"I read about it in the paper."

Amy pinned me with her piercing eyes. "I hope you also read PETA's statement that there's no justification for animal research." Her tone was that of a fundamentalist minister lecturing the congregation on the evils of drink and the devil. "When somebody commits a murder, it's a crime against society. But when animals are tortured and murdered in the name of science, it's business as usual. We can all see how immoral and inhumane Harwick's experiment is. How would he like it if somebody strung *him* up?" Her voice, which had become louder and louder, rang with the passionate energy of moral and emotional conviction. There was no doubt about it. Amy was her mother's daughter.

"Hang Harwick instead!" somebody in the crowd shouted. "Stop him from murdering innocent animals!" A chorus of voices took up the refrain: "Hang Harwick instead!" When I turned around, I saw the reason for the commotion. The TV cameraman was kneeling down with his shoulder-held camera, zeroing in on two demonstrators who had just strung up a straw-stuffed effigy of Harwick. Another danced in front of the camera with a "Save Noah's Ark" sign. It was showtime.

A soft, baggy woman with a Cabbage Patch doll face and

a straggly brown perm stopped on the stairs beside me. It was Rose Tompkins, a secretary in the biology department. "A shame, that's what it is," she muttered, feet planted apart, hands braced on her heavy hips. "Somebody ought to stop these horrible people. Dr. Harwick's experiment is causing enough trouble—we don't need a demonstration to make it worse."

I've known Rose since she signed up for my aromatherapy class. More recently, she had come into the shop to buy a wreath, an expensive one, actually. It was a gift for the Castles' wedding anniversary, she announced, from her and the department's senior secretary, Cynthia Leeds. She said this in a tone that defied any negative judgments I might be inclined to pass on the subject of Dr. Castle's marital saga.

Five or six years ago, before I came to Pecan Springs, Frank Castle went through what was popularly supposed to be a mid-life crisis. He divorced Margaret, his wife of twenty years, to marry a pretty young graduate student. The event attracted widespread attention in the close-knit CTSU community, especially among the wives, whose curiosity quickly became apprehension. If it could happen to Margaret (who'd had to get a job and move out of the expensive home she and Frank had shared), it could happen to them. The newlywed Castles had not been invited to very many dinner parties that year, and even now the "new" Mrs. Castle wasn't a popular person. University communities have long memories. But through it all, Rose had been her boss's staunch supporter.

Now, she turned to me, her plump hands fisted, her dumpling-cheeked face grim. "I'm going to call campus security. We can't have things like this going on today, with the regents meeting just across the quad. Dr. Castle is there this very minute, discussing the new science complex."

"I don't think it'll do any good to call the cops," I said. "The demonstrators have a permit."

"A permit! For *that*?" She pointed at Harwick's effigy swinging from the tree. "It's disgraceful!"

It wouldn't do any good to argue the principle of free speech with Rose, who was obviously incensed by anything that besmirched her boss's reputation or that of the biology department. "I'm here to see Dottie Riddle," I said. "Can you point me to her office?"

"First floor," Rose said. "Two doors down from the drinking fountain."

Dottie's office faced away from the quad, but the sounds of the protest were still audible.

"What do you think of what's going on out there?" Dottie asked, stubbing out a cigarette. Her office was small, but the very high ceilings gave it an illusion of spaciousness, and the tall casement window behind her littered desk swung open onto a view of the river.

"I doubt that the demonstrators will be able to convince the regents to cut down on animal research," I said, taking the chair that was obviously meant for students who were there to discuss their performance on the last quiz. "Somehow, I can't see university officials turning away grant money."

Dottie's expression grew dark. "That's it exactly, China. Money. The bottom line. In fact, that's why Castle is promoting the new complex. Better animal lab facilities will attract more grant dollars." Her tone was acid. "If we're all grubbing for grants, who'll teach the students? Which one of these publish-or-perish yahoos will take a minute from his research to pay attention to a kid who doesn't understand the basics? I'm going to keep hammering away at the principle of this thing, even if Harwick and Castle and the rest get so sick of it they want to shoot me."

I could see why Dottie was unpopular among the science faculty. But I understood her passion, just as I understood

Amy's. I tended to take their side—at least, as far as I understood the issues. But I wasn't sure the conversation was lead-
ing us anywhere. "You mentioned a letter," I prompted.

"Oh, yes." Dottie rummaged for a moment in the litter on
her desk—student exams, departmental memos, a hairbrush,
hand lotion, copies of the campus newspaper. She found what
she was looking for folded into her grade book. "This is it,"
she said, thrusting it at me. "Came in campus mail, like the
others."

I took the paper gingerly, by the corners. "You've handled
it, I suppose?"

"I had to read it, didn't I?" She passed her hand over her
eyes. "Sorry, China. The last couple of days I've felt like a
volcano. When I opened the letter, I even blew up at Cynthia."
She made a disgusted noise. "Of all people. I should have
known better."

"Cynthia Leeds?" The biology department's senior secretary.

"Dr. Castle's henchwoman," Dottie said with emphasis.
She made a face. "She's worked for him so long she knows
what he wants before he does. She knows her job, but if you
ask me, she knows too much. Anyway, she's had it in for me
for years, ever since I opposed Castle's nomination for the
chairmanship."

McQuaid says that there's a rule of thumb about staff jeal-
ousies: the more penny the ante, the higher the intensity of
feeling. It was my guess that Cynthia Leeds, like Rose Tompkins, didn't have any real power in the department. What little
she had, she used whenever she got the chance. You couldn't
really blame her for that. "You told her about the letter?"

"She was standing beside the departmental mailboxes when
I opened it. Read it—you'll see why I came unglued."

The letter had only one sentence. "Shut up about the lab

and get rid of the cats or you're dead." Short on detail but straight to the point.

I frowned down at the letter. Dottie's voice wasn't the only one raised against the lab. There was a whole crowd of demonstrators on the quad protesting Harwick's experiment and Castle's Castle. "Who else is getting letters like this?" I asked.

"Who else wants to build a cattery on the vacant lot next to Harwick's house?" she asked bitterly.

Her answer begged the question, but I didn't argue. "Do you still have the envelope?"

Wordlessly, Dottie pushed it across the desk. It was a number ten white, plain, hand addressed. I examined it. "Harwick's handwriting?"

"This time he tried to disguise it, but I'm sure it's his." Dottie leaned forward. "Can you get him on this? I mean, the others only threatened to kill my cats. This one threatens to kill *me*. That's pretty serious, isn't it?"

I looked at her. Something about this situation struck me as peculiar. I liked Dottie, and I sympathized with her. But I was beginning to wonder if I was being used. Had Harwick really sent this letter?

"I'm not the one to 'get him,' Dottie." I used her words with emphasis. "The police will have to see this letter, and the others. Do you have them?"

Dottie dropped her eyes. "Yes," she muttered. She yanked the desk drawer open and fished around in it. She pulled out two envelopes and tossed them on the desk. "This is the lot. Take the damn things. I don't want them."

I pulled the letters out of the envelopes and examined them. They looked identical to the one Dottie claimed to have received today. The handwriting on the three envelopes didn't look exactly the same, however. I'm no handwriting expert myself, but I've examined and cross-examined my share, and

I know something of the art. It was my guess that whoever addressed the first two envelopes had not addressed the third. I remembered telling Dottie that it would be easier to prosecute Harwick if he threatened her.

I put the letters back in the envelopes. "Since these came in campus mail," I said, "you should notify campus security. Because of the death threat, I'm sure they'll bring in the Pecan Springs police. They'll need these for evidence." I hoped she was smart enough not to make an accusation the evidence would not support. She could get into almost as much trouble forging death threats as she could slinging hammers.

Dottie looked at me, then away. "I thought maybe you could just kind of handle this," she said slowly. "You could talk to him. You're a lawyer. You can get people to . . . stop doing things they shouldn't. Like threatening my cats."

Now I was sure I was being used, and although I understood Dottie's motives, it made me angry. When I replied, I was terse.

"A death threat is police business. They'll examine the handwriting, the printing, the paper. They'll look at *everything* before they attempt to decide who sent the three letters." I paused and looked her straight in the eye. "If there's any indication that Harwick isn't the one who wrote them—" I stopped. I'd already made my point.

"Okay, okay," Dottie growled. She scooped all three letters into the drawer and stood up. "There's something I want to show you." She took a camera off a shelf and checked the flash. "Come on. We're going to the basement."

I stood up too, hoping I'd heard the last of that letter. However Dottie intended to take revenge on Harwick for catnapping Ariella and threatening her rescue project, framing him with a bogus murder threat definitely wasn't the way to do it.

The basement of Noah's Ark was a warren of hallways, labs, and graduate student offices. The section where Dottie

was taking me was apparently only used for storage and util-
ities. The hallway was so dimly lit that there was barely
enough light to see the cracks in the cement floor and the water
stains on the walls.

"Not very pretty, huh?" Dottie said as we ducked under a
steam pipe. "Just wait until you see *this*." We had come to
the end of the hallway. She produced a key from her pocket,
unlocked the solid-core door, and pushed it open. "I came
looking for the source of a bad odor in my office this morning,
and I found this." Her sarcasm was scorching. "I wonder
what the animal rights people will say when they get a look."

The stench of animal odor, ammonia, and disinfectant hit
me like a fist, and I took an involuntary step backward. "What
is this place?" I asked, when I could breathe.

"It's an animal holding facility," Dottie said disgustedly.

The windowless room was dark and airless and smaller than
my shop. Against one cement wall were shelves of caged
mice, hamsters, rabbits, many of the cages caked with filth,
urine and rust encrusting the wires. Along another wall were
stacked dozens of cages of guinea pigs, with three and four
animals crowded into a cage—over a hundred in all. Along a
third wall were smaller cages housing frogs, lizards and other
reptiles, even a few birds. Opened sacks of food pellets, trash
cans overflowing with litter, and boxes of supplies were
stacked along the fourth wall, some of them wet from a dripping pipe under a filthy scrub sink. A bag of apples had broken. Moldy fruit, much of it gnawed by rats, was scattered
across the floor. A shelf held a litter of file folders and
papers—animal records, I supposed.

I looked around, incredulous at the dirt, the neglect, the
wretched conditions. The sight dispelled any myths I might
have held about how scientists treated their animal subjects.
"God," I breathed. "This is *awful*!"

Dottie stepped forward, aimed the camera at the bank of

guinea pigs, and shot. The flash was blinding in the dark room. "It's worse than awful," she said, cocking the camera. "I assume that Harwick is holding the guinea pigs for his experiment. The rest—the frogs, the reptiles, the rodents—are headed for his vertebrate anatomy lab." She recocked and took a close-up of an open feed sack in which a dozen disgusting cockroaches were having lunch. "He insists on having students prepare dissections themselves, under his supervision. Which means starting with live animals."

I frowned. "What else would he start with?"

"Prepared specimens from supply houses. That's how most departments handle it." She bent over and took a shot of a cage that contained a huddle of white mice, the waste tray beneath overflowing. "Normally, only about a dozen cages are kept here. The number of animals here now is far more than the room can accommodate. They're not being cared for, either." She straightened, gesturing sharply, her anger building. "Look at this mess. The cages are unspeakable. Some of the animals have no water. The ceiling paint is flaking, the spigot leaks, the floor drain has backed up, and that vent up there in the ceiling is rusted shut. There's no air circulation at all, not even a—"

The door behind us opened. "Who are you?" a high-pitched, tremulous voice demanded. "How'd you get in? What are you doing with that camera?"

I whirled. The speaker was a slender, intense young man of twenty or twenty-one, in white tee and dirty jeans. His dark eyes had a look that bordered on panic, and the corners of his mouth trembled under a straggly brown mustache. His long, tapered fingers were closed around a pipe wrench. He raised it.

I took a step back. The kid was scared, and sometimes scared people react violently. But Dottie stood her ground, wielding a natural authority that was far more intimidating than the pipe wrench.

"*I* am Dr. Riddle," she said imperiously. "I let myself in with a key from the chairman's office so I could document this mess. Who the hell are *you*?"

The young man stared at her uncertainly, his upper lip twitching. Then he turned to the sink, dropped to one knee, and applied the wrench to the trap under the sink with a surprising strength. "My name is K-K-Kevin Scott," he said, twisting the wrench as if he were wringing somebody's neck. "I work here." I wondered if he ever cursed the fate that had saddled him with a name he couldn't say without stuttering.

Dottie's tone was caustic. "If by 'work here' you mean that you're responsible for this facility, you're doing a piss-poor job. There are at least a dozen violations of the USDA animal care code. Drainage, ventilation, lighting, sanitation, cage space, food storage—and that's not the end of it. An inspector would throw the book at you."

Kevin stood up, blinking rapidly. His face was pasty and there was a sheen of sweat on his forehead. I couldn't tell whether he was scared to death of Dottie, overwhelmed by the presence of two aggressive-looking women, or borderline psychotic. He spoke with deliberate slowness, trying to control his nervous stuttering.

"I'm only p-p-paid for t-ten hours a week. I've got to hold another job to stay in school, so I can't afford to spend extra t-time here. In t-t-ten hours, it's all I can do to feed, change the water, and clean the worst c-c-cages." He gnawed at his lip. "The c-c-cage washer broke down in January, right after I was hired. They haven't b-b-bothered to fix it."

"Why doesn't the department give you more hours?" I asked. "And repair the equipment?"

"You t-t-tell me." His glance flicked nervously to Dottie's camera, then to the cages and around the room. Clearly, he didn't want us here. Was it because he was ashamed of the mess? Or was there another reason?

"The problem is the extra animals," Dottie said. "The guinea pigs for Harwick's experiment." Her voice held an undisguised note of triumph. "If it weren't for those hundred animals, you could handle the rest in ten hours a week, easily." She fixed Scott with a sharp look. "Couldn't you?"

At the mention of Harwick, the boy's head jerked. His tongue darted out and licked at his mustache. His "P-p-probably" was almost inaudible.

Dottie's eyes narrowed. "Does Harwick know about this situation? What about Castle?"

Kevin Scott looked uneasy. "Dr. C-C-Castle has never been down here. I asked him to c-come, but he d-didn't have t-time. Dr. Harwick drops in every d-d-day or so."

"Of course he does." Dottie was bitterly amused. "I'll bet Harwick comes down here every morning to make sure that none of the animals managed to get away in the night. But he doesn't stay to clean cages."

Kevin's Adam's apple bobbled. "What are you going to d-d-do?"

"Get Castle down here. For starters. If he doesn't repond, I'll go to CULAC. If that committee doesn't act, I'll get the USDA animal health inspector here." There was an unpleasant smirk on her face. "That'll make the good old boys move their butts."

Kevin's eyes were apprehensive. "D-d-do you think you could d-d-do it without getting me in t-trouble? Like, this isn't really my fault, you know. I t-t-tried to t-tell Dr. C-Castle that something had to be done, but he said there wasn't any money to p-pay me to work more hours."

I shook my head. In the hierarchy of things, student employees aren't very far above the lab animals. Unless I missed my guess, the boy hadn't tried very hard to wring more hours out of Castle. He was probably scared of losing what little time he already had. But Dottie wasn't afraid of the chairman. And she had leverage. I looked around. This place would give her a *lot* of leverage.

"What about Harwick's grant money?" I asked. "If his grant bought the guinea pigs for his experiment, it ought to be paying for their upkeep. Why isn't it?"

"Yeah," Dottie muttered. She backed up two paces and took a picture of Kevin Scott framed against a backdrop of filthy, overcrowded cages. "Good question. Why isn't it?"

Kevin looked as if he'd like to yank the camera out of her hand but didn't dare. "I have to get to work," he said. His voice was shrill, and he tried again, bringing it down a notch. "I'm sorry to be rude, Dr. Riddle, b-b-but—"

"We're going," Dottie said, taking one last picture. Kevin almost pushed us out the door, and I wondered again why we made him so nervous.

Out in the hallway, I could still smell the stench of the holding facility, which seemed to have permeated my entire body. I felt as if I'd have to strip and stand under the shower for half an hour to wash it from my hair, my skin. But would I ever be able to wash away the ugly image of so many animals, crowded, untended, destined for a grim fate?

As we went up the stairs, Dottie was gleeful. "Boy, are *they* in trouble," she said.

I didn't think she was talking about the guinea pigs. "Harwick and Castle?"

"Right. Violations of the Animal Welfare Act. When the USDA sees that mess, they'll shut it down. Which means that Castle will have to answer a lot of embarrassing questions and Harwick could even stand to lose his grant. You don't fool around with the USDA—especially with PETA barking at their heels."

"PETA? But they're not involved with this."

"Not yet." Dottie grinned mirthlessly. "But it'll only take a minute to step outside and put in a word with Amy Roth, their organizer. Maybe she'd even like to see that hell-hole down there, after the kid is gone, of course."

I glanced at Dottie's face. I knew how much she hated Harwick. But I hadn't guessed that she was vindictive enough to turn the USDA loose on him. This was a side of her I hadn't seen. I didn't much like it.

"I'm not sure it's a good idea to go public with this before you confront Castle and Harwick," I said cautiously. "They'll probably clean things up. They won't want to risk—"

"Fuck them," Dottie said distinctly. "They knew about the problem and they've had plenty of time to correct it. *I've* got the whip hand now. And I'm not afraid to use it, either."

Never again will I slam my dreams, I thought as we reached the first floor. Outside, I could hear rhythmic hand-clapping and shouts of "Save the Ark!" and "Hang Harwick instead!" The rally was still going on.

Then, suddenly, the shrieking was *inside* the building. Rose Tompkins was running heavily toward us, arms outflung, skirt flapping around her plump knees, her Cabbage Patch doll mouth a crimped O of horror.

"Help, help!" she cried hysterically. "Get help, quick!"

Dottie caught the heavy body. "Get hold of yourself, Rose," she commanded roughly. "What's the problem?"

An erect, gray-haired woman came out of an office. "What's going on here?" she demanded, scowling. "Rose, stop making that horrible noise! You're attracting attention to yourself."

Rose was like a sack of flour in Dottie's arms. "He's dead," she moaned.

My blood chilled. "Who's dead?"

"Dr. Harwick," she cried. "He's hung himself!"

CHAPTER 6

Dottie stared, uncomprehending. "Dead? Harwick?"

Rose moaned. "I saw him hanging there. It's horrible, horrible!"

Cynthia Leeds, the soldierly senior secretary, took charge. "Stop babbling, Rose. Come into the office and sit down while I call Campus Security and the dean's office."

Protocol, I thought. Everything had to go through channels. I put my hand on Rose's arm. "Where did you find him, Rose? Are you *sure* he's dead?"

"In his office." Rose's eyes were closed. She could barely manage the words. "I went right up to him and touched his hand. It was . . . cold." Dottie made a comforting sound and tightened her grip as Rose sagged against her.

"I'll go see," I said and stepped back. "Where is it?"

"One-oh-five," Dottie said. "Across from my office."

I turned to Cynthia Leeds. "When you call Security, tell them to come in by the parking lot entrance."

"What's going on here?" A spectacled, long-haired male came up, carrying an armload of books. With him was a young woman with a box of test tubes. "Can we help?"

I was already several steps down the hall. "Stand at the quad entrance," I ordered the startled man. "Don't let any-body into the building." To the woman, I added, "Ditto the parking lot entrance. When the police come, send them to Dr. Harwick's office."

Dottie was handing Rose over to Cynthia. "I'll come too, China."

"No," Cynthia said quickly. "You come with me, Dr. Rid-dle."

Dottie turned her head to glare at Cynthia. "I don't have to take orders from—"

But I was already on my way down the hall. I didn't want Dottie with me. I was operating on the same premise the cops would: the fewer the better where a death scene is concerned.

Harwick's door was open. I stepped inside, nudging the door shut behind me with my heel, shivering, not wanting to see what I knew was there.

His slight body, slender as a boy's, was suspended by what looked like nylon rope from a pipe three or four inches below the twelve-foot ceiling. His head was pulled sharply askew by the clumsy-looking knot, his face gray-blue, his eyes wide open and bulging. He was clad in brown slacks and a rumpled white shirt with a coffee stain on the pocket and the sleeves partly rolled up. The toes of his brown shoes dangled just below the edge of the desk. It looked as if he had climbed up, pushed the rope over the pipe, stuck his head in the noose, and stepped off to dance into eternity. Watch that last step, I thought irrelevantly. It's a doozy. I touched one hand, and shivered. He had been dead for some hours.

I looked around. Two walls of the small office were lined floor to ceiling with bookshelves, but instead of books the upper shelves were filled with the gleaming ivory skeletons of small mammals displayed in a carefully graduated order and aligned a precise inch from the edge of the shelf, like art objects in a museum. Each was mounted on a black-lacquered block that bore an engraved plaque identifying the species in Latin—*Procyon lotor, Lepus californicus, Rattus rattus.* Lower shelves displayed fish and reptile skeletons, mounted with the same artful care and pride. The lowest were lined with gleaming jars containing transparent fluid and things that had once been living flesh. Everything was meticulously composed and orderly, even beautiful, and I couldn't see a speck of dust. I couldn't help contrasting the living animals downstairs, crowded, uncared for, inhumanely caged in their own excrement. Harwick's profession had been the study of the beauty and variety of living beings, but this multitude of artifacts seemed to hint at an almost pathological preoccupation with death. In this setting, his hanging body also seemed artifactual, and not at all out of place. Just another of the specimens, hung up on display.

The desk Harwick had danced off was also neat. There was a grade book and a stack of student quizzes, tidily ordered. The one on top had a big red "F" printed on it—had Harwick killed himself in a fit of depression over some kid's performance? There was also an empty cup with a coffee-colored puddle in the bottom, reading glasses, a pipe, an ashtray made—naturally—out of a hoof.

I looked again. The ashtray was filled with ash and charred bits of paper. One of the "F" papers, burned because it was too awful to read? Or something connected to his suicide? A draft of a note, perhaps, or the note itself, written and then rejected. I looked up at the body, hanging like the straw man the demonstrators had strung up in the tree an hour ago, and the flesh prickled on my shoulder blades. Their demands had been met. Harwick's animal experiments were finished. *Harwick* was finished.

I was facing the door when it was pushed open. An irate

male said, "What's this I hear about—" The sentence ended in a gurgle.

"Hello, Dr. Castle," I said.

Frank Castle's "Oh my God!" was a bare whisper. He stared open-mouthed at the apparition hanging from the ceiling. He was tall and striking in a charcoal pin-striped suit, pale pink shirt, and tasteful gray-and-pink tie. There was no softness in his face, and his gold-framed glasses and carefully trimmed salt-and-pepper hair gave him the look of a man who demanded respect. Lines of control appeared like deep parentheses on either side of his mouth, and he had the wiry, disciplined look of a serious jogger.

He closed his mouth with an audible gulp and looked at me. "Who are you?"

"China Bayles," I said. "We met at Dr. Patterson's house a couple of months ago."

"Oh, yes. The defense attorney." His eyes were once again engaged with the thing on the rope. "What are you doing here?"

"Ex-defense attorney. Miss Leeds asked me to stand guard until Campus Security gets here." I spoke gently. "I'm afraid I must ask you to leave."

He turned to me, jaw tightening, eyes suddenly fierce. He had remembered who was in charge in this building. "You've got a helluva nerve! Miles Harwick was my best friend! And this is *my* department! I ought to order *you* out." Involuntarily, with something close to fascination, his eyes skittered back to Harwick's body. "How could Miles do such a thing?" he muttered to himself, as if he had forgotten about me. "*Here*, of all places. The publicity—" He shook his head sharply, as if to clear it. "How *could* he involve the department in this?"

I couldn't help feeling that Castle's question was an ungenerous response to a friend's last desperate act—if that's what it was. "You're afraid his suicide will reflect badly on the department?"

"Naturally," he snapped, as if he were admonishing a freshman who had confused a tibia and a fibula. "Worse, it will nearly hamstring our research program. Dr. Harwick was the most promising member of the new animal research unit. His bone density project was just the beginning. He was developing an outstanding reputation and strong connections with the funding agencies. We had every expectation that over the next few years he would bring in grants on the order of a half-million dollars or more." Castle had slipped easily into an buzzword-studded style that sounded almost like a script. Perhaps it was the one he'd prepared for the regents' meeting. "In fact," he added, strengthening my suspicion, "it was the high probability of the department's success in creating a strong animal research unit that decided the regents to include the animal lab in the science complex that's about to be built."

I blinked. An outstanding reputation? Most promising researcher? But Dottie claimed that Harwick's project was redundant, frivolous, and downright stupid. Who was right? Should I believe Dottie, who was clearly hungry to see Harwick discredited? Or should I buy the department chairman's version, even though he had both a personal and a professional stake in enhancing Harwick's success? I looked at Castle, carefully coiffed, nattily dressed, and thought once again about the mess downstairs. Why hadn't he taken the time to look in on the holding facility after Kevin told him about it? How could he tolerate—perhaps even cover up—the ill treatment of animals by one of his own faculty members?

But I was distracted from these questions by another one. "The science complex is no longer on hold?"

The lines around Castle's mouth relaxed. "Right. The chairman of the Board of Regents informed the dean last week that they'd decided to go ahead. It will be announced this after-

noon.'' His voice failed him and he shook his head again. "So
sad," he said thickly. "So *very* sad. I wish the decision hadn't
been confidential. I wish the dean had let me tell Miles about
it. Maybe it would have kept him from—'' He didn't finish
the sentence.

I looked up at the figure. "Why do you think he did it?"
It was ironic that a man would take his life just as his dream—
presumably, the new animal lab *was* Harwick's dream—was
about to be realized.

Dumbly, Castle shook his head. "I suppose it was those
ridiculous charges against his research. He refused to read the
newspapers, but it was harder to avoid the calls and the hate
mail—''

"Hate mail?" I thought of the letter Dottie claimed to have
received.

"One of the activists' campaign tactics," Castle said dis-
tastefully. "Threatening letters, abusive phone calls at all
hours of the day and night, even bomb threats."

I stared at him. "I realized that the demonstrators were angry, but I didn't know they were violent."

"We managed to keep it quiet," Castle said. "We had to
evacuate the building twice, but told people that there was a
problem with the ventilating system in one of the chemistry
labs. We alerted Campus Security after every call, of course,
and they searched the building. There isn't much more we can
do." He looked back at Harwick's body. "I had to tell Miles
about the threats, of course. He was terribly disturbed. He was
also very upset about some sort of run-in he had this weekend
with one of his colleagues."

"Dr. Riddle?"

"You know about that?" His mouth tightened impercepti-
bly. "There's been bad blood between them for quite a while.
He thought she went out of her way to . . . antagonize him.
Poor Miles. Lately he seems to have thought that everyone

was against him." He fumbled for a handkerchief, turned away, and blew his nose.

I felt a certain sympathy for Castle. He had lost both his friend and his star researcher, whose golden grants promised to pave the department's path to glory. But I could also feel sympathy for those who had won the battle and lost the war. Harwick's experiment was ended and a hundred guinea pigs had been spared, but the state-of-the-art animal lab would be built after all. Scientists would use thousands of animals in their search for more knowledge, and demonstrators would continue to protest the sacrifices. Ruby, who studies Buddhism, has a term for it. *Samsara.* The endless cycle of birth and death, action and reaction. Karma.

But there wasn't time to think about Harwick's karma and his place in the endless circle that always comes round to dying. A uniformed campus cop appeared at the door and with courteous deference told Dr. Castle that the dean was waiting for him. I gave one last look at Harwick, hanging in silence, and followed Castle into the hall, closing the door behind me. Down at the end, in front of the departmental office, I saw a knot of people—faculty and staff, I guessed—talking to another cop. Then an administrator-type in a gray suit stepped forward and he and Castle disappeared into the biology office. I wondered if there was a special protocol for faculty suicides.

I stood by Harwick's door for another three or four minutes until I saw McQuaid coming from the direction of the parking lot, matching his stride to that of a stunning young blonde in a tailored black suit and silky white blouse, a pager clipped to her black shoulder bag. They were talking as they walked, their shoulders close together.

McQuaid did a double take when he saw me. "What are *you* doing here?" he asked, surprised.

"Waiting for Campus Security," I replied. The blonde's shoulder-length hair was sleek and shiny and her artfully natural makeup made me remember that I hadn't combed my hair since breakfast. "What are *you* doing here?" I asked McQuaid. "It's spring break." What was *she* doing here? Who *was* she?

McQuaid was wearing his cop look. "This is Sheila Dawson, CTSU's new chief of Campus Security. She just came on board this week. The dean asked me to give her a tour of the campus. We got as far as the library when Sheila's pager went off. Sheila, this is China Bayles."

The blonde extended her hand—skin soft and smooth, nails nicely shaped, pink, and pearly. She was not as young as I had thought at first. But young enough. Mid-thirties, maybe. A year or two younger than McQuaid. We shook hands in a businesslike way.

"Hello, China," she said. Her words were clipped, her tone authoritative. "Mike has told me about you." She glanced at the closed door. "In there?"

I wanted to ask just what "Mike" had told her about me, but she didn't look as if she had time for chitchat just now. "Yes," I said. I stuck my hands in the pockets of my denim skirt. I dig every day in an alkaline soil that eats hands alive, and my nail polish looks like Black Pearl. "Harwick's office."

"Did you find the body?" McQuaid asked.

I shook my head. "Rose Tomkins, the departmental secretary, found him. I went in to secure the scene. Frank Castle came in, too. Neither of us touched anything." Except the hand. The dead, cold hand.

"Please wait here." Sheila spoke with the quiet command that makes "no" utterly impossible. She nudged the door open with her elbow and turned to McQuaid. "Call the local authorities, Mike. We need to get them in on this right away." She went into the office.

McQuaid went down the hall in the direction of the telephone. I was left standing beside the door, reflecting that the tone of Sheila's instruction to me had been entirely different than the one she used for McQuaid. Mike.

I was still standing there when Bubba Harris arrived, accompanied by two PSPD officers. For the last decade Bubba has been in charge of law and order in Pecan Springs, and he's used to having things his way. He's a hard-fisted, heavy man, with graying hair, drooping jowls, and a belly that sags out over his belt as if his internal stuffing has shifted. He sucked in his breath when he saw me, almost sucking his unlit cigar with it. The cigar is a fixture. I've rarely seen him without it, although I've never seen it lit. He narrowed his eyes under bristling black brows.

"What are *you* doing here?" It was McQuaid's question, put with animosity rather than surprise, in the tone of a man who suspects the worst and is disappointed if he doesn't get it. He likes his ladies sweet and southern style. He doesn't much like me.

"I've been keeping out the hoi polloi."

He scowled. "You find the body?"

I was about to explain the sequence of events when Sheila Dawson opened the door. "You must be Chief Harris," she said, with precisely the right blend of sweetness and deference, southern style. "I'm so *relieved* to see you! I'm Sheila Dawson. I've just taken over Campus Security. We have an unfortunate situation here, and we need to keep it as quiet as possible."

Bubba's scowl went away. "Yeah, sure," he said quickly. He turned to me. "Go down to the biology office and give your statement to Dominguez," he said, and stepped through the door, leaving me to reflect that Sheila Dawson was one smart cookie.

Dominguez finished with me twenty minutes later. Dottie and I walked out onto the quad together, where clumps of people—demonstrators, faculty and staff, curiosity seekers—

were still standing around, stunned.

"I hated him," Dottie said wearily. "Probably everybody hated him, in one way or another. But what I hate more is the thought of him doing that to himself." Her face was gray and saggy. "I hate the thought of him hanging in that room since God knows when. Why did he do it? Was it because of all this?" She waved her arm in the direction of the A-frame. It was empty, but the sign was still there. "Hang Harwick Instead."

"What do you think?" I asked. "Why *did* he do it?"

"I don't know. I'm sure his reputation meant a lot to him, but I wouldn't have thought a little embarrassment would drive him to kill himself. Especially when he and Castle were so close to getting what they were after. The new science complex, I mean. The lab."

So Dottie had heard the big news. "Maybe it was personal," I said. "Did Harwick live alone?"

"Yeah. I don't think he had many friends. Occasionally I'd see a car parked in front of his house, but not often." She looked at me. "You were in the office. Was there a note?"

"If there was, I didn't see it." I leaned forward, lowering my voice. "About that letter you showed me—"

Her jaw tightened and she flushed red. "Let's forget about that, okay? The man's dead. He's no threat anymore. There's no point in bringing it up."

"*I* can forget it," I said. "I wonder about Cynthia Leeds."

"What do you mean?"

"You showed her the letter. If somebody comes up with the idea that this wasn't a suicide—"

"But it *was* a suicide. Wasn't it?"

I was saved from answering by Amy Roth, who appeared beside us still carrying her clipboard with the words STOP SENSELESS MURDERS! written on it in red. "Is it true?" she asked, breathless. "Did Harwick really hang himself?"

"I have to go," Dottie said, already two steps away. "I'll call you, China."

"Well, did he?" Amy demanded. She seemed almost exultant.

"That's what it looks like," I said. What kind of woman was Ruby's daughter, to rejoice at someone's death?

Her eyes widened. "Are you suggesting that maybe he didn't—"

"Of course not. I just meant that . . ." I sighed. "Look, I used to be a lawyer. Lawyers can't agree to anything without qualifying it all to hell. It looks like suicide."

She shook her head. "What a cop-out. But that's like the guy. He could dish it out, but he couldn't take it."

I looked at her. "Couldn't take what?"

She seemed to recollect herself. "The criticism, I mean. Being in the newspaper, having people protest his research."

"Well, you *did* say some pretty nasty things." I nodded in the direction of the A-frame. A boy was taking the sign down as several others stood silently and watched.

Amy looked nettled. "That's what we're here for. To say nasty things. Things that make people think about the harm they're doing to defenseless animals." The nettled look became openly contemptuous. "But the guys we go after usually have more guts. *This* guy wasn't just a murderer, he was a coward."

"Wait a minute," I said. "He hadn't started that research project yet, had he? How can you call him a murderer?"

She made a vicious noise. "Have you seen those skeletons in his office? Those are animals he killed and stripped himself, for the fun of it. The man was a butcher, I tell you! A sadist!"

I found myself thinking that even if this was my best friend's daughter, I didn't like her. As if she had read my thoughts, she said, in a much calmer voice, "You're going to be at that party at my . . . mother's house tomorrow night?''

I frowned, surprised by her ability to turn her rage off and on so quickly. "Well . . ."

"Going to hedge on that one, too?"

"I'll be there."

"I'm not sure I will." Her face took on a taut, wary look. "Why is she doing it? Asking all those relatives in to meet me, I mean."

"Because she cares, I guess." I was uncomfortably aware that I wasn't too sure of Ruby's motives. "I've never been a mother. I don't know about these things."

She wasn't going to let me off the hook that easily. "You're a daughter, aren't you? You've got a mother?"

That made me even more uncomfortable. "She wants you to be part of the family," I said.

"But what if I don't *want* to be a part of the family?" She turned her face away. "What if I'm happy with the family I've got?"

"Then why did you look her up?"

"Because I wanted—" She stopped. Her slender shoulders were hunched, heaving. "I had to know why."

"She told you?"

The word was flat, without inflection. "Yes."

"And that's enough for you? Just knowing?"

"Yes," just as flat. "It's enough."

"It isn't for her," I said.

She whirled, chin thrust forward, Ruby in the set of her mouth. "What's that supposed to mean?"

I spoke more softly, trying to take the sting out of the words. "Sometimes when we start the ball rolling, it doesn't stop where we want it to. Did you expect to sashay in and say 'Hi, Mom. Why, Mom? 'Bye, Mom' and dance out again?"

The anger was back, overlaid with sullenness. "I didn't expect to be overrun by a hoard of sisters and grandmas and aunts and family friends.''

I shrugged. ''A couple of hours, big deal. Who knows? You might like us.'' *Us*? But I was, after all, the family friend.

She snorted. ''Give me a break,'' she said, and walked off.

CHAPTER 7

I was ready when McQuaid showed up at the kitchen door that evening for our house-hunting expedition. I hadn't given any conscious thought to a certain stunning blond person, but I had spent a few extra minutes on myself, even going so far as to put on some makeup and dig out a pair of beige pants and an oversize blue sweater I hadn't worn in a while.

"Hey, nice," McQuaid said. "I like the way you've got your hair fixed, too."

"Thanks." That's a man for you. Put on a little lipstick, and he likes your hair. Mine is straight and kind of dingy brownish-blond, and there's a wide gray swath down the left side. Short of coloring the gray and getting a perm, there isn't a lot I can do with it. Of course, I could always go blond. "How many houses are we going to see?"

McQuaid's glance at me was uneasy. "I've been thinking about this, China. I really don't want to force you to do something you don't feel is right."

I paused, my hand on the doorknob, wary. "Are you getting cold feet?"

He chuckled, an uncomfortable chuckle. "What makes you think that?"

"Well, first you're all hot to get a place together and then you sound lukewarm. Feels like cold feet to me."

"*You're* the one who's been lukewarm."

I opened the door and stood aside. "Look, McQuaid," I said. "Are we going to fight, or are we going to look for the circus?"

He stepped through the door and I locked it behind us. "The circus?"

"It's the only place I can think of big enough to hold us." We were silent out to the end of the walk. "By the way," I asked, as we got in the truck, "what happened this afternoon after the PSPD showed up?"

"The usual," McQuaid said. "You know the routine." He frowned. "I have to say, though, that Bubba was pretty thorough. Something about the crime scene seemed to bother him."

"Oh, yeah? What was it?"

"It had to do with the pipe Harwick slung the rope over," McQuaid said. He turned the ignition key. "They took the body down and Bubba himself got up on the desk for a look." I was about to ask him what was so interesting about the pipe when he grinned. "Now that was something to see. Bubba Harris's belly at eye level. Up front and personal." It's okay for McQuaid to joke about Bubba, of course. McQuaid may be an ex-cop, but he's still a member of the fraternity, an old boy. I wondered what happened when girls joined the fraternity and how that changed the chemistry of the situation.

"So Sheila Dawson is the new Security chief," I said casually, as if the thought had just occurred to me. "Where did she come from?"

"University of Texas, Arlington campus. Academy training, strong street experience. Excellent overall background in law enforcement. Highly recommended.''

Yeah. Rave reviews, I'd bet. "What does she think about Harwick?"

"I didn't get a chance to talk to her, actually," McQuaid said. He slid me a glance. "I hung around for a few minutes after you left, but I had to do a couple of errands." He raised both eyebrows. "Hey, you're not jealous, are you?"

I hooted loudly. Too loudly. "Jealous of a stunning blonde who also happens to be one smart cookie?" I told him about Sheila's maneuver with Bubba and we both laughed. He laughed harder.

"Seriously," he said, sobering. "Are you?"

"We-e-ll," I said.

"Don't be." He put his arm around me and pulled me over against him so that we were sitting like a couple of teenagers on a date. "She's engaged."

"She's not wearing a ring." I would have noticed *that* right away.

"He lives in San Antonio. They're getting married next month. Anyway, Smart Cookie isn't my type. She's pretty tough. And I've never cared for blondes."

I swiveled to look at him. "I'm tough. And Sally's a blonde."

He shook his head. "You're not tough like Sheila's tough— not these days, you're not. And Sally wasn't blond when I married her. That didn't happen until after we were divorced. It was part of her search for the real Sally." He said it with sadness. Even though they aren't married, Sally's psychological troubles have been hard on him. And hard on Brian, too.

I raised myself to look in the rearview mirror, eyeing the gray. "I've sometimes wondered if the real China is blond."

McQuaid pulled me down. "Don't even think it," he growled. "On you, gray is sexy."

We didn't find the circus. The first house was almost okay,

but it was located on a busy street and had no yard, which meant that Howard Cosell would have no shrubbery to dig up and Khat would have no trees to climb. The second house had a lovely big yard with bushes for Howard Cosell and trees for Khat and an enormous garage that would accommodate McQuaid's gun hobby—but only two bedrooms and one bath.

"I don't think this will work," I said, picturing the morning traffic jams outside the bathroom.

"Neither do I," he said regretfully, "now that I give it a closer look. But that garage is sure terrific."

The third place had three bedrooms and two baths, there was a large garage, and the yard was lovely, but the lot backed up to I-35. As we stood on the front porch, the rumble of the traffic was deafening.

"No," I said. A big rig hit its air horn and I put my fingers in my ears.

"Right," McQuaid said with a sigh. He thanked the landlord and we got back in his pickup. "How about going over to Bean's for a beer?" he asked.

I sat back, surrounded by the truck's familiar smells—vinyl seats, basset hound, gun oil, McQuaid's Old Spice. "A beer sounds good," I said. "Bean's sounds good, too. I'm sorry about the houses."

"Me, too," he said, as we drove off. "There were certain things I liked about each of them, but I guess I just didn't put it all together." He turned right onto Cedar. "Should I keep looking?"

"How else are we going to find a house?"

"I just meant that . . . You didn't like any of these. I thought maybe—"

"*We* didn't like any of these," I said. "I wouldn't mind seeing a few more." I glanced at him sideways, liking the rugged look of him in his plaid shirt and jeans and cowboy boots. Not handsome, necessarily, but nice looking, craggy.

Definitely sexy. I thought of a certain stunning blond engaged person and half smiled.

His hand slid over mine on the seat. "You're sure you're not just agreeing because you think it's what I want to do?"

"Let's not complicate this," I said. "I'm agreeing because you want to do it and I want to do it and *we* want to do it. Anyway," I added practically, "you and Brian need a place to live. And I need more room at the shop. If we can find the right place, it makes sense to do it together." So I'm rational. Does that *have* to mean I have an issue around intimacy?

The laugh lines crinkled at the corners of McQuaid's eyes. "Yeah," he said. "It makes sense. I'll start over again tomorrow. There must be *someplace* we can live." He turned onto Guadalupe. "I'm hungry. How about some fajitas to go with that beer?"

Bean's Bar & Grill, which is located on Guadalupe between the railroad track and Purley's Tire Company, used to be called Lillie's Place. It's a down-home Texas eating and drinking hangout with a pool hall in the back. Plastic baskets of tortilla chips and crockery mugs of fiery salsa are plunked down without ceremony on plain wooden tables. A chandelier made out of a real wagon wheel wound with lights shaped like red and green jalapeño peppers hangs from the ceiling, and a fake cigar-store Indian stands in the corner with a politically correct sign in one hand, requesting that people refer to him as a Native American. The restroom doors are labeled "Bulls" and "Heifers," and favorites on the jukebox are "Mamas, Don't Let Your Babies Grow Up to Be Cowboys" and "Your Cheatin' Heart."

Bob Godwin, the owner of Bean's, was behind the bar, where he usually is at this hour of the evening. When McQuaid and I sat down, he came over to the table, bringing a pitcher of Lone Star and two mugs. We do this so often that he doesn't need to ask what we want to drink.

"What're ya eatin' tonight?" Bob is paunchy and snaggle-toothed, with thinning red hair, a spider tattoo on his forearm, and a stained white apron tied over his jeans. He and one of his Vietnam buddies bought the bar a couple of years back. The buddy was killed in a hunting accident, and Bob inherited his share.

"Fajitas for me," McQuaid said, filling our mugs. "Chicken." The menu is written in hieroglyphics on a chalk-board, under a hand-lettered sign that says "7-Course Dinner = A Six-Pack and a Possum." We don't need to consult a menu. We always have fajitas. Unless we're having enchiladas or chicken-fried steak.

Bob grinned at me. "Hey, don't you look purty tonight, China. Big date?"

"Been house hunting," McQuaid said, casually. My head jerked up. I wasn't sure I was ready to go public just yet.

"No kiddin'," Bob said incredulously. "You two?"

I frowned. "Does that strike you as odd?"

"Hey, no offense." Bob flapped his apron at a fly. "I just meant that ya'll seem kinda, well, not romantic enough. If you know what I mean." His shoulders were apologetic.

"Is romance the only reason for two people to live to-gether?" I asked crisply.

"No, ma'am." Bob grinned, showing a broken tooth. "If you ain't got romance, a little sex'll do just fine." He lifted his order book. "What're you havin' tonight, China?"

"Fajitas," I said. "Beef."

"Guacamole's extra good." Bob waggled his eyebrows suggestively. "How about a double order?"

McQuaid looked at me and we both shrugged. Bob, who's skilled at reading the small signals people send one another over the table, said, "Guarantee you won't be sorry. Organic avocados."

"Okay," McQuaid said, deciding for us both.

"What's an organic avocado?" I asked, but a George Strait song overpowered me, and anyway, Bob had already pocketed his order book and headed for the kitchen. At the table beside us, a family was trading jokes in rapid-fire Spanish, punctuated by laughter. At the table on the other side, two men in suits and cowboy boots were bent earnestly over a calculator, copying numbers onto their napkins—a business deal in progress. At the end of the bar, a group of guys were throwing darts at a poster of the governor in a white cowboy outfit, astride a white motorcycle—a blowup of the cover of a recent *Texas Monthly*. The governor, too, has been known to stop in from time to time. Last month the *Enterprise* ran a picture of her throwing darts at herself and her white motorcycle. Bean's draws all kinds.

Another George Strait and two Willies later, Bob was back, loaded with plates of chicken and beef, tortillas, sour cream, cheese, onions, refried beans, and rice, and a huge red pottery bowl of guacamole—all balanced on his forearms. Bob scorns trays. He says that wearing an apron is bad enough; carrying a tray makes him feel like a butler.

"Hear ya'll had a little excitement up th' college this afternoon," he said to McQuaid, setting down a bowl of grilled chicken for the make-it-yourself fajitas.

"Yeah," McQuaid said, refilling my mug.

"Too bad 'bout Harwick," Bob said. He put down the tortillas. "Any idea who did it?"

McQuaid sloshed beer onto the table. "What do you mean, who did it?" he demanded testily, grabbing a handful of paper napkins to stem the tide. "The man hung himself."

"Not 'cordin' to Bubba," Bob said, arranging sour cream, onions, and cheese around the tortillas. "He was in here at happy hour with some real purty blond gal. I heard 'em talkin'. Kind of interestin', I thought. Almost never see Bubba in here durin' the day. He mostly comes in to catch the Spurs on tee vee, play a little pool. Don't know who the gal was. *Real* purty, though. High class.'' He set down the guacamole and began wiping up the rest of McQuaid's puddle. "You folks ready for another pitcher?''

I stared at him. "Aren't you going to tell us what they said?''

Bob stopped wiping, perplexed. Then his expression cleared. "Oh, you mean 'bout Harwick.''

"Yeah,'' McQuaid said. "About Harwick.''

The jukebox started again, and Bob raised his voice to be heard over Waylon Jennings. "Didn't catch it all, but it had somethin' to do with a pipe. Bubba was sayin' that Harwick lacked a foot of bein' able to reach up to this pipe that the rope was slung across. Said the guy couldn'ta done it himself. Little short fella, y'know.'' Bob held his hand at shoulder height. " 'Bout so high. Cocky. Sorta like a kid, or a banty rooster. Not much to crow about, but he loved t'rare back on his heels an' let 'er rip.''

"Oh, so you knew him,'' I said.

"You bet.'' Bob wiped his hands on his dirty apron. "Used to come in, get a beer on Saturday nights, talk to a few of the guys. One in particular, as I recall. Some friend of his, Max somethin' or other.'' He frowned. "Wonder where Max's been hangin' out lately. Haven't seen him.''

"Maybe Harwick couldn't reach the pipe,'' McQuaid said, "but he could have thrown the rope over it.'' He began to load chicken onto his tortilla.

"Not so fast,'' I objected, remembering. "There was only a two- or three-inch clearance between the pipe and the ceiling. It'd be tough to toss a rope through.'' The skin on my arms prickled. "You know, I didn't think about it,'' I said slowly, "but Bubba's right. The ceilings in that old building are high, twelve feet, at least.'' I did a rapid calculation. "Harwick was about a foot shy of reaching that pipe. There's no way he could have knotted that rope around it.''

McQuaid looked at me. "Maybe he put something on the desk to stand on.''

"If he did, he didn't leave it on the desk,'' I said. "Or on the floor.'' I was suddenly intrigued, thinking of the chants and the signs in the mall that afternoon. "Hang Harwick instead.'' Was it possible that sombody *else* had hanged Harwick? He was a small man, and he might not have been fully conscious when he was hanged. If he had been subdued first, the autopsy would indicate how it was done. A blow to the head, maybe. I thought of the brown liquid in the bottom of the coffee cup on his desk. Or a sedative.

McQuaid looked up at Bob. "Has Bubba got a suspect yet?''

"The way Dottie tells it,'' I said, "nobody liked him. There'll probably be a flock of suspects.''

Bob raised his shoulders and dropped them in a *quién sabe?* gesture. "Don't think so.'' He grinned. "Unless maybe it's that blonde. He was sure watchin' her mighty close.''

"She's the chief of Campus Security,'' McQuaid said, lathering sour cream onto his chicken.

Bob's eyebrows were two bushy red arches. "No *shit*.'' He whistled. "Boy, I tell you, you can lock me in her jail any ol' time.''

"Forget it,'' McQuaid said. "The guy she's engaged to is one big sonofagun. Real John Wayne type.'' I grinned, imagining Smart Cookie married to the Duke. It would serve them both right.

Bob shook his head sadly. "Story of my life. How 'bout that pitcher?''

An hour later, after the fajitas, a second pitcher, and a fast round of pool, McQuaid and I adjourned to my place. What happened after that was slow, sweet, and deeply satisfying.

"Romantic enough to suit you?'' McQuaid asked, dislodg-

ing Khat from the corner of the bed and untangling his long
legs from the sheet. Khat flicked his tail to indicate his dis-
pleasure with the entire sequence of events and jumped up
onto the top of the wardrobe, where he licked one paw and
gave us the evil eye.

"I'm with Bob," I remarked, stretching lazily. "If you ain't
got romance, a little sex'll do just fine."

McQuaid got up, straightened the sheet and the blanket and
tucked them in at the foot of the bed. He climbed back in and
pulled me against him.

"How about a *lot* of sex?" he asked, his voice muffled.

As I was drifting off to sleep a little while later, snuggled
up against McQuaid's warm back, I reflected that living together had certain fringe benefits. It might not be so hard to
get used to, after all. Sleepily, I said, "I love you," to
McQuaid's back.

He reached a hand around and patted the first thing he
touched, which happened to be my hip. "Me, too," he mum-
bled.

Bob was right. No romance.

The party at Ruby's the next night reminded me of a re-
union of sharks. Amy arrived late, clad in black baggies and
a black tee with the words "Cows Cry Louder Than Cabbages" on the front and "Eat Your Veggies" on the back.
The short red hair over her ears was freshly clipped and the
little tail in back was tied with a string and decorated with a
black feather. She was sullen, responding to most questions
with a muttered "yes" or "no" and inclined to snap. She
pointedly refused Ruby's roast beef and concentrated osten-
tatiously on carrots and string beans.

The other guests behaved with about the same degree of
civility. Ruby's mother, a thin-lipped, sharp-chinned woman,
never once spoke directly to her newfound granddaughter and

spent the entire evening looking as if she smelled something she didn't like. Shannon, Ruby's other daughter, seemed to suspect her stepsister of planning to make off with the family silver. Ruby's sister Ramona made a half-effort to engage Amy, and when she was rebuffed, lapsed into a pout. Ruby tried to paper over everybody's surliness by laughing too loud and being too cheerful, while I attempted to steer the combatants toward neutral territory. By nine-thirty, I was ready to call it an evening.

"It isn't going too well, is it?" Ruby said to me in the kitchen, where we were putting the dessert plates into the dishwasher. Shannon, Ramona, and Ruby's mother were settling down to Trivial Pursuit. Amy had been in the bathroom for ten minutes.

"I'm afraid not," I said. "Your mother and sister don't seem crazy about adding onto the family, and Shannon thinks Amy is a cat burglar."

Ruby slammed the dishwasher defiantly. "They can think whatever they damn please." She poked the buttons and the dishwasher began to hum. "Amy's *my* daughter. I'm not going to let my family come between us again."

I swiped the counter once more. "I wish you'd go slow," I said. "Don't charge into a relationship that might not work out."

"Why shouldn't it work out?" Ruby demanded. "There's plenty of room here for two people. She could have her own private entrance."

I stared at her. "You're thinking of asking Amy to move *in* with you?"

A pan in her hand, Ruby opened the cupboard. "Why not?"

"Doesn't she already have a place?"

Ruby shoved the pan in and slammed the door. "Sure. But you know what apartment rents are like. Living with me wouldn't cost her anything. She could finish school, get a job—''

"Ruby," I said quietly, "you are moving *very* fast. Give yourself a little time, for crying out loud. What if she isn't the person you think she is?"

"Of course she is who I think she is." Ruby was brisk. "She's my daughter. I have a copy of her birth certificate."

"That's not what I mean," I said. I thought about the vicious Amy I had met that afternoon, the one who had called Harwick a sadist, a butcher. She might be Ruby's daughter, but there was something deep within her—some savage hatred, some ferocity—that Ruby had yet to witness. What was at the root of it? Was it her mother's abandonment that fueled Amy? Was it Ruby herself that Amy hated?

Ruby sounded weary. "I don't know why you're always so negative, China. I've never done anything for Amy. Giving her a place to live seems like a nice way to start."

"I'm not negative," I said, irritated. "I'm realistic. It's not a good idea to jump into a living situation, especially with somebody you don't know. And might not like if you—''

Ruby slammed her hand on the counter. "What's *wrong* with you, China?" she burst out angrily. "Don't you have any *heart*? Can't you imagine what it's like to care enough to *want* to live with somebody? You know, sometimes I really feel sorry for you, stuck forever in that head of yours. Just look at this business with you and McQuaid."

"What do you know about me and McQuaid?"

"I know what you've told me. Here you are, faced with the biggest decision of your life, and all you can think of is how many bathrooms you need. What's so important about bathrooms? Where's *love*?"

"It's not necessarily the biggest decision of my life," I said, beginning to feel angry, too. "The biggest decision of my life was deciding to go to law school."

"You didn't decide on law school," Ruby reminded me. "Your dad did."

She was right. My father made that choice for me. But even if he hadn't pushed me, I would have jumped. There never was any question who had the power in my family, so there wasn't any choice of role models: I would grow up to be as nearly like my father as possible, to the point of rejecting relationships, softness, the feminine. As the feminists say, I was male identified to the max. Changing hasn't been easy. But I wasn't going to give Ruby the satisfaction of agreeing with her.

"I am perfectly capable of making my own decisions," I snapped. "Then and now."

"Bully for you," Ruby said sarcastically. "So am I. And in this case I am making the *right* one, so I'll thank you to butt out."

We glared at one another. Ruby and I don't argue often, and when we do, it's queen size. It can go on for days while we hiss and sputter like twin volcanos, until some sort of earthquake moves one of us to change her position and relieve the pressure. Or until we both explode and bury ourselves in fallout.

"Excuse me," Amy said from the doorway. "My ride's picking me up out front. Thank you for the dinner. It was lovely." Her acid smile and caustic tone gave the lie to her words.

Ruby rushed over to her daughter. "I'm *so* glad you could come," she said with exaggerated enthusiasm, putting her arm around Amy's shoulders. "And *don't* forget about that lunch. It will be such *fun* to get together. Won't it?"

I gritted my teeth. Ruby's tone was so sickeningly sweet, it could have attracted flies. I wouldn't have been surprised to hear her call Amy "darling" or "honey."

Amy tossed out a nonchalant "I'll let you know." She glanced at me. "See you."

"I'm leaving, too," I said stiffly. "Thank you for the dinner, Ruby. Please tell your mother and sister how *much* I enjoyed their utterly *fabulous* company. It was an evening I won't forget for a *long* time."

Ruby gave me a hard look. "Don't mention it," she said. "I'm sure Mother and Ramona were enormously *thrilled* to see you again. They admire you so *tremendously*, of course."

It really was time to go. The conversation had deteriorated into the satiric hyperbole of feuding fourteen-year-olds.

Outside, I took a deep breath of the clean March air, spiced with the scent of the junipers along Ruby's driveway. I was glad I had walked over, because walking back would give me a chance to burn off some of the negative energy I generate when I fight with Ruby. Actually, our arguments are always the same argument—not the same subject, of course, but the same two positions, over and over again. Her passion against my rationality. Her right brain against my left. Her impulsiveness against my caution. The hostilities are high voltage because the conflict is so deep seated, so fundamental. On the surface, our arguments are trivial; underneath, they go straight to the heart of who we are.

Amy walked down the gravel drive beside me, silent. She seemed to be turning something over uneasily in her mind. Finally, she stopped at the sidewalk under the streetlight. When she spoke, her voice was thin and taut.

"Is it true what I heard about Harwick? Did somebody really string him up?"

A campus is like any other small town. News gets around fast, even during spring break. Still, the question surprised me. From suicide to murder in six hours or less. "Where did you hear that?"

"This girl who works with me on PETA projects." The

narrow triangle of her face was grayish blue in the mercury light and her freckles stood out like flecks of metallic snow. "She heard it from her uncle. He's a custodian at the campus police station."

"You know as much about it as I do," I said. A van rumbled past, then a motorbike, the small engine revving shrilly in the quiet night. The smell of oily exhaust tarnished the sweet cedar. "Probably more, in fact."

Amy thrust her hands into the pockets of her baggies. She looked like a tall, sad clown with her punk clothes and hair, her face washed with blue light. "I heard your boyfriend was a cop. I figured that he'd have an inside track."

"He isn't a cop anymore." Where was she getting all this information? "What did you hear about Harwick?"

She turned halfway away from me. "That he was doped up when he died." Her voice was so low I could hardly hear. "That he was keeping a roomful of abused animals in the basement under his office." She laughed harshly. "Funny, huh? He planned to hang all those guinea pigs, and *he's* the one who gets hanged."

"Doped? With what? How?"

"In his coffee." She shrugged. "That's just what I heard. You don't know anything more?"

"I didn't know that much." I sifted through the rest of her information. "Who told you about—"

"Here's my ride," Amy said, as a yellow Camaro, one fender bashed in and rusting, pulled up in front of us. "I have to go." She opened the door and climbed in.

"Wait," I said, catching the door before she closed it. "Who told you about the animals?"

"I just heard it," she said. "You know how people talk." She turned to the driver. "Let's go."

"Ok-k-kay," the driver said, and let out the clutch fast, squealing the tires.

I stared after the Camaro as its taillights disappeared around the next corner. I could figure out who had told Amy about the room in the basement, but the answer left me even more puzzled. Amy the animal activist and Kevin the animal keeper—an odd combination. How long had they known one another? What had brought them together?

My right-brain emotions had simmered down enough to allow my left brain to get logical, and the argument with Ruby wasn't the only thing I mulled over as I walked home through the dark. Ruby, me. Ruby, Amy. Amy, Kevin. Harwick, Kevin, Amy. I wasn't sure I liked all of the possible connections.

When I got home, I called McQuaid. I was greeted, as I expected, by Brian's taped announcement: The captain and first officer of the Starship McQuaid were in hot pursuit of the Klingons through another galaxy and would the caller please leave a message after the beep. I knew McQuaid had driven down to Sally's to pick Brian up and take him for a weekend visit to the elder McQuaids' farm outside Seguin, a little town about thirty miles east. He wouldn't be home until the next day.

"Greetings, Captain McQuaid," I said to the machine, and got down to it without preamble, phrasing my question so it would be suitable for eleven-year-old ears if Brian got to the answering machine first. "Star Fleet wishes you to ask Smart Cookie whether there's any truth to the rumor that Harwick's coffee had something in it. Brian, if you get this message, please write it down. Live long and prosper, you guys."

What's the good of being intimate with an ex-cop if you can't exploit his connections once in a while?

CHAPTER 8

Saturday was one of those days that happens every now and then in a one-person shop. It wasn't the herbs, of course. Plants are pacific and naturally good-natured. They are never rushed or impatient or snappish. But people are all of the above, and that day *I* was, too, partly because I had Ruby on my mind (we were still doing our volcano act and weren't speaking), partly because of what Amy had told me, and partly because I was coping single-handedly on what was shaping up to be the busiest weekend of the year.

I was working by myself because Laurel had gone off to a meeting of the Society of Ethnobiology at the Smithsonian in Washington, where she was giving a paper on capsicums— cayenne and chili peppers. To a botanist, a pepper is a fruit; in the produce market, it's a vegetable; dried, on the shelf, it's a spice, like cayenne. What gives capsicums their personality is a unique alkaloid called capsaicin (cap-SAY-a-cin), which is so potent that a human taste bud can respond to as little as one part per million. *Muy picante*. When somebody is so foolish as to actually eat, say, a habañero, which is the red-hot mama of all hot peppers, the capsaicin irritates pain cells in the mouth. The brain responds with endorphins, the body's natural painkiller. The more habañeros, the more endorphins, until you end up with a habañero high. But you don't need to be a chili junkie to reap the benefits of this savage process. If you suffer from chronic pain, you might try rubbing on some capsaicin cream. If you're a hiker in grizzly country, you can repel the beast with a capsaicin spray called Counter Attack. And if you're a woman who walks dark streets, you can arm yourself with pepper gas instead of Mace. Capsicums aren't just for chiles rellenos.

Hot also described the traffic. The store was crowded, almost without respite, from the minute I opened until the minute I closed. By midafternoon I had completely sold out of the most popular potted culinary herbs—parsley, basil, sage, thyme—and the herb gift baskets my friend Cara had made. It had rained early that morning, and I worried about how the paths were holding up in the gardens. But I didn't have much time to worry. I didn't even have time for lunch. Maggie Garrett stopped in about one, saw my predicament, and sent over a Magnolia Kitchen takeout box containing a generous slice of quiche and a serving of lemon verbena flan. I ate on the run. It kept me going the rest of the day.

At five minutes to closing time, there were still two women, elderly sisters, left in the shop. One of them—the one with Lady Clairol blue hair rolled in little blue sausages all over her head—wanted an herbal remedy for the ailment suffered by their cocker spaniel, Pretty Baby. When I asked her to describe the problem, Lady Clairol was delicately evasive.

"It's . . . you know," she said, gesturing vaguely. "In Pretty Baby's intestines."

"The vet gave her something," the other sister offered, "but it made her . . ." Her prim little mouth drew tighter. "Well, you know, all over the carpet. She was so humiliated, and we feel we can't subject her to such torture ever again. But we do have to get rid of the . . ." The mouth got tighter and more prim.

Some people are squeamish. "Have you tried garlic?" I asked. I was describing its traditional uses as a treatment for internal parasites when the door opened and Dottie Riddle came in. Her brown hair was loose and untidy, and there were lines around her mouth and navy smudges under her eyes.

"I don't think Pretty Baby would like the taste of garlic," Lady Clairol objected, shaking her head. "She's really quite finicky about what she eats."

"Then you might try making up some pellets." I opened the top drawer of the file cabinet behind the counter and found a copy of my recipe for garlic and rosemary worming pills. "This is something people have used for a long time." The law forbids me to prescribe herbal preparations, but it doesn't keep me from offering information about traditional herbal practices.

A few minutes later, the sisters had what they needed and were on their way to alleviate Pretty Baby's suffering. With a sigh of relief, I hung up the "Closed" sign, locked the door, and turned to Dottie.

"What's up?" I asked.

"I need to talk to you," she said. She took a cigarette out of her purse. "I need some advice. Legal advice."

"If you want to smoke," I said quickly, "let's go outside." A lot of the people who come into my shop are concerned about health. They don't want to smell cigarettes.

"If you don't mind," she said. She followed me out to the fountain, where we sat down on the stone bench. She lit her cigarette and I surveyed the area around the fountain, making a mental note to loosen up the soil around the bronze fennel and dig in a little compost. I glanced around, thinking that there was more work here than I could handle myself. Maybe it was time to break down and admit that I needed a gardener. Not full time, I couldn't afford that. But ten hours a week would help a lot.

Dottie pulled in a lungful of smoke and pushed it out again. Her forehead was shirred, her voice gritty. "Chief Harris came to my house this morning and questioned me. He brought the new head of Campus Security with him. A woman named Dawson. But Harris asked all the questions. The woman just listened."

I abandoned my mental list of possible gardeners. "They were there to talk about Miles Harwick?"

"Yes. How long I had known him, how well I knew him, what kind of person he was, who his enemies were. That sort of thing."

I frowned. "They seem like pretty ordinary questions to me. You worked with Harwick. You were his next-door neighbor. You're the logical person to ask." But Bubba is a busy man. If he was convinced that Harwick's death was a suicide, he wouldn't bother to interrogate the neighbors. I thought about the pipe that was out of Harwick's reach and the coffee that might have been doped. "What else did he ask?"

"Where I was on Wednesday night from seven until eleven."

"And you said—"

"That I was trucking around the campus, feeding stray cats, from seven to nine. I do it every night. After that, I was home. By myself. I went to bed about eleven."

Seven to eleven. A pretty big slot. That must have been when Harwick died. "What else?"

Dottie pulled one ankle over the other knee and nervously fiddled with the tassel on a black loafer. Her navy slacks were shaggy with cat hair. "He asked about Harwick and me. How we got along. He wanted specifics. He said he already had the general picture."

I raised my eyebrows. "Who gave him that?"

"Castle, probably." She pulled hard on her cigarette, peevish. "And Cynthia Leeds."

"Did he ask about—" I paused and let her finish it for me.

Her eyes flickered. "The letter? Yes." Wary, she ran her teeth over her lower lip. "He seemed to know what it said. I guess Cynthia told him." She flashed me a look. "Unless you did."

I shook my head. We were getting closer to the truth. But first there was something else. "Dottie," I said, "let's make a deal. Before you say anything else, I want you to give me some money. A couple of bucks'll do it."

She frowned. "Why?"

"So I can't be compelled to discuss our conversation." Things looked serious. If I was going to help Dottie, I had to know whether she had done anything that could result in criminal charges. In return for letting me in on the extent of her culpability, she would get the assurance of my silence. She would also get my advice about when, and under what conditions, she should tell the truth.

Dottie looked at me, half understanding. "Oh," she said. "You'll be my lawyer?"

For the last four years, I've said "no" to that question every time it came up. For Dottie, I was willing to say "yes, but."

"In a limited way," I said. "I won't represent you in court. But if you're in trouble, I'll give you the best advice I can."

"Oh," she said again, and fumbled for her wallet. She found it and fumbled with bills before she sorted out a five. "This is the smallest I've got."

I took the five. "Tell me more about Chief Harris's questions. Did he ask you for the letter that turned up on Thursday, or for the other threatening letters you received?"

She looked down. Her "yes" was rough, reluctant.

"What did you tell him?" It's not easy to dig information

out of somebody who is either ashamed or afraid to tell the truth. I was guessing that Dottie was both, which made it harder.

She began talking, too fast. "I told him I threw all three letters away after Miles' body was found. I said that making a fuss about the threats at that point would have been..." She raised her eyes to mine, didn't quite make it, and dropped them again. "There wasn't any point. He couldn't harm me or the cats. I'd only be blackening his reputation, for no purpose."

"I see. What did the chief say to that?"

"Nothing." She got up and began to pace back and forth in front of the fountain, gesturing with her cigarette. "He just sat there, making notes in a little blue book, giving me this look like he didn't believe me." I'd bet. I was sure that Bubba wanted Dottie to notice his skepticism, aiming to make her more nervous. "He knew about Miles trapping Ariella," she added, "and the hammer. I guess the sheriff told him."

That would be my guess, too. Blackie and Bubba regularly cooperate on cases. The interesting—and thought-provoking—question was how they had gotten together so quickly on this one. Had Bubba gone fishing for information? Or had Blackie heard about Harwick's death, recalled his Monday morning trip out to Falls Creek, and decided that Bubba needed to know about the catnapping, hammer-slinging episode? The latter was more likely. In law enforcement circles, a hammer attack on somebody who turns up dead soon after is considered interesting, especially when the death is not a natural one.

"I see," I said again. I waited, watching her, not letting her off the hook.

Dottie dropped her cigarette in the fountain, then caught my eye. Sheepish, she fished it out, holding it as if she didn't know what to do with it. "The truth is," she said nervously,

"I kind of . . . well, came unglued." She sat back down, wrapped the wet cigarette in a tissue, and dropped it into her purse. "The chief was being pushy. He wanted to know why I threw the hammer. He kept asking me what I'd done with the letters. I didn't want to say anything, but he just sat there, like a stupid fat toad waiting for a fly. Finally I told him."

"I see," I said for the third time. As a technique of inter-rogation, waiting somebody out works more often than you might think. People get nervous. They think you know more than you actually know, and they tell you so they won't look like they're hiding anything. Bubba does a pretty good fat toad.

She began to worry her lower lip again, with more energy. "I threw the letters in my office wastebasket. On Friday." She shook her head. "Stupid," she muttered. "Why didn't I burn them?"

I agreed with her, because I knew Dottie well enough to believe that those letters—more specifically, the third letter—were irrelevant to Harwick's death. But Bubba didn't know Dottie from Eve. It was my guess that he'd already formulated a theory of the case, and he needed the letters in order to test it. I calculated. If the custodian had picked up Dottie's waste-basket last night, the letters were probably still in plastic bags in the dumpster behind Noah's Ark, waiting for pickup. Or, more likely, Bubba either already had them or was on his way to get them. In which case, he might consider his theory sup-ported, which might lead him to frame his facts into an alle-gation.

"Do you think . . ." She cleared her throat and tried again. "Do you think I should go look for them? I mean, they might still be there, in the dumpster."

"I doubt it," I said. "Chief Harris probably has them al-ready—or soon will. Anyway, it wouldn't be a good idea for you to be seen rooting around in the dumpster. It would look like you had something to hide.''

Dottie shifted uncomfortably. ''I didn't mean . . .'' Her voice trailed off and she dropped her eyes.

I phrased my next question carefully, not wanting to lead her. I wanted her to tell me, as accurately as she could remember, the tack Bubba had taken in his questioning. ''Did Chief Harris mention anything related to the conditions surrounding Harwick's death?''

''The conditions surrounding—'' She fiddled with her purse, trying to decide whether she'd look like a nicotine fiend if she smoked another cigarette. ''Well, yes. He asked if I knew of any good reason why Miles would hang himself. Is that what you mean?''

Close enough. ''What did you say?''

''That I thought Miles did it out of spite.'' She stopped worrying about appearances and dug out another cigarette. ''He was that kind of man, you know. Petty, mean, vindictive, like a little kid. He was always trying to make himself look good by getting other people in trouble.'' It took two matches to get her cigarette going. ''I can certainly imagine somebody killing him—plenty of people had it in for him. But if he wanted to kill himself, it would be just like him to rig it so somebody else got blamed.''

That wasn't as bizarre as it sounded. A friend of mine once conducted the defense in a similar case. A man set up his own successful suicide—a barbiturate poisoning—so it looked as if his ex-wife had done it. He gave her everything the cops needed for a murder charge: motive, means, and opportunity. He even left a few helpful clues, all pointing to her, of course. The case was so persuasive that the dead man almost got away with it. It took an appeal to overturn the first guilty verdict.

Dottie laughed harshly. ''If Harwick wanted to do it that way, he wouldn't have to try very hard to create a motive. Anybody who served on a committee with the sonofabitch probably wanted to do him in—not to mention the animal rights people.'' She frowned. ''Or maybe one of them actually did it. The animal rights people, I mean. It seems kind of farfetched, but I suppose it isn't out of the realm of possibility.''

Dottie didn't seem to have a clear sense of her own danger. ''Did the chief want to know anything else?'' I asked.

''Just to see my cattery, so I gave him the grand tour. Then he left.'' She ran a hand over her hair. ''He asked me not to leave town without letting him know. Does that mean anything?''

''Not necessarily.'' The cattery? That was odd. I couldn't imagine Bubba being overly fond of stray cats.

She was going to gnaw that lip raw if she didn't stop. ''It's that letter I'm worried about, China. The last one.'' She hesitated. ''To tell the truth, I wrote it.''

''I figured that out,'' I said. Bubba would, too, but not right away. In the meantime, the death threat gave Dottie a convincing motive for murder. It looked as if she had decided to kill Harwick before Harwick killed her.

''You already had the other two threats, which were genuine,'' I said. ''Why did you need a death threat?'' I was asking for the record. I already knew that, too.

Dottie looked sheepish. ''Actually, I got the idea from you. If I wanted to take legal action against Miles to keep him from harassing me about the cattery, you said I needed more ammunition than the first two letters.'' She kicked her foot back and forth, back and forth. ''I guess I was being pretty childish, huh?''

''Yes,'' I said, not cutting her any slack. ''You were. You *know* I didn't mean that you should manufacture evidence.'' I let that soak in for a minute. ''But it's already done, and we have to assume that Chief Harris got what he went looking for.''

"What should I do?"

I hesitated, considering. Should Dottie tell Bubba what she had done, or wait until he asked? I usually subscribe to the view that it's a bad idea to volunteer incriminating information. But this was different. If Bubba knew that Dottie had written the letter, he'd probably scratch her off as a suspect. Not even a total nincompoop would forge a death threat from a man she was about to murder. On the other hand, I couldn't be sure that Bubba had the letters, or even that he suspected Dottie. I came down on the side of waiting. It couldn't hurt.

"For right now, my advice is to sit tight," I said. "Go home, pour yourself a stiff drink, climb in a hot bath, and relax. Sooner or later, you'll have to tell Chief Harris what you did. But let him ask first."

She ran her fingers through her hair, looking frazzled. "I can't go home. I borrowed a friend's truck and I'm on my way to the animal holding facility."

"A truck?" I stared at her. "What *for*?"

"I have to pick up the guinea pigs." At my look, she added defensively, "I can't just leave them there to suffer, can I? I dragged Castle down to the basement and made him look at the situation. He admits it's pretty awful. Something has to be done."

"Why didn't he do something before?"

"He said he didn't think it was that bad. Anyway, it was Miles' turf, and he didn't want to interfere. He said he'd dispose of the guinea pigs—sell them to another lab, probably. But I told him I'd make room in the cattery. I guess he didn't care enough to argue."

"Dottie," I said, "what the *hell* will you do with a hundred guinea pigs?"

She tapped the ash off her cigarette, frowning. "Do with them?"

I pictured a hundred caged guinea pigs, which would, in the

natural course of guinea pig events, soon be a hundred and fifty, and then three hundred, and then—

"Do with them?" she repeated slowly. She sounded as if she might be asking herself that question for the very first time. "Why are you asking?" She looked at me. "Why do you have that expression on your face?"

I shrugged. "It's a reasonable question, isn't it? Well? What *are* you going to do with them?"

Her jaw was working. "I don't know. I guess I hadn't thought that far." There was another long silence. Finally she shook her head. "I *really* don't know, China. Maybe I shouldn't be talking to a lawyer. Maybe I should be talking to a shrink."

I stood up. "I can make a referral," I said. "Come on. I owe you three bucks."

"Pentobarbital sodium," McQuaid said. "According to Sheila, it was in Harwick's coffee."

We were in the truck again, on Saturday evening, on our way to see another house. McQuaid hadn't previewed this one, but it sounded big enough to house the three of us plus our respective toys and animal companions, with a separate shop for McQuaid and three (count them) bathrooms. It belonged to an English prof who was taking an extended sabbatical.

"Pentobarbital sodium?" I repeated dubiously. "That's a new one on me."

"Not a very common barbiturate," McQuaid said, stopping for the light.

"The dose was big enough to be lethal?"

"The M.E. didn't think so. Could've made Harwick pretty groggy, though. By the way, he died on Wednesday night."

I nodded.

We turned the corner onto Limekiln Road, which heads west out of town, up and across the abrupt escarpment of the

Balcones Fault. You can see the escarpment from I-35, which parallels the fault zone as you head from Austin to San Antonio. The older, harder rocks of the Lower Cretaceous rise to the west along the rim of the Edwards Plateau, while the younger, softer rocks of the Upper Cretaceous, deeply eroded and layered with what the farmers call "black gumbo," drop toward the east and the Coastal Plain. It was this topography that the Spaniards called Los Balcones. That's what it looks like, a balcony—right now, a balcony planted with flowers. The shoulders of Limekiln Road were heaped with meadow pinks and prairie phlox and wine cups, like mounds of pink and magenta shells cast up along a beach. The sun was setting over the hills, and the variegated pinks of the western sky matched the flowers, shading into saffron close to the horizon and into deep, rich lavender as it arched eastward over our heads.

But lovely as the landscape was, I hardly saw it. I was more interested in what McQuaid had just told me, and what had been on my mind since Dottie had gone off to rescue her hundred guinea pigs.

"Dottie had a visit from Bubba today," I said. "He asked where she was on Wednesday night and questioned her pretty carefully about her relationship with Harwick. He also asked about a threatening letter she claimed Harwick wrote her." I sketched the details. "By now, he's probably dug up all three letters."

McQuaid whistled under his breath. "Not real smart of her, under the circumstances. If Bubba decides that Harwick was murdered—"

I finished it for him. "—Then Dottie's going to look like a logical suspect."

"Not 'look like,' China. From what you've told me, she *is* a logical suspect. Maybe *the* suspect."

"But only if you don't know that she forged that letter," I

pointed out. "Why would she do that, if she planned to kill him? It doesn't make any sense." A whitetail doe bounded out of a cedar brake and across the road in front of us, followed by a fawn as fleet as a shadow. "Anyway, I know Dottie," I added. "She'd rather punch the guy out than kill him. Once he was dead, she wouldn't have anybody to go up against." As I heard myself saying it, I knew it was true. Dottie was confrontational, but it was up-front confrontation she thrived on. She might kill somebody in the passion of hand-to-hand combat, especially in defense of her animals, but murder by stealth wasn't her style.

McQuaid shook his head, frowning. "You're seeing it from your angle, China. Look at it from Bubba's. Physically, Dottie could've strung the guy up. Does she have an alibi?"

"She was feeding strays," I said.

He looked at me and shook his head.

"Innocent people don't go around building airtight alibis," I said defensively.

He picked up the hand-drawn map that lay on the seat and squinted at it. "Looks like our turnoff should be coming up any moment, on the left. A sign with flowers painted on it. Meadow Brook."

"Bubba's angle be damned," I said spiritedly. "Dottie didn't do it. I was with her when Rose Tompkins came screaming down the hall that Harwick was dead. I'd been with her for almost the whole hour before that, looking at the animal holding facility in the basement. *Harwick's* animal holding facility. She was planning to use that situation to discredit him, and she expected to have a lot of fun doing it. She had no idea he was dead."

"We must be almost there," McQuaid said, peering down at the odometer. "Four miles from the crossroads."

I pointed. "There's the sign. Meadow Brook. I'm telling you, McQuaid. She *didn't*."

"I hear you." McQuaid turned onto a gravel lane. "But if you're right, that leaves only two possibilities. One, Harwick really did kill himself, although that doesn't seem likely, given the circumstances."

A split-rail fence ran along both sides of the road. Behind it, a flock of wild turkeys was picking sedately among the grasses. "Dottie suggested that he might have committed suicide with the intention of pinning it on somebody else," I said. "Don't frown," I added. "It's been done."

"Yeah, sure. There's nothing new under the sun. Harwick was the type to do it, too. I served on the library committee with the guy last year. But that still wouldn't explain how he managed to put the rope over that pipe. He's too short to—"

"Maybe he meant that to be a clue," I said. "He could have put some books on the desk, climbed up, pushed the rope over, and then put the books away again. That's how I'd have done it if I wanted to make it look like murder."

"Aren't you unnecessarily complicating this?" McQuaid asked. He slowed down to cross a cattle guard. "If Harwick was serious about framing somebody, he'd have planted an *obvious* clue."

I gave him a somber look. "Maybe he did."

"Like what?"

"Like pentobarbital sodium," I said.

"Maybe." He sounded doubtful. "The other possibility is that somebody else did him in. He had more than enough enemies. Some of the members of his own department wouldn't speak to him."

"I wonder if anybody actually *liked* the guy," I said. "Castle, maybe. They were pals. Although it's hard to tell whether he liked Harwick or simply found him useful."

"Any family?"

I shook my head. "As to friends, I only know of that guy Bob mentioned. Oh, *look*!"

We had turned a corner, and the gravel lane was doubling back on itself in a circular drive in front of a two-story Victorian painted in period colors of blue, gray, and mauve. It had a gingerbread-trimmed porch and a three-story turret crowned with an iron horse whirligig. Forsythia—exactly the bushes Howard Cosell preferred above all others—bloomed yellow around the house, and there was a large pecan tree in the middle of the carefully tended lawn, exactly what Khat required for his daily tree-climbing exercises.

McQuaid parked the truck and leaned his forearms on the steering wheel, looking around. "What do you think?"

I didn't want to tell him that in my childhood imagination I had built a house just like this one, where on winter nights I could curl up before the fire with a big bowl of popcorn, a mug of mulled cider, and a book. "It's big," I said, carefully noncommittal. "Probably an acre of floors. It'd be a job to keep them clean."

"Sure would," McQuaid said. He eyed the turret. "And I'd hate to fix that roof. Probably fall off and break my neck."

"Probably," I agreed. The lawn curled around the house like a green velvet shawl, separated from the woods beyond by a rock wall. Yellow desert marigolds and huisache daisies were scattered along it like little chips of summer sunshine in the springtime grass. In the back, I could see a large sunny yard, perfect for an herb garden.

McQuaid had one hand on the door. "Do you want to go in? Or is it too big?"

"Well, we're here," I said, very casual. "I guess it won't hurt to take a look."

CHAPTER 9

"The rent's too high," McQuaid said. We were back in the truck, heading for town. "I wasn't expecting to shell out *that* kind of money. And it's really too big for us."

"And it's a two-year lease." I hadn't gotten past the first week, let alone *two years*. What would happen if we signed the lease, moved in, and discovered that proximity killed intimacy? A lease would cast in concrete what had been flexible, open, free. A lease could kill us. Why hadn't I thought of that sooner?

McQuaid was silent for a minute. "But I have to admit to lusting after that shop," he said finally. The English prof fancied old automobiles. The shop was a converted three-car garage, more than adequate for a mere gun hobby.

I didn't answer. For my part, I had to admit to lusting after the gracious rooms, the polished wood floors and woodwork, the high ceilings, and the cozy window seat in the round room on the third floor of the turret. And there was the sunny yard behind the house, sloping to the willow-shaded brook, and the barn, and the—

Hey, wait. Not very long ago, I was in the habit of coming home sometime between ten and midnight to an elegantly modern condo whose furniture and accessories had been selected by a decorating service, whose interior was spiffed up by a maid service, and whose lawn was mown and vacuumed by a lawn-mowing service. With a great deal of psychological restructuring, I had graduated to the neat four rooms behind my herb shop. To take on a rambling Victorian in the country was too much, even if . . . It was too much, period.

"We need a house that costs less and doesn't have a lease," I said. "And fewer bedrooms." I had counted five. Five! Who needs five bedrooms?

"Right," McQuaid said. "So we keep looking."

"Right," I said.

He sneaked a look at me. "Too bad. I've never seen a shop like that one."

I thought of the window seat. "Let's go to Bean's and have a beer," I said.

Bean's was crowded. Somebody had punched up a medley of Dolly Parton songs, the dart-board gang was firing on the governor and her white motorcycle, and the bar was jammed. It took Bob ten minutes to bring our pitcher. When he did, he had something on his mind besides beer and chips.

"See that guy at the bar?" he asked, out of the side of his mouth. "That's Max."

"Max who?" McQuaid asked.

"Max Wilde," Bob said. "Makes wood furniture over around Wimberley. You know, stuff like wooden beds with the bark still on, stuff like that."

"Not interested," McQuaid said. "We haven't found a house yet. It's too early to think about beds, with or without bark." He dipped a chip into the salsa, tasted it, and winced.

108 Susan Wittig Albert

"Hot enough to melt teeth," he muttered happily, and dipped again.

"I'm not talkin' beds," Bob said. "I'm talkin' information. As in Harwick."

"Oh," I said. "*That* Max." The man to whom Miles Harwick had occasionally talked on Saturday nights. I stood up and peered over the crowd. "Which one is he?"

"The one in the leather—" Bob started to point and broke off. "Shit. Musta just left."

I sat back down. "He was a friend of Harwick? A close friend?"

Bob shrugged. "Dunno 'bout *close*. Don't think anybody was close to Harwick. The guy was kinda a strutter, 'fya know what I mean. But Max was sayin' a minute ago that he figgered he knew Harwick about as well as anybody. Said they had some kinda business deal goin' a while back."

I sipped thoughtfully at my beer. "Where around Wimberley?" Wimberley is a small town about twenty miles northwest of Pecan Springs. The first Saturday of the month, the Lions Club hosts a huge flea and craft market that attracts people from as far away as San Antonio and Houston and creates a humongous traffic jam on FM-2325. Wimberley is also famous for being an artists' colony. The two facts are not unrelated.

"Dunno," Bob said. "Shouldn't be too hard to find, though. Wimberley ain't that big."

"Thanks," I said. "Maybe I'll look for him."

When Bob had returned to the bar, McQuaid cocked an eyebrow at me. "You're not turning lawyer again, are you?"

"Not on your life," I said fervently.

"Then why would you go looking for Wilde?"

"Because I'm curious. According to Dottie, Harwick couldn't research his way out of a paper bag. Castle claimed he was the academy's best and brightest. You say that nobody at the university liked him. Maybe Wilde will be a little less biased." I gave him a cocked eyebrow. "Want to help me shop for a handcrafted wooden bed with the bark still on it?"

McQuaid dipped into the salsa again. "We don't have anywhere to put it," he said. He shook his head pensively. "Did you see the size of that master bedroom? We could sleep an army in there. Great view, too, out over the meadow."

"Not to mention a great rent," I reminded him. "A great *big* rent. With a great big *long* lease. And we're not an army."

"Yeah," McQuaid said. He looked at his watch. "Fifteen more minutes, and I've gotta split. I promised Brian I'd be home by ten." He grinned at me. "When we find that house, we can go home together. That'll simplify things, won't it?"

Actually, it would. But it might have been nice if he'd put it a little more romantically. And I wasn't sure I liked the thought of being expected home by ten by somebody who had not yet attained puberty.

Sunday morning is my fooling-around time. Sleep late, do the laundry, cook something fun for breakfast. I woke up early, thinking of driving to Wimberley to look for Max Wilde. But it was too early to start, so I put in a load of sheets and towels and let them wash while I rounded up two eggs, what was left of a jar of caviar Ruby had given me, some yogurt, basil, and chives. I was getting ready to whip up an omelet when the phone rang. It was Dottie, with news that made me postpone breakfast.

"I've been arrested, China." Her voice was so low, so tightly controlled, I could hardly make out what she was saying. "For Miles' murder. You're my lawyer. You've got to—"

"Whoa," I said quickly. "When did this take place?"

"Chief Harris woke me up about six-thirty." There was a note of something like incredulity in her voice, as if she still didn't quite believe it. "He had two other policemen with him, and a policewoman. The men searched the house and the cattery while the woman made me sit in the living room. After about forty minutes, he arrested me."

The cattery? What did Bubba expect to find in the cattery? "Did you sign a consent-to-search form?"

"A consent-to—No, he had a warrant. He brought it with him."

"Do you know what they found?"

"No," she said. "If they found anything, they didn't tell me."

I had kept my voice neutral, but I was concerned. The fact that Bubba came armed with a warrant to search the house *and* the cattery suggested that he was looking for something specific that would link Dottie to Harwick's death. In order to get the warrant, he had to go before a judge with a sworn affidavit describing the areas he wanted to search, the items he intended to search for, and the reason he expected to find those items in that place. Judges don't hand out search warrants on a whim, especially on Saturday night, which was most likely when Bubba had requested it. So I had to assume that he knew what he was after and where he was likely to find it. He must have probable cause—the letter, most likely.

"He's charging me with murder," Dottie said. She was making an effort to stay in control, but I could hear the panic cutting into her voice as the reality of her situation began to crowd out the incredibility. "You've got to—"

"It's okay, Dottie," I said quietly. "Has the chief asked you for a statement yet?"

"Yes, but I said I wanted my lawyer here, so he told me to call you. Please, China, come just as quick as you—"

"Tell him that your counsel will be available later in the day. You'll give him a statement then. And refuse to talk to him until your lawyer is sitting right beside you."

"Later in the day? But—"

"I can give you legal advice, Dottie, but I won't represent you. For that, you need somebody who's in the courtroom regularly."

"China!" She made a noise like a stifled wail. She was beginning to lose it. "If you won't, who will I—"

"I'm going to call a friend," I said, cutting off the hysteria. "Go back to wherever they're keeping you, sit down, and have a cigarette. I'll be in touch. And don't forget—no statement until your lawyer is present." The minute Dottie hung up I pulled out my Rolodex, looked up Justine Wyzinski's number, and dialed.

Justine and I sat next to one another in first-year criminal law at the University of Texas. Everybody called her The Whiz because she could whip a complex tangle of issues into a comprehensible legal theory faster than anybody else. I was insanely jealous of her, which made me work like hell to keep her from getting too far ahead—which of course earned me the nickname of Hot Shot. This madness went on until we both made it to the relative security of *Law Review* and could relax and let our rivalry ripen into a wary mutual respect. When I left the law, The Whiz publicly expressed the conviction that I was non compos and ought to be committed, while I privately thought she was bananas to stay with it. But aside from that minor difference of opinion, we were more or less friends. Justine had her own criminal law practice in San Antonio, where if I remembered correctly, she had once brought a charge of animal abuse against the owner of a big boarding kennel. If the gods were on my side, she'd be home this morning, have a hole in her calendar, and be willing to take on Dottie's case.

The Whiz is not an early riser. She answered the phone on the seventh ring, still groggy. "She strung him up for beating up on a cat?" she asked when I had outlined the plot. There was an unmistakable note of admiration in her voice. "Must be one helluva woman."

"She is, but not because she strung him up," I said. "I mean, that isn't what happened. That's why she needs you. Tell you what. Why don't you wash your face and make some coffee and call me when you can focus without blurring."

Fifteen minutes later, I was explaining the situation to a more functional woman. "A warrant, huh?" I could hear her gulping coffee, revving up her motor. The Whiz doesn't move at a speed lower than Mach 2. "What was he after?"

"No idea," I said. "I've given you all the information I have." I thought of McQuaid and Smart Cookie. "By the time you get here, though, I might have more."

"You think I ought to take the case?"

"I hope you will," I said. "I don't know what the chief has tucked up his sleeve, but I know Dottie Riddle. She's nutty about cats. But she didn't kill Harwick."

"Tell her I'll be there in a couple of hours. I've got one or two things to tidy up here first." If I knew The Whiz, that didn't mean she was going to make her bed. It meant she had two briefs and an interlocutory to write before breakfast. She paused. "If your friend didn't kill him, who did?"

"No idea," I said. "He might have killed himself, with the intention of deliberately shifting the blame to Dottie. Or if it was murder, there are plenty of suspects." I thought of the chanting crowd on the mall, the "Hang Harwick Instead" signs, the bomb threats. "A cast of thousands. All we need is Cecil B. deMille and we're in business."

The Whiz was brisk. "I'd settle for Paul Newman and a few dozen viable suspects to take the heat off. I hope you have plenty of time to spend on this case. I'll need a good investigator and help in preparing the defense."

I was dubious. Working for The Whiz might recharge some of those old competitive urges. Or I might resent being demoted from Hot Shot to gofer. I gave her a less revealing reason. "I don't think I can take time off. I've got a business to run."

"Excuse me, Hot Shot," The Whiz said firmly, "but Pecan Springs is your turf. I'd be crazy to get mixed up with a small town murder without a good local backup who knows the accused, the cops, and the terrain. You don't have to appear in court if you don't want to—*if* this gets to court, which with any luck it won't. But somebody has to run down witnesses, take depositions, handle the day-to-day contact with the client. I can't manage all that shit. If you're not on board, I'm not either. Got it?"

I got it. But I wasn't going to give her the satisfaction of hearing me say it.

"The shop is open one to five. Drop by when you're finished at the jail." I hung up.

Sunday afternoon in the shop was a lot like Saturday. Maybe it had to do with the light drizzle that dampened the outdoors or the fact that spring seems to encourage people to learn something new. Whatever, it was a day to sell books. Herb gardening books, cookbooks, herb craft books—they walked out of the store faster than I could put them back on the shelves. I also sold out of the Moth Attack blend that I grow and mix myself—southernwood, wormwood, rue, and santolina. I guess it was also a day to think about mothproofing winter wools.

But while my hands were busy, my mind was with Dottie and The Whiz in the PSPD's interrogation room, which is painted a nervous burnt orange and furnished with gray tables and chairs. I wanted to hear the questions Bubba asked Dottie, listen to The Whiz's whispered advice, think strategy, plan moves. But I couldn't, so I did the next best thing. I called McQuaid.

"Dottie was arrested this morning for Harwick's murder," I said. "Justine Wyzinski has agreed to represent her and wants me to help build the defense. I need some information. Could you phone Smart Cookie and ask her—"

"I was just going to call you," he interrupted. "Sheila says that Bubba went in with a warrant looking for the pentobarbital sodium. He found it in the medical supply cupboard in Dottie's cattery. Beuthansia-D Special, used to euthanize animals. He located one partially used fifty-millileter multiple-dose vial, and one full vial."

"Uh-oh," I said.

"Yeah. He also took a hairbrush. He intends to match Dottie's hair against some hairs he found in the noose around Harwick's neck."

I sighed. "You've made my day."

"Not yet," he said. "He also took a length of nylon rope he found in the garage. For what it's worth," he added, "Sheila thinks that Bubba's barking up the wrong tree. That's why she's leaking the information."

"Tell her thanks," I said heavily.

"Sure. Listen, I've turned up a couple more possibles. Houses, I mean. Want to see them this evening?"

I wasn't exactly in the mood, but maybe househunting would help. "Okay," I said. "Sevenish?"

"Yeah. Oh, by the way, the English prof phoned. If the rent's a problem on Meadow Brook, he might come down."

"How about the lease?"

"Afraid not. He's hanging tough on two years." McQuaid sounded regretful, thinking, no doubt, of that enormous garage.

"As far as I'm concerned, it's nothing doing unless he backs off on the lease," I said. "Even then, the place is too big. What would we do with five bedrooms?"

"Yeah," McQuaid said. I could hear the grin in his voice.

"Did anyone ever tell you that you're hard to please?"

I made lavish kissing noises into the phone. "See you at seven."

When we hung up, I began to go through my game plan for the week ahead. I was glad that Laurel would be back on Tuesday. I might need to ask her to pinch-hit for me in the shop. For additional backup, I could ask Ruby.

Ruby. My redheaded twin volcano. I hadn't heard any rumblings from that direction since Friday night. Was it because I'd been too busy to listen, or because the elemental fire had died down? Could I count on her to help with the shop? I probably could, if only because she'd want me to be free to help Dottie.

I was about to risk an inquiry into the matter when the door opened and Amy came in. She seemed paler and more wary than before, but it was hard to tell. Hypervigilance seemed to be her normal style. As usual, she didn't beat around the bush.

"I heard that Dr. Riddle has been arrested for Dr. Harwick's"—she licked her lips—"murder. Is it true?"

I forgot for the moment that Amy was Ruby's daughter and therefore almost one of the family. I looked at her, remembering that she had called Harwick a sadist and a butcher, remembering that she had known about the doped coffee before I did, remembering that she had driven away from Ruby's party with the young man who took care of Harwick's animals.

"I'm curious," I said. "Why is Harwick's death so important to you?"

Patches like rust stains spread across her cheeks, and her mouth looked strained. "I just want to know, that's all," she said. "Why do I have to have a reason?"

"Because there's a murder investigation going on. Because anybody who has any information about the way Harwick died—"

"I don't *have* any information," Amy said. "That's what

I'm asking you for.'' There was a note of desperation in her voice, laced with fear. When you've worked with people who are afraid of the truth, you learn what a lie smells like. Amy was afraid, and she was lying.

"There was a link between you and Dr. Harwick," I said. "What was it?"

Amy flinched and turned her head. "You know what it was. He was abusing his research animals."

"No, not that. Or rather, more than that. Why are you so interested in his death? What is there about it that makes you afraid?"

Amy pulled herself up. "You're wrong," she said. "And I didn't come here to get harassed. I came to get information."

There was a noise behind me. I turned. Ruby was standing in the connecting door between our shops, her feet wide apart, her hands planted on her hips.

"If that's what you want, Amy," she said, pointedly ignoring me, "I'll be glad to tell you anything you want to know."

Amy's eyes slitted. "You will?"

"Of course, dear," Ruby said. She smiled, but she still didn't look at me. "You don't have to go behind my back to—"

"I don't think," I interrupted tactfully, "that we're talking about what you think we're talking about, Ruby."

Ruby exploded. "I don't give a shit what you think, China Bayles!"

"Mother," Amy said, "Please don't—"

"You stay out of this, Amy," Ruby said.

"Ruby," I began, "I wish you wouldn't—"

Ruby's face was as inflamed as her hair. She spoke with the kind of passionate indignation that only she can summon. "Why do you have to keep trying to get between me and my daughter, China? Don't you *care* that we're trying to piece together our lives? Or is it because you don't have any idea what love is all about?'' She began to ooze scorn. ''Or is love for you always a matter of how much private space you'll have to yourself?''

I cast a look at the door. ''Ruby,'' I said, ''the shop is still open, for pete's sake. There are people in the garden. Please lower your voice.''

Ruby stamped her foot. ''I will *not* lower my voice! I don't care if the whole world hears me! China Bayles, you are an icecold, stone-hearted, insensitive—''

''Mother!'' Amy roared. ''Will you shut up? You're making a fool of yourself!''

Ruby stared at Amy, her fists clenched, her eyes filling with tears, the tears spilling over and running down her cheeks.

Amy closed her eyes and spoke into the silence. Her voice was rough. ''I didn't come here to ask China anything about you, or about us. I came here about . . . something else entirely. Something that doesn't have anything to do with you.'' She opened her eyes, so vulnerable, so filled with pain, so like Ruby's. ''In fact, I almost didn't come, because I didn't want to see *you*.''

''Didn't want—'' The words came out like a small cry, and Ruby put one fist to her mouth, holding them back.

''No.'' Amy spit it out. ''I didn't.''

Ruby put out a hand. ''But you can't mean that, Amy. You went to all the trouble to find me. You *cared* about me. You can't just turn away and pretend I'm not—''

''Yes, I can!'' Amy shouted furiously. ''Looking you up was a stupid idea! I should have known better!'' She wheeled and almost ran for the door. When she reached it, she turned. ''I want you to forget about me, okay?'' she cried. ''Just forget I ever existed. Go back to thinking I'm dead, or lost, or whatever it was you thought before I came along and messed up your life!''

I stared at her. Ruby's explosion I could attribute to her misunderstanding of the situation. Amy's was inexplicable. Nothing Ruby had said could account for her reaction.

"Amy," Ruby whispered, pleading.

"Just forget me!" She slammed the door behind her so hard that the glass shattered all over the floor. Ruby stood rooted, wordless, her eyes streaming tears.

"I'm . . . sorry," I said. The words were so meager, so inadequate, that I immediately wished I hadn't said them. I stepped forward and put my arms around her. "I'm *so* sorry," I said again. Two times inadequate is no improvement, but I couldn't think of anything else.

"Why?" Ruby sobbed brokenly, onto my shoulder. "Why is she doing this?"

"I don't know," I said. "I wonder if it's because—" I didn't finish the sentence. Ruby didn't want to hear what I was wondering. Neither did I. It would only make both of us feel worse.

CHAPTER 10

Whatever else it accomplished, the fight between Amy and Ruby had vented the passion that fueled *our* fire—Ruby's and mine, I mean. Closing was half an hour away, but Ruby hung up our "Closed" signs and locked both doors while I nailed a piece of plywood over the empty pane. Then we adjourned to my kitchen. Ruby sat down at the table and dropped her head in her hands.

"She's right. I was a fool to think we could mean anything to one another."

"You're a mother," I said. "Sometimes mothers just don't know when to quit."

I hadn't meant to come out with it that way, but it was true. My mother recently decided that she and I should become best friends and make up for all our lost years. The new intimacy she clearly hopes for has been hard for me to take. I spend a lot of effort finding excuses not to see her or return her calls. I could sympathize with Amy—on that score, anyway. But my heart—yes, my stony, icy, insensitive heart—went out to Ruby.

Ruby raised her head. "All I want is for us to get to know one another. Is that too much to ask of a daughter you haven't seen since the day she was born? Well, is it?"

I looked at her. Ruby is truly a wonderful person, but she has an unfortunate tendency to obsess. My experience as her best friend has taught me that the best antidote to obsession is diversion. Ruby needed something else to think about.

"Ruby," I said, "it's tough about Amy. But something much worse has happened. Dottie Riddle was arrested this morning for killing Miles Harwick."

Dottie was Ruby's friend before she was mine. "Omigod," Ruby breathed. "Tell me about it."

Ah, diversion. I related what I knew of the situation, up to the point where The Whiz had asked me to investigate. I had just finished the story and was wondering where to go from there when synchronicity knocked. It was The Whiz herself, with a briefcase in one hand and a bottle of sherry in the other, one sensibly shod foot tapping out the ten seconds it took me to get to the door and open it.

"I hope you've got time for business," she said, not wasting any breath on a greeting. She stepped inside and stopped, casting a questioning look at Ruby. "Oops. Didn't know you had company."

"Ruby isn't company," I said, suddenly inspired. "She's my assistant investigator. Ruby Wilcox, Justine Wyzinski. Dottie's lawyer. Otherwise known as The Whiz."

Ruby's eyes flew wide open. I gave a warning shake of my head.

"Good work, Hot Shot." The Whiz put her briefcase on the table, opened it, and began to thumb through her notes. "Judging from what turned up this afternoon, there's enough to keep two people busy. Glad you're here, Ruby. This way we won't waste any time." The Whiz had switched from impulse power to warp drive.

"I'm glad too," I said. "Time and tide wait for no woman."

"Absolutely." Scraps of paper were flying right and left as Justine sorted. "I have to be back in San Antonio fifteen minutes ago, so we'll get right down to it. Ruby already knows the facts of the case, I assume."

"Right," I said.

Ruby stared at me as if she'd lost her tongue. her mouth soundlessly formed the words "Assistant investigator?"

I bent over her and whispered into her ear. "Be cool." Out loud, I said, "I'll locate something to go with that sherry." I headed for the refrigerator to find the caviar that had escaped being tucked into an omelet that morning.

Physically, the Whiz reminds me of Janet Reno, upon whom may the heavens heap blessings for being so forthright about the difference between appearance and substance and the incontestable significance of the latter as compared to the former. Justine is sturdy, with broad shoulders and ample hips. Her usual costume is a dark, baggy jacket with the lining hanging a half inch below the hem, a dark skirt (wrinkled), and a white blouse (untucked). Her chestnut hair looks as if she combed it before the hurricane, and her glasses are always crooked because she takes them off and swings them by the temple, using them to punch out her words. She does not dress for success. She doesn't have to.

Notes sorted, more or less, she sat down and yanked off her glasses. "Number one, the warrant. Your police chief was after a drug, a hairbrush, and a rope. Why did he want all that crap?"

"The drug was pentobarbital sodium." I put caviar and wheat crackers on the table. Ruby was getting up to open the sherry and locate glasses. "One empty fifty-milliliter multiple-dose vial of Beuthanasia-D Special, and one full vial. Both were located in the medical supply cupboard of Dottie's cattery. The M.E. found the same substance in Harwick, and the lab identified it in the dregs of his coffee. Not a lethal dose. Just enough to render him groggy. Groggy enough," I added, "to submit to being strung up."

Ruby put down the sherry glasses, being cool. "Beuthanasia used for—"

"For euthanizing animals," I said. I poured sherry.

The Whiz reached for her glass. "How'd you find all this out so fast?"

"Superior intelligence," I said. Ruby giggled, then remembered what we were talking about and straightened her face.

"Seriously," The Whiz said.

"Hey," I said, injured. "No insults. Or you won't get the rest of it."

The Whiz sighed. "Let's not waste time."

"He wanted the rope for comparison to the one that hung Harwick."

"But why the hairbrush?" Ruby asked.

"There were some hairs caught in the noose," I explained. "Bubba's trying for a match. The leak," I added, "is the chief of Campus Security." I grinned. "Smart Cookie. She doesn't think Dottie did it."

"Hubba hubba." The Whiz grinned back, appreciative. "Keep that leak dripping, Hot Shot." She sat back, sipping her sherry. "Beuthanasia," she mused. "If not Dottie, then who? Harwick himself?"

Good question. If Harwick was trying to frame Dottie, Beuthanasia was almost as good as a fingerprint. But Dottie wasn't the only one who might have had access to the drug.

"Harwick was planning to euthanize his research animals when he was finished with them," I said. "There ought to be some Beuthanasia, or something close to it, in his lab or in the animal holding facility in the basement of the science building. If that's true, Harwick had access to it. And so did one or two other people."

Other people. As I spoke, my stomach tightened. Other people, like Kevin the animal keeper, who could have taken it from the holding facility. Did he have a motive to use it? Or had he given it to Amy? I pulled in my breath. I had congratulated myself for diverting Ruby's attention from Amy to Dottie. I hadn't stopped to think that the investigation might circle back to Amy.

"Other people." Justine was slathering caviar on a wheat cracker. "Yeah, right. Uncover as many suspects as possible. Five, ten, a dozen. Let's people the landscape with possibilities. Confuse the D.A. with options."

Ruby sat down and sipped her sherry, looking thoughtful. "The thick plottens, as Kinsey Millhone says."

"Kinsey Millhone?" The Whiz was blank.

"A famous P.I.," I said, and hastily added "fictional" before The Whiz could suggest that we hire her.

"Oh." Justine dismissed famous fictional detectives with a wave of her hand. "The problem is," she said, "that we don't know diddly-squat about Harwick. That's a good job for you, Ruby. Check him out, top to toenails." She began rattling things off. "Who he buddied with, what he did for fun besides torturing beasties, what his colleagues thought about him, who his mother was, what he wanted for his birthday. Get your hands on anything and everything worth knowing about the guy. And do it lickety-split. I'm hoping to head this one off before it gets to the grand jury. Got it?"

Ruby's "Got it" was crisp, incisive. She was already practicing her new persona.

I looked at Justine. "Did Dottie come clean in the interrogation about the letter she forged?"

"You bet," she said. "I doubt if the chief believes her, though. He can't afford to. The letter is his motive."

"He'll believe her when he brings in a handwriting expert," I said.

"We need our own expert. See who's available." She loaded another cracker with the last of the caviar. "You eat like this all the time?"

"I've gone totally decadent since I left the rat race," I said. "So what you want from Ruby and me—"

"Is anything you can dig up on Harwick." She stuffed the cracker in her mouth. "And Riddle."

"On Dottie?" Ruby asked dubiously. "But she didn't do it."

"So?" Justine was imperative even with her mouth full. "You believe that. But the cops don't and the prosecutor probably won't either. So talk to her. Dig out what she knows." She banged the knife on the table to emphasize her words.

"Okay," I said mildly. The Whiz obviously relished the opportunity to order us around like legal clerks. "We'll come up with a game plan. When will you be back?"

"For the preliminary hearing tomorrow afternoon." The Whiz chugalugged the rest of her sherry and fished among the papers in her briefcase, coming up with a dozen business cards. She handed them to me. "Put your names on these and use them," she instructed. "And just remember. A woman's been accused of murder. If we do right by her, she might not have to stand trial. If we don't, she might wind up in Huntsville. Simple as that." She turned to me. "And if we gotta go to court, let's get a not-guilty on the first go-round, okay, Hot Shot? I hate monkeying with appeals."

With that final rah-rah, The Whiz banged her briefcase shut and charged out the door.

Ruby looked at me. "Hot Shot?"

I rolled my eyes.

"Oh." Ruby took several cards, pensive. "Well, all I've got to say is if anybody can get Dottie off, she will."

"Yeah," I said, almost grudgingly. Maybe The Whiz's exhortation to the troops would have had more effect on me if I hadn't heard it a half-dozen times from my senior partner. But I had to admire the drama.

The door opened again. "Excuse me," The Whiz said, somewhat abashed. "I forgot to give you a message from Dottie. She wonders if you'd feed her animals and shoot Ariella, whoever *that* is." She frowned. "I hope it's legal."

"Ariella's a diabetic cat," I said. "The Lioness of God. She gets shot every day."

"We'll take care of it," Ruby said. "Feeding won't take long."

"Are you kidding?" I asked. "That woman's got over a hundred and fifty cats. Plus a hundred guinea pigs—maybe two hundred, by this time. It'll take hours." I looked at The Whiz. "It'd be faster with three of us."

"I bill at one fifty an hour." The Whiz replied. She looked at me. "By the way, what are you and Ruby billing at? I need to factor it in."

"Who's paying?" Ruby asked quickly. "You or Dottie?"

The Whiz was aghast. "The client *always* pays."

Ruby and I traded glances. "It's on the house," I said.

"That's what I call loyalty," The Whiz said, and shut the door.

It took thirty seconds to shoot Ariella and ninety minutes to feed the cats and the guinea pigs. I got back just in time to meet McQuaid. We came up empty-handed again. One of the houses had a kitchen the size of my refrigerator and the other was across the street from the middle school, which in my view made it the House from Hell. Anyway, feeding Dottie's cats and dealing with her problem, on top of a half-day's work in the shop, had left me as edgy as if I'd been sacking rattlesnakes. McQuaid dropped me at my door with a quick kiss and a cheerful promise to keep me up to the minute on Sheila's leaks. Friendship is easier to live with than romance.

Thank heavens the shop is closed on Monday. Ruby and I rendezvoused over the phone at eight A.M. to lay out Monday's game plan. I would head for the jail to interview Dottie, then to the university to see what I could dig up. Ruby would shoot Ariella, then drive to Wimberley to scout out Max Wilde, the elusive woodworker, who might be of some help in piecing together Miles Harwick's background. We would meet at Dottie's at three to feed the animals—although by that time, The Whiz might have gotten Dottie bailed out so she could feed them herself.

I had a reason for dividing our efforts this way. I wanted to keep Ruby occupied while I located Kevin and talked to Amy. If Amy was involved in this thing, I wanted to know it up front and as soon as possible. I couldn't shield Ruby from unpleasant information about her daughter, but at least I could see which direction the fire was coming from.

So instead of hotfooting it to the jail, I tucked my notebook into my purse and drove to the campus, where I sweet-talked a visitor's permit and gate card out of the surly guard at the kiosk and drove to the lot behind Noah's Ark, letting myself in through the card-controlled gate. The students were back en masse, tanned and hung over from a solid week of boozing at the beach. But Rose Tompkins, one of the women I had come to see, was alone in the departmental office suite.

The sizable reception area contained two desks, Rose's next to the entrance and Cynthia Leeds's squarely in front of Dr. Castle's door. Rose was studying a piece of paper on her desk, her round face squeezed, worry lines furrowing her forehead. She looked up and saw me and was distracted for a moment from what she was reading.

"Hello, Rose," I said. "I hope you're feeling better." I didn't think she was. Her face was gray and her eyes were puffy. I could detect the scent of rosemary, coming from a small diffuser on her desk. In aromatherapy, rosemary is a pick-me-upper.

Rose's breath came out in a puff of a sigh. "It was such a shock. I can't get the sight of Dr. Harwick out of my mind." She gave a little grimace, her eyes going back to whatever it was she was reading. She looked up again. "Miss Leeds said I made a terrible fool of myself. She said I embarrassed the department."

"That's easy for Miss Leeds to say. She didn't walk in on a dead man. And I don't know why the department ought to be embarrassed." I nodded at the diffuser. "You've chosen the right scent, Rose. It should make you feel better."

Rose sat up straighter. "You're a friend of Dr. Riddle's, aren't you? Could you let her know something for me? I would have called, but I wasn't sure . . ." She left her sentence unfinished, but I got the meaning. She wasn't sure how to get a message to Dottie in jail.

"I'll be glad to," I said. "What do you want me to tell her?"

She spoke absently, as if a quarter of her attention was on me, three quarters somewhere else. "Tell her we've canceled her Monday classes, because . . ."

This sentence stalled out too, and her eyes went to the paper she had been studying. Either she didn't want to say something as blatantly rude as "because she's in jail," or she was preoccupied with what was on the paper, or both. I tried to read upside down. It looked like a letter. Another threat from the animal rights people? But surely that kind of thing had stopped with Harwick's death.

Rose looked up with an effort, recalling her attention to me. "I'm sorry. I'm slightly distracted this morning. Miss Leeds isn't in yet, and I've been dealing with everything myself. We've cancelled Dr. Riddle's classes for the week because we don't have anybody available to cover for her while she's . . .''

I hate unfinished sentences. Three in a row were too much for me. I finished this one for her, since her meaning was so clear.

"While she's in jail? That won't be too much longer. I'm expecting her to be out on bail momentarily, so don't bother to cancel her classes."

She looked shocked. "I don't handle that. Dr. Castle phoned Miss Leeds from Boston, where he's attending a meeting. He told her to cancel Dr. Riddle's classes, period. He'll hire a replacement as soon as he gets back."

I frowned. Castle was jumping the gun. He could at least hold off until Dottie was indicted, which wasn't going to happen, if I had anything to do with it. But that's the way this business works. The minute somebody's arrested, the popular imagination renders a guilty verdict. Forget the trial, the evidence, the jury—go straight from "charged" to "guilty" in one fast move.

"Boston?" I frowned. "I guess that means I can't see him until he gets back. Which is when?"

"Wednesday. If you'll let Miss Leeds know when you want to see him, she'll make an appointment for you."

"You can't do that?"

Her eyes widened. "Me? Oh, *no*. Miss Leeds takes care of Dr. Castle's calendar, and she's at the dentist this morning, getting a new crown." She paused. "I don't suppose there's anything I could do for you." Her remark was so diffident that it invited a "no, thanks," but I tried anyway.

"I'm anxious to talk to the young man who's employed in the animal holding facility. His name is Kevin Scott. I need his address and phone number, and his work schedule."

Involuntarily, her eyes went to the paper in front of her. "Kevin?" She was suddenly flustered. Without looking up, she slid the letter under a purchase order. "We . . . we don't have anybody by that name working here. Perhaps you should try the chemistry department.''

I knew Rose well enough to suspect that the best way to get something out of her was to pull rank. I straightened up, organized my face into the most lawyerly look I have in my repertoire, and tuned my voice to match. I felt like Clark Kent emerging from a phone booth.

''I spoke to Kevin last week. He identified himself as a part-time employee of this department. It is imperative that I talk with him again. I believe him to have important information regarding the death of Dr. Harwick, with whose murder my client is charged.''

''*Your* client?'' Rose's eyes were as round as her face, and fixed on me with a new awareness. Suddenly she wasn't talking to the friendly owner of her favorite herb shop. She was talking to a lawyer, and the thought of it scared her. I pushed.

''I am a member of Dr. Riddle's defense team. At this preliminary stage, our investigation is informal. Later, we will subpoena the evidence and the testimony we need.'' I let that sink in for a moment, then let my eyes wander to the purchase order lying on top of the letter. ''I assume you are willing to cooperate?''

An interruption saved Rose from answering my question. The man came into the office, tall, gray-haired, bearing himself with the authority of a full professor. ''I need thirty quizzes run off,'' he barked. ''Right away, if you don't mind.''

Academic departments are like law offices. The people at the top expect the people at the bottom to jump when they give an order, reasonable or not. The people at the bottom are trained to jump, convenient or not. Rose was torn for a moment between defending her desk and doing her job. If the request had come from an assistant professor, she'd have balked. But in this case there was no contest. She jumped.

''Of course, Dr. Schmidt,'' she said, getting up and going

swiftly to the door. Hand on the knob, she turned, glanced at her desk, then at me. Habits of social intercourse die hard. She could not bring herself to say something as rude as "Come with me so I can keep my eye on you," or even "Wait outside until I get back," much less "Keep your filthy hands off that letter on my desk." She settled for a meek "I'll be back in a shake."

"I'll wait," I said helpfully, mentally calculating the time it would take her to warm up the copier and run off thirty quizzes. It would certainly be longer than a shake. Rose and Herr Doktor Schmidt were scarcely out of the office when the letter was in my hand.

It was a dot-matrix copy in draft mode, dated ten days before Harwick's suicide, with a salutation but no closing and no signature. It took thirty seconds to read it, and about four times that long to scrawl it into my notebook.

Dear Dr. Harwick:

You don't know me, but I know you, and what you did ten years ago. You may think you've gotten away with it, but you haven't. Unless you abandon your research, the whole world will know what you did, and your career will be totally ruined. You have one week from today in which to decide. If you have not announced by then that you are giving up your project, you can expect to read about your crime in the campus newspaper. And just in case you're thinking that a research project might be a cheap price to pay to get off the hook, think again. This is only the beginning. You should pay the highest penalty for what you did.

At the top of the letter was written, in pencil, a seven-digit number and the name "Kevin Scott."

I stared at the letter. It was exactly what The Whiz was hoping for, of course—evidence of a clear motive for suicide. She could argue that with blackmail hanging over his head like a heavy sword, Harwick had chosen to kill himself rather than face public embarrassment. Or worse. I reread the last three sentences, wondering how I would feel if someone vowed to dog my heels forever for something I had done ten years ago.

But suicide was not the only possibility raised by the letter. The deadline had passed several days before Harwick died, and he hadn't recanted his research plans. Had the letter writer decided that public exposure wasn't punishment enough? Had the blackmailer turned murderer and exacted the "highest penalty" for Harwick's crime? What crime? What could the man have done that had festered in somebody's heart long and deeply enough to produce such a deadly poison?

I looked again at the name at the top of the page. If Kevin had written the letter, how did he come to know about something Harwick had done ten years before? He couldn't have been more than nine or ten at the time. If Kevin knew, did Amy know too? And if Amy knew that, what *else* did she know? But maybe Kevin hadn't written it. Amy's words ran in my mind. Sadist. Butcher. Maybe Amy—

I stopped. Yes, this letter was exactly what The Whiz was looking for. But as I put my notebook back in my purse, I knew it wasn't what *I* was looking for. In fact, I was wishing like hell I hadn't found it.

The door opened and Rose scurried into the office, breathless. "I'm sorry I had to—" she began. She broke off when she saw the letter in plain sight on her desk. Her plump hand went to her throat. "You had no right to read—"

I was stern. "You can't withhold this, you know. It's evidence in what might be a murder case."

"I . . . I wasn't going to withhold it." Her Cabbage Patch cheeks flushed and she shifted her bulk awkwardly. "I was waiting for Miss Leeds to get back from her dental appointment. She has to see it before—"

I didn't let her finish that one. "Before you turn it over to the campus police," I said. It would be good to bring Sheila into the loop. At the least, it would slow things down. I needed a little time so I could get to Kevin and Amy before the police did.

"No," Rose said, stubborn. "Dr. Castle has to be told about it first. Miss Leeds will speak to him this morning when he calls in for his messages."

"Tell me how you got it."

"I . . ." She sat down heavily, and her chair creaked. "I found it. Just now. In the departmental computer."

I sat down across from her. "You printed it out?"

She nodded. "It was a backup file, not the original." She licked her lips. "The original had already been deleted."

It figured. Whoever composed it had been smart enough to erase the file but dumb enough to forget about the backup.

"Did you write Kevin Scott's name at the top of the page?"

"Yes."

"What's the seven-digit number?"

Her nostrils flared out, pulled in. "I copied it from the ac- counting log. It was the only one of our accounts active when the letter file was created. It's Kevin Scott's access code." The corners of her mouth turned up. "Actually, I'm the only person who understands that log. Not even Miss Leeds or Dr. Castle know how to use it."

"Where is the computer?"

"In the supply room." She gestured with her head. "Miss Leeds and I have a work station there. Dr. Castle also has one, and there's another in the computer room in the basement."

The computer room in the basement. Handy to the animal holding facility, no doubt. And accessible to anybody who knew what he—or she—was doing.

"I need Kevin Scott's address and phone number," I said again. "And his schedule."

She fiddled nervously with a paper clip. "I really don't

think I have the authority to . . .''

I leaned forward. ''The information can be subpoenaed, Rose. If it is, *you'll* be subpoenaed too.''

She put down the paper clip. ''We don't have an address for him. He was moving when he came to work here. He was supposed to give it to us, but he never did.''

''Do you have a phone number?''

She didn't say anything, but her eyes signaled yes.

''Could you get it for me?''

She worked her mouth nervously. ''I really would rather you asked Dr. Castle. Or Miss Leeds.''

I looked at her silently. She shifted several times, then finally got up and went to a file cabinet, where she took out a file and made a note on a slip of paper. She came back to her desk and handed it to me.

I tucked the slip into my purse. ''If you're not going to tell the police about this letter right away,'' I said, ''I suggest that you lock it up.''

She frowned. ''Well, I suppose. Miss Leeds may have a better place to put it, but for now, I'll lock it into the bottom drawer of the file cabinet.''

''I'd also make a copy of the computer file on a floppy disk and lock up the disk,'' I said. I stood up. There was one thing more. ''I need to check on a departmental purchase. Can you help?''

''Maybe,'' she said, a little more brightly now that I'd announced my intention to leave. ''Miss Leeds is the only one with the authority to sign purchase orders. But I make sure that they're filled out correctly before she sees them.''

''Of course,'' I said, wondering briefly how many hands any given piece of paper passed through before it reached its final destination. ''But this is such a small detail—I hate to put you on the spot. You probably won't remember.''

She smiled, proud of herself in one respect, anyway. ''Actually, I have a pretty good memory."

"Good luck with this one," I said, as if Rose were a contestant on a quiz show. "What I'm looking for is called Beuthanasia. Has it been purchased lately?"

"That's easy." Her answer came so quickly that I was sure she didn't know the significance of my question. "Two fifty-milliliter vials were ordered about three weeks ago for Dr. Harwick's animals. The shipment arrived early last week." She made a face. "I remember, because I don't like the idea of animals suffering unnecessarily. I was glad he was putting them to sleep."

"I don't suppose you happen to remember," I said offhandedly, "who prepared the purchase order. Was it Dr. Harwick?"

"Well, no, it wasn't, actually," she said. Her eyes went back to the letter.

"Was it Kevin Scott?" I asked. She nodded nervously.

"I see," I said. I let the silence hang for a moment. "Is Kevin working today?"

She shook her head.

"Tomorrow?"

She shook her head again.

Cynthia Leeds spoke from the doorway, making us both jump. "You won't be able to speak with Kevin Scott at all. He turned in his resignation on Friday."

"Oh," Rose said. She ducked her head. "I'm sorry," she said to me. "I didn't know." She spoke again to Cynthia Leeds. "Ms. Bayles was asking some questions about Dr. Harwick's—"

"We've heard enough about that," Miss Leeds snapped. She sniffed the air and turned, frowning. "What is that horrible smell?"

Rose reached for the diffuser, but Miss Leeds was too quick for her. She snatched it up. "I thought I told you last week,

Rose. You aren't to use perfume here. This is a university office, not a boudoir.''

''But that was jasmine,'' Rose protested feebly. ''I thought rosemary would be less . . .''

Another unfinished sentence. It was my cue to leave.

CHAPTER 11

The pay phone was at the end of the hall, beside a glass case that displayed a grinning skeleton suspended in an eternal *danse macabre*, every bone labeled for easy reference. When I punched in Kevin's number, I got a not-in-service recording. I tried Information and struck out again. No listing.

I wasn't surprised. Kevin had gotten himself hired by the department back in January, and he'd concealed his address and given a phony phone number. Clearly, he'd been planning the blackmail scheme for some time. Kevin may not have killed Harwick; the man could easily have been compelled to suicide by the fear of having his guilty secret—whatever it was—broadcast to the world. But the boy was no doubt running scared, afraid that somebody might connect him to the death. He might even be running. For all I knew, he was already in Mazatlán or Juarez.

Which left Amy. I didn't know her phone number, and neither did Information. Ruby probably knew it, but she was unreachable. So I got in my Datsun, surrendered my parking card to the surly guard as I left the campus, and drove to the Pecan

Springs Mall at I-35 and Juniper Hills Drive, where Ruby had said Amy worked in a pet store. It turned out to be something called PetPlaza, an upscale pet supermarket that stocks the heart's desire of every animal companion under the sun. It's all there: a mind-boggling shop-till-you-drop half-acre of fleece-lined doggie beds, kitty toilet seats, high-intensity continuous-acting ultrasonic flea eliminators, and one (only) top-quality, made-in-America brass-trimmed oak doggie casket, white satin blanket and pillow included, marked down to $149.99 for a limited time, sorry, no discount. The casket could have held two dozen guinea pigs.

Amy was on her knees stocking cat toys in an aisle called "Your Pet's Funtime." Vigilant as usual, she spotted me coming, got up, and started to walk away. I cornered her at the end of the aisle between a display of Fabulous Feline Fun Furniture and a bin of Tabby Teaser Toys.

"Kevin Scott?" She shook her head when I asked her, but she didn't quite meet my eyes. "I don't know him." She started to push past me. "I've got to get to work. I have to get that box unloaded before the boss comes back."

I stepped in front of her and looked up. She was as tall as her mother, and the determined set of her shoulders reminded me, painfully, of Ruby. "Of course you know him," I said, softening my tone. "The guy who picked you up on Friday night. The yellow Camaro with a bad case of bashed fender."

She shook her head, stubborn. "That was my friend Lou. He was driving his roommate's car."

"I've met Kevin. I've heard him st-st-stutter. I heard him say Ok-k-kay when you got in the car."

I had to give it to her. She was tough. And quick. "Lots of people stutter," she said. "Lou stutters. It's so bad that the only kind of job he can get is one where he doesn't have to talk to people."

It was time to stop pussyfooting around. "Amy," I said

quietly, "in another day or so, it won't be me asking about Kevin Scott. It will be the police. Kevin is a material witness to Dr. Harwick's death."

"Material witness?" Her hazel eyes—Ruby's eyes—opened wide, the pupils dilated and dark. She stood for a moment, caught. Between what and what? Between what she knew and what she feared? Or—

I watched her, a thought circling around in my head like a demented dog going after its tail. Anybody who knew Kevin's computer code could have walked into the basement terminal room and used it to gain access to the computer. Who had written the letter? Was it Kevin? Or Amy?

"Sorry," she muttered. She was so wired that she almost vibrated. "I can't help you." She stepped around me and went back to the box of furry cat toys she'd left on the floor. She knelt down and began to take small black fuzzies out of the box, eyes down, motions quick and jerky.

I stood looking down at the top of her head, the clipped hair stubbly over her ears, the little red tail at the back of her head poking out over the collar of the blue PetPlaza shirt she wore over her jeans. Amy knew what I needed to know. I had to dislodge her. Tough as she was, I could only do it with scare tactics. I'd hate myself afterward—worse, Ruby might hate me. But the truth had to be jarred out of her.

"I've seen the blackmail letter," I said.

She froze in mid-motion, her hands full of black fuzzies. But only for an instant. She dropped the toys on the floor and began to arrange them on the shelves, one at a time, paying careful attention to lining up their little black paws as precisely as if she were assembling them for a parade. "Blackmail letter? What are you talking about?"

"The letter to Harwick, threatening to reveal what he did." I paused, giving her anxiety a moment to ripen into fear. "Telling Harwick he'd have to pay the highest penalty. What did the man do, Amy? What crime did he commit?''

A toy fell out of her hand. She didn't pick it up. She didn't get up, either. She crouched, her face hidden.

I had been trained to hone my words sharp enough to slice away any resistance. I used that training now, ruthlessly. ''Dr. Riddle's lawyer is very tough, very aggressive. Her law school buddies called her The Whiz. Perry Mason in drag. She'll pounce on that letter like a panther on a rabbit. She'd be a fool not to use it to get her client off the hook. You know where that puts Kevin, don't you?''

She crouched, still resisting, still silent. The back of her neck looked young and vulnerable. I went on.

''And of course The Whiz will be tickled to learn that Kevin's name is on a purchase order for two vials of the chemical that the medical examiner found in Dr. Harwick, and in his coffee. Which puts Kevin up shit creek, Amy. Without a paddle. Without even a canoe.''

It was enough. Amy scrambled to her feet. Her face was torqued tight, body taut, fists clenched. She looked like an out-of-control skier seeing a sheer drop-off dead ahead, twisting, pulling, but knowing that at the end there'd be nothing but free fall into open sky.

''Kevin didn't do it.'' She closed her eyes and said it again, harder, the energy of denial charging every word. ''He . . . didn't . . . do . . . it.''

''The Whiz won't care whether he did or not.'' I was cold, deliberate. ''I know her. I know what a sharp criminal lawyer can do in a situation like this. She'll use every trick in the book to defend Dr. Riddle, which includes digging up any other suspect who might take the heat off. If you're right and Kevin's innocent, maybe he can use his information to gain some leverage with the cops and the D.A. Maybe I can help him do that. But when word gets to The Whiz about the letter and the purchase order, he can kiss that advantage goodbye.''

There was a long silence. Long enough for a tear to squeeze out from under Amy's coppery lashes. Long enough for me to remember what it was like to twist the truth for a living, every day of the week, every week of the year, without thinking twice. I was thinking twice now, and I wasn't sure whether the truth I hoped to wring out of Amy justified the spin I was putting on it right now. Offering absolution and the promise of protection or help in return for full confession is the oldest trick in the book, turned by parents, priests, psychologists, cops—and lawyers. That doesn't make it clean or good or right, especially in this case, where my offer of help might be the fatal bait that hooked a frightened kid. Two frightened kids. I felt like crying myself.

Amy opened her eyes. ''I'll have to . . .'' Her voice was so low I could barely hear her. She swallowed. ''I mean I can't just . . . I need to talk to him.''

I fished in my purse for one of my Thyme and Seasons cards and wrote my personal phone number in one corner. ''If I'm not there, leave a message. I'll get back to you. Do it *soon*, Amy. He's only got a few hours of clear space until the biology secretary shows the letter to Castle and they turn it over to the cops. After that, I can't help him.''

''That's where it is?'' she asked. ''In biology?''

I started to say yes and thought better of it.

''I'll tell him,'' she said, and stuck the card in the pocket of her shirt. I left her there, head bowed, shoulders hunched, red tail sticking out over the collar of her blue shirt. She might be a six-foot woman, but she looked like a little girl. Ruby's little girl.

As I got back in the car and headed for the jail, I found myself thinking that I had left the practice of criminal law because what I did in the name of right was sometimes terribly wrong. Yet here I was, at it again. I wasn't guilty of lying to Amy, but I wasn't wholly innocent of deception.

The best I could hope for was that Amy's information was worth what both of us paid for it.

The Pecan Springs jail isn't a fancy place. Seeing Dottie meant sitting on a stool in a windowless, green-painted room about as big as a bathroom and redolent of floor wax and disinfectant, in front of a window with a grid in it. Janette James, who had recently been promoted from meter attendant to prisoner attendant, brought Dottie into the matching room on the other side of the window and seated her in a folding chair.

On the way to see Dottie, I had sorted through the questions surrounding the blackmail letter. Harwick had once been involved in something so awful that its ten-year-old scars had not yet healed. What crime could have left such a legacy of hatred? Was it connected to his death? If so, how? To answer those questions, I had to know more about the man.

Dottie felt the pocket of her front-zip uniform jumpsuit and frowned. "Janette, did you remember to get those Salems for me when you went out for lunch?"

"Oh, yeah. Almost forgot." Janette stepped forward and pulled a fresh cigarette pack out of the pocket of her gray polyester slacks. Her bleached hair was a yellow halo around her head, and her fire-plug-red nails matched her lipstick. "Need a light?"

"Of course I need a light." Dottie peeled the cellophane ribbon around the top of the pack. "I guess they figured I was planning to burn the place down. They took my lighter." She tapped out a cigarette, put it in her mouth, and Janette flicked a lighter to the tip. Dottie sat back, inhaling deeply, and Janette disappeared through the door, presumably to stand guard in the hall.

"How are you doing?" I asked.

Dottie shrugged. "How should I be doing? I'm in jail, aren't

I?'' She frowned. "I wish they'd hurry with that bail hearing. Who's covering my classes?''

"Castle canceled them," I said uncomfortably.

"Canceled them!" She sat up straight. "What a jerk! He can't do that!''

"Calm down, Dottie," I said. "We'll take care of it." I put my notebook on the shelf under the window. "I need some information about Miles Harwick.''

Dottie took another pull on her cigarette. "What kind of information are you looking for?''

I opened my notebook. "When did Harwick first come to CTSU? Where did he come from?''

She stared up at the ceiling, counting soundlessly. "Eleven years ago. No, ten.'' She frowned and ran one hand through her wispy gray hair. "Yeah, ten. CTSU hired him as an associate professor from the UT San Antonio campus. He got tenure after a couple of years and promotion to full prof the year after that.'' She paused to drag on her cigarette. "The promotion was way early, but Castle was pushing him hard and nobody but me cared enough to object.'' Her half-grin was ironic. "Nobody but me *ever* cares. Castle's got the department in his pocket. He makes sure that everybody owes him a favor and he's not shy about collecting.''

"Do you know how long Harwick taught at UTSA?''

She pulled a beanbag ashtray toward her, its metallic tray already half full of stale butts. "Three or four years, I guess.'' She tapped off the ash. "Castle recruited him. He thought his animal research was hot stuff.''

I made a couple of notes. "So Harwick was doing animal research when he was first hired?'' Maybe his ten-year-old crime had to do with animal abuse. That might tie him and Amy together. I frowned. No, that didn't make sense. Ten years ago, Amy wasn't more than fourteen or fifteen.

"Some, but it was pretty small-time.'' Dottie blew a stream

of smoke from her nose. "Castle might dream big, but the department didn't have the facilities or the money to support a real animal research program. That kind of thing soaks up money like a sponge. You've got to reel in the big grants to keep it alive." She gave a short, bitter laugh. "But of course, when the new complex is built, Castle will be two-thirds there. All he'll need are two or three good researchers to bring in the grants."

"Will he have the money to hire them?"

Dottie raised one shoulder, let it fall. "Five senior people are retiring in the next three years. And there's Harwick's salary, too, of course. That'll give Castle a nice bundle of salary money to wheel and deal with. He ought to be able to buy anybody he wants." She laughed again. "A real shell game, huh? Build the lab, hire the big guns, and watch while the big guns knock down the big grants. Them that has, gets. That's the way it works."

What Dottie was saying about the grant business was revealing, but her bitterness toward Castle was pulling us off the mark. "What kind of animals was Harwick using ten years ago?" I asked, still trying to pin down any possibility that he might have been guilty of animal abuse.

"Rats. He and Castle teamed up to test the toxicity of cosmetic products. It was a pretty small project, compared to what Harwick was into recently."

"Was there anything questionable about their work? In terms of the use of animals, I mean."

She made a quick motion with her head. "Only if you question the LD 50 test."

"LD 50?"

"It's a methodology used to establish degrees of toxicity, to protect users of a product from poisoning. The researcher administers the drug or chemical or cosmetic to all the test animals, in increasing dosages. The LD 50 standard is reached when half of them die. Harwick and Castle went through quite a few white rats back in those days.''

"Is that a common procedure?"

"Too common. The trouble with it is that the extrapolation of research results from rodents to humans is highly unreliable. What kills rats may or may not injure people. Furthermore, there's a great response variability among animals, depending on sex, age, weight, and stress level. And even if you have good data and you can reliably extrapolate it, you can't apply the information to most human poisonings because you usually don't know how much or even what kind of substance the victim has ingested.'' She glanced up at me with a wicked glint in her eyes. "So don't eat your lipstick. The fact that it only killed half the rats doesn't mean it won't kill you.''

"I don't wear lipstick," I said hastily. "At least, not very often. What happened to that project?"

"Harwick and Castle were working for some company in San Antonio. Harwick brought the money with him.''

"Meaning?"

Dottie was patient. "Meaning that when CTSU hired him, Harwick moved his research funding with him. That's one reason why the university was glad to hire him. His grant paid part of his salary.''

I jotted a note. "Ten years is a long time. I don't suppose you'd remember the name of the company that was funding him?"

She shook her head. "The records are probably around someplace, though. It was a small company, but as I remember it, there were a couple of big names on the board. Come to think of it, that's how Castle got the chairmanship.''

"Oh yeah?" I was intrigued. "How'd that work?"

She cocked her head to one side. "The president of the company promised the president of CTSU that they'd fund a lab and put money into ongoing research. There was a string attached, of course. Two strings, actually. One was that the research would be *their* research. The other was that Castle would be appointed chair. I suppose they wanted him because they knew that his ambitions were in line with their goals.''

My jaw dropped. Deals like the one Dottie was describing came down every day in the real world, but somehow I'd thought that academics were above trading on influence. ''Does that sort of thing happen often?''

''What do you think?'' Dottie's grin was bleak. ''University types aren't really any holier than thou. The difference is that our dirty deals don't usually make it into the media. In fact, I probably wouldn't have found out about Castle's quid pro quo if Beulah Bracewell hadn't told me. She was the department secretary back then. Castle didn't like her, so when he was appointed chairman he got the dean to transfer her. She went to Personnel, and Castle hired Cynthia Leeds.''

''Did you tell people what you found out? About how Castle got his chairmanship, I mean.''

''Sure, I did. I raised a stink. But I'm a woman, and I'd just gotten tenure. My say wasn't worth much with the senior professors, and they were the only ones who could have gotten in his way.'' Her shoulders were eloquent. ''They were all pretty busy, anyway, trying to figure out how to put the make on Castle to get what *they* wanted.''

''And all this happened about the time Harwick was hired?''

''Yeah. But Castle's big idea got shot down not long after that.'' She smiled in wry appreciation of a cosmic joke. ''He'd only been in the job a few days when the company that rigged his appointment was bought up by Revlon—that's a name I *do* remember. And Revlon was already tied into an animal research program at some other university—Penn State, maybe. Yeah, I think that's where it was. Anyway, Harwick's funding dried up like Mineral Wells in August. Castle's lab evaporated along with it.''

"And they've spent the last eight or nine years trying to get it back?"

"Right. Castle's positioned Harwick for every possible grant." Her mouth was skeptical. "Although if you ask me, Harwick was a pretty poor excuse for a researcher—not nearly the hotshot Castle thought he was. Both of them busted their butts to get the regents to include an animal lab in the new building. But you know about that." She stabbed out her cigarette with quick, jerky motions. "And now Harwick's dead, and Castle's got what he wants."

I was fascinated, but unenlightened. None of this seemed to have a bearing on Harwick's death. "How about Harwick's personal life?"

"He didn't have one. Not much of one, anyway. No family that I know of. No girlfriends to speak of, either, although he dated one of the secretaries in Education for a while—Vannie Paige." I started to write a note but Dottie shook her head. "Don't bother. That was four, maybe five years ago. Vannie married the assistant football coach last year. I don't think it broke Miles' heart."

"What about men friends?"

Dottie gave me a shrewd look. "If you're thinking he was gay, maybe. He kind of had that look, don't you think?"

"What do *you* think?"

She propped her chin on her hand. "Well, if he was, he stayed in the closet. When he first bought the house, right after he got hired, some guy used to stop by every few weeks. But that didn't last long. I remember him because the first time or two he had this beautiful greyhound with him."

I started clutching at straws. "Did Harwick travel? Did he have any addictions? Any hobbies?"

"Sometimes in the summer he'd close up the house and take off a few weeks. Addictions, I don't think so, if you mean was he a boozer or a druggie. Hobbies, ditto." She paused.

"No, wait a sec. It wasn't exactly a hobby, but he was involved at one point with some sort of furniture-making enterprise. Up around Wimberley somewhere."

Ah-ha. "Did it involve a man by the name of Max Wilde?"

"That was it. Wilde made furniture that Miles liked. He had several pieces, and for a while he may have been involved financially. But I got the impression that Miles and Wilde got into some kind of hassle about it."

I made a couple of notes, then looked up. "A few more questions. One, do you know who might have phoned the department last week, threatening to bomb the place if Harwick didn't close down his project? And two, do you have any idea who leaked Harwick's research protocol to the campus newspaper?"

She shook her head. "No, on both counts, if you mean do I *know*, specifically. The animal rights people were obviously behind the bomb threat. But the protocol leak puzzled me, too. All I can think of is that somehow a copy got into the hands of somebody who had something against Harwick, and who couldn't pass up the opportunity to get even. That could be just about anybody in the department." She looked alarmed. "The police don't think it was *me*, do they?"

"If they do, I haven't heard about it." I closed my notebook. "One more thing. If I wanted to get a look at an employee's personnel record, would Beulah Bracewell be in a position to help?"

"Sure," Dottie said. "That woman knows everything that goes on at CTSU, and she's got an opinion about three-quarters of it. Are you going to ask her about Miles' records?"

"Yes. And Kevin Scott's, as well." The department couldn't be the only place where staff addresses were kept. "You remember Kevin," I added. "The nervous young man who took care of Harwick's animals."

Dottie frowned. "You think he has something to do with this?"

"I don't know, but I want to talk to him." I put the note-book in my purse. "Something else. Do you remember a piece of white nylon rope in your garage?"

Dottie looked blank. "Rope? Not offhand. I remember re-cently looking for rope to tie cages together, and having to settle for wire. Why?"

"Just asking," I said. I pushed my chair back. "Let me know if you think of anything else. Oh, by the way, we learned about Wilde last night. Ruby's in Wimberley right now, play-ing Nancy Drew."

Dottie leaned forward, her face serious. "I'm grateful to both of you. It's nice to have friends at a time like this." Then she sat back quickly, as if she were half ashamed of having given in to a sentimental female impulse. "If Miles didn't kill himself, have you got any idea who murdered him?"

I thought of the blackmail letter and Kevin—and Amy. "Hey," I said. "You're supposed to leave the detecting to Ruby and me. Didn't Justine Wyzinski tell you to think pos-itive?" That's what I would have told her, if she were my client.

"Yeah, she did, but I'm not very good at it." She pushed back her chair and stood up as Janette came into the room. "How're the cats and the guinea pigs?"

I got up too. "On the increase," I said. "You now have one hundred and ten guinea pigs and seven new kittens."

"A hundred and ten *pigs*?" Janette echoed, incredulous. From her look, I could see that she thought Dottie ought to be permanently incarcerated, probably in the psycho ward at the hospital.

"*Guinea* pigs," I said. "They're like big white rats." Ja-nette recoiled.

"I'm glad Beetle had her kittens," Dottie said. "I'm only

sorry I wasn't there to help." She looked at me. "Make sure Ariella gets her shot." Her half-smile was wistful, yearning. "Tell her to be patient. I'll be home as quick as I can."

"It had better be *soon*," I said. "Somebody needs to separate the boy guinea pigs from the girl guinea pigs."

CHAPTER 12

It was noon. I went home and found three messages on the answering machine. Laurel was back and available if I needed her. Leatha, my mother, would love to hear from me when I had a spare moment and if I didn't I'd be hearing from her (no surprise). McQuaid reported that the English prof was willing to come down to eighteen months on the Meadow Brook lease. There was no word from Amy, also no surprise.

I phoned McQuaid at his office. "Eighteen months, huh?"

"That seems pretty reasonable," he said. "And I'm running out of leads. That house may be the only one around that's big enough for us."

"But it has *five* bedrooms," I objected. And a tower with a window seat, and wild turkeys, and space for a big herb garden. I closed my eyes and saw the yellow desert marigolds and huisache daisies splashed along the rock wall.

"The place across from the middle school is still available." He was serious.

I shuddered. "Do you want to look at Meadow Brook again?"

"Do you?" he countered.

We were a couple of wary teenagers, dancing the do-you-don't-you two-step. "Well, maybe. If you do."

McQuaid chuckled. "Pick you up at seven. Wear walking shoes, and we'll take a hike along the creek." He paused. "Aren't you the least bit excited?"

"To tell the truth," I confessed, "I'm scared." It wasn't just the eighteen-month lease, either. It was actually living—day to day, moment to moment—with McQuaid and Brian and (oh, God) Howard Cosell. Suddenly five bedrooms didn't seem like enough. Maybe ten would do it. Or fifty.

"Yeah," he said, sober. "Me, too. The thing with Sally was bad. I'd hate to go through that again." There was a pause. "But I guess that's the chance we take. No pain, no gain."

Spoken like an ex-quarterback who still jogged five miles every morning and worked out with weights three times a week. But his response pointed up the essential difference between us. Never having been married, I was focussing on the difficulty of day-to-day living. Having been married and divorced, he was focussing on what might happen at the end. Either way, it was scary.

"Not to change the subject," he went on, "but I talked to Sheila a few minutes ago. Got your bucket?"

I sat up straight. "Another leak?"

"It's not going to make you happy. Remember the hairs Bubba found in the noose? There were three, stuck in the knot, as if they'd been caught when it was tied. The hair from Dottie's hairbrush looks like a match. Ditto the nylon rope from her garage."

"You've made my day."

"What do you think? Harwick sneaked into her house, stole some of her hair and a clothesline, and used them to frame her for his death?"

"Could be."

"Sure," he said skeptically. "How could Harwick be sure that the hair in the knot would be spotted? Somebody could have cut him down and destroyed the evidence. That's how the prosecution will rebut, you know. With the hairs and the Beuthanasia, the case against Dottie is pretty solid."

I set my teeth. "You've made my *whole* day. Let's hope the evening is better."

"I was just giving you the other side."

"Yeah," I said, "thanks." I tried to make it lighter. "Tell Sheila I really appreciate it, huh?"

"I will. She's a little miffed just now. She thinks Bubba's closing her out of the loop and she doesn't like it."

"I can understand that," I said. "After all, it happened on her turf. But I'm sure Smart Cookie will find a way to put things right."

He laughed. "She likes the nickname. Said it was a real compliment. She's got one for you, too."

I wasn't sure I wanted to hear it. "Oh, yeah?"

"Sage Woman," he said.

I put down the phone, grinning.

Lunch was an avocado-and-sprout sandwich and milk. While I ate, I phoned Laurel to find out how the pepper paper had gone and to ask if she could mind both my shop and Ruby's for the rest of the week, in case the thing with Dottie was still unresolved. She was happy to do it. What's more, her sister would be available, too, if business was more than Laurel could handle alone.

I had just finished eating when the phone rang. It might be Leatha, making good on her promise. I let the answering machine screen the call, but when I heard the voice, I picked up the phone myself.

It was Amy.

"I need to see you," she said, low and tense, as if she didn't want to be overheard. I heard somebody laughing behind her. Maybe she was calling from work.

"Have you talked to Kevin?"

"No." She hesitated. "This has nothing to do with Kevin." She repeated herself, for good measure. "Nothing. Really."

I didn't believe her. "Where do you want to meet? When?"

"Can I come to your place? Say, six? I don't get off work until five-thirty."

I rapidly calculated the time it would take to feed a clowder of cats and a plague of guinea pigs. "Six ought to work," I said. "See you then."

Beulah Bracewell's office was in the administration building, on the other side of the quad from Noah's Ark. The Spanish-style buildings on the campus, most of which are more or less ersatz, at least have some historical referent. They connect to places and people and ideas. The administration building connects only to itself. It has no personality. It's nothing but a big pink brick box, with a fake colonnade across the front and seven floors of offices concealed behind reflective windows that insiders can see out of but outsiders can't see into—a perfect metaphor for what happens in bureaucracies.

I found Personnel on the third floor, in a large multistation, open-plan office that took up the whole south side of the building. Beulah's desk was in the far corner, behind a bank of lateral file cabinets topped with an impressive set of large ring binders and a lanky philodendron whose leaves were green on the side that faced the window and yellow on the other side.

Beulah was sixtyish, white haired and slender, with soft pink skin, a low voice, and a contained manner. She reminded me of my grandmother, whose improbable name my father had bestowed on me. She had the look of someone who would go quietly about her work while everybody else was searching for towels to throw in. She motioned me to a chair, her shrewd gray eyes sizing up my denim skirt, blue plaid blouse, loafers, and grubby nails. She was probably measuring me for one of the openings described in the brochure on her desk: *Job Opportunities at CTSU. People Working Together for Higher Education, Good Citizenship, and Strong Stewardship.* The title sounded like something hammered out by an undergraduate marketing class. It had enough buzzwords to make your ears ring.

"Perhaps you've heard that Dr. Riddle was arrested yesterday," I said, after I introduced myself. "I'm working with her lawyer to try to fill in some of the details of the case."

"Of course I heard it," Beulah said. She made an impatient gesture. "Last week everybody was talking about Dr. Harwick. This week it's been nothing but Dottie." Her mouth turned down at the corners. "How's she holding up?"

"About as you'd imagine," I said. "She's mostly concerned about her cats."

Beulah's dark eyes snapped. "Those cats! I love Dottie, but I'll never in the world understand why she spends so much time and energy on animals." She frowned. "Is anybody taking care of them while she's in jail?" Beulah had no trouble with the word.

"Ruby Wilcox and I are helping out."

She looked at me, eyes flinty. "China Bayles. Aren't you the one who runs the herb shop? Why are *you* working with Dottie's lawyer?"

"I used to be a trial lawyer in a former life," I said. "I'd like to help Dottie clear up this misunderstanding."

"Well, I certainly hope to God *somebody* straightens things out," Beulah said, pushing up the sleeves of the gray sweater that topped her tailored white blouse. Her tone was testy. "How Bubba Harris can be fool enough to arrest that woman is totally beyond my comprehension. Somebody's getting away with murder while he's wasting time picking on an in-

nocent person. In fact, I told Bubba's wife Gladys that *very*
thing when I ran into her at the post office this morning. I told
her to tell Bubba too.'' She frowned. ''Now, how can I help
you?''

''I'm hoping to trace out a lead or two.''

She picked up a pencil and twirled it like a miniature baton.
''What exactly are you looking for?''

''Miles Harwick's personnel file. I'm specifically looking
for the name and address of next of kin, information about
prior employment, and address at the time of initial application. At this point, I'm making an informal request for the
material,'' I added, to show her I meant business. ''Dr. Riddle's attorney will subpoena it later.''

She shook her head. ''I'm sorry, but you're too late. Sheila
Dawson, the new head of Campus Security, came up on Friday
and took it.'' She pressed her lips together. ''I believe she
planned to turn it over to Bubba Harris.''

''I see,'' I said. I wasn't surprised. Maybe I'd have better
luck with my second request. She furrowed her brow and
stood up when I gave her Kevin's name.

''Terminated last week? Let me check.''

She was gone about five minutes, while I sat, listening to
the buzz of voices in the open office behind me. When I came
in, I had noticed the spirit of good-natured camaraderie that
energized the office—telephones ringing, people moving from
desk to desk, lots of chitchat. The clerical staff was almost a
hundred percent women, of course. In any bureaucracy,
they're the ones who keep the paper-stream flowing, input the
data into the computers, and do the nitpicky things that make
institutional life halfway bearable for everybody else. The
trouble is that they're usually pretty much invisible. People
count on them, get used to them, fail to notice them. I'd bet
it would take three, maybe four of the female clerical staff to
equal the salary of the male personnel director. He'd certainly

miss them if they left. I wondered if anybody would miss him.

When Beulah came back, she was carrying a manila folder. She laid it on the desk and glanced at her watch. "I usually take a break right about now."

I looked up at her, grateful for her tact. "Thank you," I said.

"Don't mention it," she said with emphasis.

Kevin Scott's file was pretty thin. But it did contain a Pecan Springs address, which I copied down. I also copied his social security number, the rest of his personal data, and the name, address, and phone number of his parents, Anne R. and Charles I. Scott, who lived on Mesquite Drive in San Antonio. I put the folder on Beulah's chair with a hastily scrawled thank-you, and threaded my way through the busy office to the elevator, where I punched the down button.

Campus Security is located on the first floor of the administration building. The elevator and the quad entrance open onto a lobby where students and faculty can apply for IDs and parking stickers and pay their parking fines, a revenue source which no doubt covers the salaries of half the Security force. A young girl with deeply waved chestnut hair was sitting behind the counter, concentrating on a computer monitor. She stood up when I came in, and I noticed that she was wearing a button with the catchy slogan "God Is Coming and Is She Pissed." When I told her who I was looking for, she took my name, sauntered through a door between a file cabinet and a computer station, and came back a minute later.

"The chief says to come on in. She's in her office, third door on the right."

I knew where the chief's office was because I had been there once with McQuaid, who was a buddy of the man who preceded Smart Cookie. When I opened the door, I saw that the office had undergone an extraordinary change. The gray metal desk, green plastic sofa and chair, and beige tile floor were gone. In their place was a polished wood desk topped with a tasteful gold reading lamp, across from a soft coral upholstered sofa and chair, on a forest green carpet. On the wall was a poster depicting a giant green pea pod, with the caption "Give Peas a Chance." The north-facing window sill was crowded with pots of pink and mauve African violets, one of which sported a heart-shaped "I Love You" balloon.

Behind the desk, Sheila looked up and smiled. "What do you think?" she asked, with a gesture that included the African violets.

"Bob Dylan was right," I said. "The times really *are* changing."

"Maybe, maybe not," Sheila said. She stood and came around the desk. "He said that almost thirty years ago. And there's more to it than redecorating." Her silky cream blouse was a mute contrast to her beige suit, her shiny blond hair was smoothed back beneath a beige hairband, and her nails and lipstick matched. "Mike told you about Chief Harris making the hair match?" She took the upholstered chair and motioned me to the sofa.

I nodded and sat down. "Any possibility that Dr. Riddle's hairs could have been planted?"

"That was my first thought," she said, showing a length of slender thigh as she crossed her legs. "But if it was a plant, it was carefully done. I saw the hairs myself when we took the body down. They were tied in with the knot."

"Yes," I said. "So McQuaid told me."

She looked at me. "McQuaid? I thought you two were like that." She held up two fingers, close together.

"We met professionally," I said. "I was on one side of a case, he was on the other. We got used to last names. But to answer your question, yes, we *are* like that. We're looking for a house together." That last sentence surprised me when I heard it. I hadn't mentioned our househunting to anybody but

Ruby. Had I told Sheila because I wanted to make sure she knew where the boundaries were?

"It's a big step," she said.

"Is it ever," I said fervently.

She kicked both beige pumps off and wiggled her stockinged toes in the carpet. "Look. I'm trained as a police officer, but I've learned to rely on my intuition. When I listened to Riddle's answers to the chief's questions Saturday morning, I got the very strong feeling that she didn't have anything to do with the crime, although she certainly was antagonistic toward the victim. That's why I've been willing to help."

"Do you have an alternative theory about Harwick's death?"

"I guess I lean toward planned suicide, with an attempt to frame Riddle for murder. It seems consistent with Harwick's personality and his relationship to Riddle. He lived right next door. If he had wanted to set her up, it wouldn't have been hard for him to get into her house. All he needed was some hair, which would never be missed, and a length of rope. Or he could have brought the rope and planted it in her garage, keeping enough for his purpose." She hesitated. "Unfortunately I haven't yet turned up Harwick's motive for killing himself."

Wait until she saw the blackmail letter, I thought, thinking I'd show it to her as soon as The Whiz had seen it. It gave Harwick a *very* strong motive for suicide. But I still had to dig into the connection between Kevin and Harwick, which troubled me deeply. I took out my notebook. "I talked to Beulah Bracewell in Personnel a few minutes ago. I understand you have Dr. Harwick's file."

Her face was bland. "Chief Harris requested it."

I cocked my eyebrows. "You wouldn't happen to have copied it, would you?"

Her mouth twitched. "What makes you think that?"

"Because that's what I would have done if I were in your shoes." I glanced at the dress-for-success pumps she'd kicked off. Mine had gone to Goodwill, along with my power suits.

Sheila got up, padded to the desk, and took a file out of her bottom drawer. "Riddle's attorney will get this sooner or later," she said, handing it to me. "You may as well have a look at it now."

The file held an application form, a copy of Harwick's W-4 listing only himself as a deduction, and the usual college transcripts. There was also a computer check-sheet showing which bank his paychecks were automatically deposited to, which health and life insurance packages he had opted for, how much he paid into his retirement fund, and how little he gave to United Way. I noticed that a couple of years ago he had changed the beneficiary of his life insurance from a Mrs. Letitia Harwick, Mother, to Central Texas State University, with the cryptic note, "bio. exper. acct. only." At the same time, he had increased the benefit from a fairly standard seventy-five thousand to a cool million. The "bio. exper. acct.," whatever that was, would be receiving a nice round sum.

I shuffled copies. Harwick's transcripts were from Texas A&M, where he earned both his undergraduate and graduate degrees. His grades were mostly As and Bs, although in two nonconsecutive undergraduate semesters he had earned Cs and Ds, even an F. I made a note of his student ID and the relevant years and turned to his employment application, which showed that at the time he was applying to CTSU he lived at 202 Mesquite Drive in San Antonio. I did a double take, and flipped to the previous page in my notebook.

There it was. Anne R. and Charles I. Scott, 204 Mesquite Drive, San Antonio, Texas.

Ten years ago, Miles Harwick and Kevin Scott had been next-door neighbors.

*   *   *

On the way to Dottie's to meet Ruby and feed flocks of starving animals, I drove by the address Kevin had put down in his personnel file. It was west and south of campus, in a neighborhood that had been developed twenty years ago, when Pecan Springs was first beginning to respond to the growth of CTSU, the town's largest employer. Most of the houses were the kind you see advertised now as "starter" homes—two-bedroom, one-bath bungalows with detached garages, stucco or lap siding, built on narrow, nondescript lots. There was a smattering of newer duplexes occupied by young families, judging from the tangle of bikes and balls and play equipment that littered the porches and sidewalks. It was past midafternoon, but there wasn't a child to be seen. My generation would have been taking naps. These kids were probably watching Maury Povitch.

There was a "For Sale" sign stuck in the middle of Kevin's front lawn. When I went up to the front door, I noticed several pieces of mail in the mailbox. My hand—a creature of old, inquisitive habits that I haven't quite outgrown—reached out and grabbed them. One was a junk-mail coupon flyer for Kevin. Two were letters addressed to Carl Wendt at the same address. Kevin's roommate, maybe. I tucked the mail back in the box and hit the doorbell. I could hear it ringing. But there wasn't another sound inside, and the closed drapes denied me a look into the living room. After a while I gave it up and went back to my car. I drove down the street, pulled around the block, and parked two doors down from Kevin's, where I sat for a few minutes, watching and thinking. But the front door remained shut, and after five minutes I drove off again, still thinking.

I was mulling over the same subject when I pulled up behind Ruby's Honda in front of Dottie's house. One of my questions had been answered, but the knowledge didn't take me far enough. I was left with at least five more, all of which had to be resolved before I could assure myself that I had arrived at something like the truth.

What was the connection between Kevin's blackmail letter—if it actually *was* Kevin's letter—and Harwick's death?

Had the man committed suicide or had he been murdered?

Either way, how did Dottie's hair come to be caught in the knot? How did the rope get into her garage—or out of her garage and around Harwick's neck?

How was Amy involved?

Of all these questions, the second was the most fundamental, and the most troubling. There is no crime as horrible as murder. There is nothing any human being can do to another that wreaks more moral havoc and shatters more completely our fragile connections to one another. When one person willfully and maliciously deprives another of life, all of the energies of the law, of society, must focus on justice.

But suicide, while it breaks the social contract just as irrevocably, is a special kind of murder, and we are ambivalent about it. We may mourn the loss of a human life and blame ourselves for not being able to prevent it. We may feel compassion for the individual whose last desperate act was self-annihilation. But there is no justice to be sought, for the killer has acted as judge and jury and pronounced the final sentence. If Harwick had killed himself, there was nothing to be done.

But I was not yet convinced. The answer to this enigma did not lie in the direct evidence, which was ambiguous at best, but in the hearts of those involved. And that took me back to Harwick, and to Kevin, and to Amy.

Amy. I glanced at Ruby's car parked in front of me. Bringing Ruby into this mess when I knew her daughter might be involved had been thoughtless and stupid. I had to find a way to divert Ruby to the periphery of the case, away from the center, away from Kevin and Amy.

I got out of the car and went around the back of Dottie's

house. I found Ruby in tight jeans, loose blue chambray shirt, and cowboy boots, dispensing cat food to a hoard of furiously hungry felines. I yelled at her through the fence.

"Have you shot Ariella yet?"

"I was hoping you'd do that," Ruby called, stepping out of the way of a giant Persian making a beeline for a food bowl. Ruby can spend hours getting acupunctured, but the thought of giving a shot makes her want to throw up.

I went into the kitchen, located Ariella's insulin in the refrigerator, filled the syringe with six units, and finally found Ariella asleep on top of the refrigerator. Giving her the injection took less time than finding her. After I put her food down (she has a special diet, of course, being diabetic), I went to talk to Ruby through the cattery fence.

"Did you locate Max Wilde?"

Ruby straightened up, a ten-pound sack of Alley Cat hugged in her arm. Her smile was lyrical. "Oh, yes, I located him. What a *fascinating* man. His woodworking business is called Wilde-Works. Isn't that a clever name? And did you know he lives in a log house?"

"I don't know anything about him, Ruby," I said. "Not a smidgen. That's what you went to find out." Now that I'd connected Kevin and Harwick, Wilde was probably irrelevant. On the other hand, judging from Ruby's reaction, he might be the diversion I needed. Her last boyfriend, a photographer named Andrew Drake, had moved out of town. Max could be helpful, especially if the situation with Amy got out of control.

Ruby shoved a full bowl aside and bent over to fill another one, the outline of her blue-jeaned butt a graceful curve. "A *big* log house about three miles out of Wimberley," she said. "With a loft. He built it himself, next to Cypress Creek. And it's absolutely *crammed* with the most fascinating *things*! Chairs and tables and cupboards he's made out of cedar, and bowls and carvings and antique tools and pottery—"

"What about Harwick? Did Wilde know him?"

"And animals!" Ruby snagged the last bowl with her toe and began to fill it. "There are animals all over the place. Peacocks that roost on the porch railing, and ducks and geese. And chickens. He scrambled eggs for lunch, with eggs we found in the chicken coop. Would you believe it? And we had wine that he made himself, from grapes he grows right there on his property."

I refrained from asking whether he had trodden out the grapes barefoot. Instead I asked, "Did Max Wilde know Miles Harwick?"

She straightened up, looked around to see if she had missed any cat bowls, and came toward the gate. "Of course he knew him," she said. "They were business partners."

Great. Now we were getting somewhere. "They were in the furniture business together?"

"Well, sort of." She came through the gate and latched it behind her, shaking it to make sure the catch held. "Harwick didn't have anything to do with making the furniture. Max did all that. All Harwick did was put up some money so Max could build an inventory and put pieces on display in various shops. But that was a while ago." She looked at me. "Have you done the guinea pigs yet?"

"I was waiting for you." We headed toward the room behind the garage where Dottie kept the food and other supplies. "This furniture business—how long ago was it?"

"Four years or so. Max said he didn't like being partners with Harwick, so as soon as he could he paid him off and eased out of the relationship." Ruby opened the door and flicked on the light. There were two buckets of guinea pig food in the corner. She took one and I took the other. "Max says he kept on running into Harwick at Bean's. But he doesn't know much more about him than we do, apparently. He didn't even know Harwick was dead." She grinned. "He doesn't read the newspapers, and he doesn't have a television set.''

We went out and closed the door behind us. "That's it?" I asked.

"Not quite," Ruby said. "When I asked him if Harwick had any enemies, he mentioned that there was some guy Harwick absolutely detested. Max even heard Harwick threaten to kill him once. Max thinks the guy had something on Harwick and was using it to get money or something. Max said when he heard Harwick was dead, this guy was the first one who came to mind.''

"Wonderful," I said. We opened the cattery gate and went toward the guinea pig cages. "Maybe you should follow it up. What's the guy's name?"

Ruby put down her bucket. "Max didn't know. All he knows is that the guy lives in New Braunfels. But he shouldn't be too hard to find. He has dogs." She pointed to a cage. "Oh, China, look! Another litter of babies! Aren't they absolutely precious?''

"What do you mean, easy to find?" I asked crossly. "New Braunfels is *full* of people with dogs." I counted the downy bodies nestled against the mama guinea, who already looked harassed. "Twelve," I muttered. "Good God.''

Ruby began dipping dry food out of her bucket into the feeders on the cages. "I don't think it'll be too hard to locate *these* dogs," she said. "Max says they're greyhounds. Retired from the race track.''

I looked at her with a new interest. "Dottie mentioned that a man with a greyhound used to visit Harwick. Must be the same guy.''

"I can check him out," Ruby offered helpfully. "I used to know a woman who adopted a greyhound. Most of them come through the Greyhound Rescue people in Houston. They must have some kind of registry. I'll call and find out.''

I began to dip pellets into a feeder while the animals in the cage chattered happily, anticipating dinner. "I'm following up another lead."

"We must be making progress," Ruby said. "What kind of lead?"

I quickly scanned my answer for obvious connections to Amy. There didn't seem to be any, so I gave it to her. "The student who took care of Harwick's animals sent him a blackmail letter a couple of weeks ago, threatening to reveal something terrible that Harwick was supposed to have done ten years ago. When I checked it out, I learned that the student's parents live in San Antonio, next door to where Harwick lived when he applied to CTSU."

Ruby looked up, eyes widening. "Hey, that's great! It sounds like you're really onto something! What does Bubba have to say about the letter? Doesn't it practically destroy his case against Dottie?"

"He doesn't know about it yet," I said, moving to another cage. "The biology secretary discovered the letter in the computer. She's the type who doesn't make a move without checking it out with the boss. She'll show it to the police after Castle sees it. That won't be until tomorrow, I guess."

"So we're going to San Antonio this evening?"

"*I'm* going to San Antonio," I said. "But it can wait until morning. Tonight McQuaid and I are going to look at a house."

"Have you found something you like?"

"Maybe. But it's too big, it costs too much money, and the lease is too long."

Ruby's eyes crinkled at the corners. "Other than that, Mrs. Lincoln?"

"Don't be tacky," I said. "Are you available for investigative work tomorrow?"

"Just try to keep me out of it!" Ruby said. "I'll have to find somebody to mind the shop, though."

"I've already asked Laurel. If she can't handle it alone, she'll get her sister to help. I want you to chase down that guy in New Braunfels. When you've located him, we'll go talk to him." Tracing the greyhound owner would keep her busy for a good part of the day, while I resolved the other, stickier business involving Kevin—and Amy.

Ruby smiled and began on another cage. "Sounds fine to me," she said. "But I have to be back by six o'clock tomorrow night."

"What's happening at six o'clock tomorrow night?"

She smiled happily. "I'm having dinner with Max Wilde."

CHAPTER 13

I stopped at Kevin's once again after I left Dottie's, but there was no answer to my ring. Someone had been there, however. The closed drapes were now open and I could see into a living room that looked exactly as you would expect if it were regularly occupied by two males in late adolescence. Laundry was piled on the sofa, newspapers littered the floor, and beer cans, potato chip sacks, and McDonald's sacks spilled off every flat surface.

It was a few minutes after six when I got home. Amy was sitting on my kitchen stoop, her arms clasped around her knees. The unpredictable spring sky had turned a pearly gray and a chill breeze blew out of the north, where snow lingered in the Panhandle. Amy was shivering in thin gray sweats.

"Sorry to be late," I said, unlocking the door. "My errand took longer than I thought." Just to see her reaction, I considered telling her that I had dropped by Kevin's, but discarded the idea. No need to let her know that I had located him.

The kitchen was warm and cozy against the outdoor chill. "Sit down," I said. "I'll make us some tea. Would you like a sandwich?"

"I don't want to sit." Amy's voice was truculent. "I don't want to eat, either. I'm in a hurry. I just want to say what I have to say and get it over with."

"Well, *I'm* sitting down," I said. "I'm a lot older than you are. I'm tired." I sat in the rocking chair beside the window and pulled off my loafers. Amy stood uncomfortably for a moment, then perched on the edge of a kitchen chair a couple of feet away and planted her sneakers flat on the floor, as if she were planning to spring up momentarily.

"What I want to say is," she said loudly, "that I killed him."

I stared at her. "You did?" This was something I hadn't bargained for.

She pulled her right ankle onto her left knee. Her face was expressionless. "Yes. *I'm* the one. *I'm* guilty. So you can stop badgering Kevin."

"I see," I said. I pushed the rocking chair with my foot, setting it in motion. "Maybe we'd better talk about this for a minute."

She put both feet on the floor again. "I don't want to talk. I said what I had to say. Now I'm going to the police." She stood up, her shoulders determined. "It's not fair for Dr. Riddle to suffer for something I did."

I locked eyes with her. "Sit down," I commanded.

She pulled her gaze away and took a step toward the door. "I said I'm going to the—"

"You're not going anywhere until I've heard your story," I said firmly. "You owe me that much, anyway. And your mother."

"My mother's got nothing to do with this," she said, but she hesitated. After a moment, she sat. "What do you want to know?" she asked, without enthusiasm.

"I want to know how you killed him, and why."

She closed her eyes. "I killed him because . . ." There was

a pause. Her eyes opened. "Because he abused animals," she said. The words began to come faster. "He was a cruel, sadistic man who tortured and maimed and totally destroyed living beings! When people kill other people, they're held to account. There's justice. But people can murder animals and get away with it! And not just murder, but torture—endless, unspeakable torture! Miles Harwick subjected helpless, defenseless animals to excrutiating tortures, and got nothing but praise for it. I did what I did to stop him, to expose him for what he is, an immoral, heartless *butcher*! I did what I did for the sake of *justice*!"

"I see." I looked at her. "Did you write the blackmail letter?"

She lifted her chin, defiant. I saw Ruby in the gesture. "I stole Kevin's computer access code number. I used the computer in the basement of the science building to write the letter and print it out. Then I deleted the file to cover my tracks. But I didn't know about the backup file." Her mouth twisted bitterly. "I was stupid, I guess. But I'm not sorry I was found out. I want the world to know what I did, and *why*. I made sure that Dr. Harwick paid for his cruelty. I'm prepared to accept the consequences of my action."

"Very laudable. And what was the crime that you were holding over Harwick's head?"

Her hands were clasped between her knees. She twisted them nervously. "That's where I screwed up. I thought I could scare him, but I couldn't."

"The crime?"

She sighed. "He had a lab at UT in San Antonio. I was just a teenager then, but a girl who used to babysit me was taking a class from him. She took me to the lab, and I saw what he was doing to animals. It was awful. Even back then, people were protesting. I thought I could use that old stuff to get him to give up the guinea pig project."

"Your scheme didn't work?"

Her glance flickered at me, then away. "When I saw that he was just going to ignore the letter, I knew I had to kill him. He deserved it, so that part wasn't hard. I don't have any remorse. But I never in the world imagined that Dr. Riddle would be charged with my crime. I can't let an innocent woman go to jail. Anyway, I want the world to know what I did!" Her voice rose. "I want them to know *why*!"

I looked at her thoughtfully. "And just how was it you killed him, Amy?"

Her jaw tightened and she shifted her feet. Her answer, when it came, was less positive than her claim to be a murderer. "I stole Kevin's key and took the stuff—Beuthanasia, it was called—out of the supply cupboard in that awful place in the basement where Harwick kept his animals. I read the directions on how much to give by body weight. I didn't want to give him enough to kill him, just enough to knock him out. I wanted him to hang, the way he planned for those poor animals to hang. I thought it would be a beautiful irony if he died with the same stuff in him that he planned to kill the animals with."

"When did all this take place?"

She hesitated. "Early Wednesday evening. I saw the light in his office, so I knew he was working late. I knocked at the door and told him I was thinking of enrolling in his class next semester, and that I had some questions about it. We started talking, and when he wasn't looking, I dumped the Beuthanasia into his coffee. He got groggy pretty quick. I had the rope in my bookbag. I climbed up on his desk, put it over the pipe, and hoisted him up." She looked at me as if testing my response. "It wasn't hard, you know. I'm tall, and I'm pretty strong. He was a shrimpy little guy. He didn't struggle a lot."

I rocked back and forth for a moment, digesting her story. "What kind of rope was it?"

Her hand came up and she rubbed her mouth. "Just ordinary rope."

"I see," I said, still rocking. I watched her for a moment, letting her watch me, letting the tension build. Still rubbing the corner of her mouth, she looked at me, then away, then back again. Finally I said, "As a former criminal attorney, I have some advice, Amy. Would you like to hear it?"

She dropped her hand and shifted uncomfortably. "I guess. Yeah, sure. I'm going to need a lawyer. I might as well hear your pitch."

"Forget about going to the police."

She blinked, startled. "But I've got to tell what I've done! There's no point to Dr. Harwick's death if people don't know *why* he died. And I've got to clear Dr. Riddle!"

"Your cock-and-bull story won't clear Dr. Riddle. If you persist in it, it can only incriminate the person you're trying to shield."

Amy looked at me. Her face was pale, her freckles translucent, her mouth so much like Ruby's that my heart ached. She made a quick, nervous gesture. "The person I'm trying to—"

"Kevin," I said.

She jumped to her feet. "That's crazy! I'm not trying to sheild anybody! I did it! I killed Harwick! I'm the one who has to pay!"

"I'm not going to tell you which of your lies will trip you up," I said quietly. "Just take my word for it. If you hand this crock of shit to the cops, you'll be charged with obstruction of justice, not murder. You can't help Kevin by trying to take the rap for yourself."

"But I did it!"

I was rocking again. "Go home, Amy," I said wearily. "Just go home."

She stared at me, teeth working, jaw clenched tight, fighting tears. Then she got up and went to the door. She turned, her handle on the knob.

"Kevin is totally incapable of killing anybody."

"Maybe," I said. "But if *you* don't believe that, how do you expect anybody else to?"

She stared at me. Then she whirled, jerked the door open, and ran out.

I sat there for a few minutes, rocking and thinking. It was possible, of course, that Amy had helped Kevin, but peripherally, without knowing all the details. If Kevin was charged, she would probably be charged as an accessory, especially if she continued to insist on her guilt. There was no way around it. If Kevin was guilty, so—to some extent, anyway—was Amy.

I was still sitting in the rocking chair, thinking about Kevin and his would-be rescuer, when the phone rang. I picked it up, expecting McQuaid. It was The Whiz.

"You won't have to feed any more cats," she said. "Dottie's out on bail, as of six P.M. Seventy-five thou."

"I'm glad that's over with," I said. Dottie is well known in the community, has a responsible professional position and has other obligations to fulfill—namely, taking care of her animals. She isn't the kind of suspect a magistrate is likely to remand to jail without bail. But where murder is concerned, you never know.

"So how'd the day go?" Justine asked. "You and Ruby come up with anything?"

I told her. "Complicated, isn't it?" I asked, while she was still chewing over my narrative.

"Rich," she said happily. "Riddled with opportunity, so to speak. You got a theory yet?"

"Hey," I said, "I'm hired to come up with the facts. *You're* hired to come up with a theory. If I give you both the facts *and* the theory, what the hell are you getting paid for? Except to make lousy puns."

Her laugh was careless. "Just thought I'd ask. Won't hurt to have two theories to work on. Suicide *and* murder, for instance, with at least a couple of good suspects for the murder. Locate that New Braunfels greyhound guy. Talk to the parents in San Antonio. Keep flossing—this is a dirty one. And give me a ring tomorrow afternoon so we can see what else you've pulled out."

"Yessir ma'am," I said.

The Whiz tch-tched. "Don't be a grouch. It's not becoming."

I hung up without answering and sat for a long time, rocking and thinking, thinking and rocking. Khat came in through his cat door to inquire about dinner. I warmed up some cooked chicken livers in the microwave and put the stuff in his bowl. He pushed it around with his nose to make sure I hadn't adulterated it with something unmentionable—dry kitty food, for instance. Assured that it was indeed pure liver, he flicked the tip of his charcoal tail and addressed it with gusto.

For myself, I found some leftover mashed potatoes in the fridge and made mashed potato soup—not as good as the real thing, but hot and tasty, with fresh parsley chopped into it and cheddar cheese grated on top. I was sitting at the table, working on my first bowl, when McQuaid showed up.

"There's some soup on the stove," I said.

He picked up a spoon and tasted mine. "Not bad," he said. "Think I will." He found a bowl, ladled it full, and laced it with catsup. He sat down across from me. "Ready to take another look at Meadow Brook?"

"Can we talk first?" I looked away from the catsup with a shudder. "I'd like your professional opinion." I pushed back my empty bowl, folded my arms on the table, and gave him a condensed version of the day's events, down to Amy's confession and Dottie's release.

"Are you asking me whether I think Kevin Scott killed Harwick?" he asked.

"Yes." I frowned. "But I have a problem with that."

"Right." He tipped up his bowl and spooned out the last of the potato-and-catsup (ugh!) soup. "Riddle's hair in the noose. The rope in Riddle's garage."

"So we're back to suicide with a murder frame-up."

"Not necessarily," he said.

"You're saying that Kevin could have planted the hairs in the knot to implicate Dottie Riddle?"

"Kevin, or Amy."

"But why would either of them want to implicate Dottie? She's on the side of the animals."

"I guess you're right," he said, licking soup off his mouth. "The girl couldn't have been in on it, anyway. If she had, she'd have known what kind of rope was used."

"Amy thinks Kevin did it, or she wouldn't be trying to cover for him. And she could be charged as an accessory if she helped compose the note or assisted in the break-in." I scowled. "But I was there when Dottie met Kevin in the animal holding facility. I'd absolutely *swear* he didn't know who she was. And he wouldn't be likely to frame somebody he didn't know."

"So we're back to suicide," McQuaid said.

"Maybe not," I said, pushing my spoon around in the empty bowl. "Maybe this guy in New Braunfels really *did* have something to do with Harwick's death. Or maybe the killer is somebody who isn't on our list of suspects." I was beginning to wonder whether the key to Harwick's death might lie in the frame-up, in those clues that seemed to point so emphatically at Dottie.

"Or maybe," McQuaid said quietly, "Riddle really *is* the killer."

"No," I said.

He leaned across the table. "Look at the facts, China. She had the motive, the means, and the opportunity. Not to mention that there are three strong clues pointing directly at her. That's what the D.A. is going to jump on. In comparison with some of the cases he gets, this one is airtight. Believe me. The chances for a true bill are very damn good."

"When will the next grand jury be empaneled?" Adams County is a small county. Unlike the larger counties, where two grand juries with staggered terms sit continuously, Adams has one grand jury that sits only three days a month.

"The middle of next week," McQuaid said. He stood up. "That gives you at least a week to wrap up your case. How about if we go look at a house?"

"I'm not sure I have time," I said. "Maybe I ought to drive to San Antonio to see Kevin's parents tonight, instead of tomorrow morning. Maybe I ought to call Ruby and—"

McQuaid shook his head, firm. "Look, Bayles. Ruby has things to do. Riddle's already out on bail. The cats have been fed. We've had dinner. Everything else—including Kevin's parents and the greyhounds—will keep until tomorrow." He held out his hand. "Come on."

Just before sunset, the gray clouds lifted like a curtain at the western edge of the sky, and the sun gilded the meadows with pure gold. But it wasn't the sunset view from the master bedroom that finally swayed me, or the discovery that the soil in the garden was rich and thick (hill country topsoil is usually six inches deep, on top of six hundred feet of limestone), or the large, bright kitchen with the window facing east to the rising sun. Or even the window seat in the top floor of the turret, just the right size for Khat and me. It was the little waterfall at the foot of the yard, where the creek splashed noisily over a limestone ledge and into a dark, clear pool beneath, bordered by clumps of maiden hair ferns. Somewhere nearby, I heard a poor-will call into the twilight, slow and haunting. A nighthawk raked swiftly, erratically across the sky. Ruby would have said it was a romantic scene, but it wasn't romance that held me there. It was the sense of having found a habitable wilderness, of standing on the margin between the wild and the tame. In one sense, it was very peaceful. In another, it was very dangerous.

"Well, what do you think?" McQuaid asked, standing a little apart. "Should we or shouldn't we?"

I looked down at the waterfall. A large leopard frog snapped at a bug. "I think we should," I said. "I guess." The frog got the bug on the second try.

He chuckled. "That's what I like. A woman who knows her own mind."

It was *very* dangerous.

CHAPTER 14

Laurel showed up at the shop at eight the next morning, as I had asked, and after giving me a run-down on the meeting at the Smithsonian and the reception of her pepper paper, went out to the garden to put in an hour of light housekeeping. It was too early for annual transplants—we can get a frost up to the last week of March—but it was time to clean off the dead leaves and trim the perennials. The comfrey and rue needed cultivating, and the bronze fennel was already sending up licorice-scented plumes. The parsley was up too, prettying the path with its frilly green lace.

I was giving last-minute instructions to Laurel when I heard the phone ring in the kitchen. I almost let the answering machine take it, but I thought it might be Ruby so I dashed inside. It was Rose Tompkins.

"They're gone." She was breathless, tense, holding herself in. "The letter, the disk, they're both gone. You've got to help me, China. I'm in *trouble*."

"Somebody broke into the locked filing cabinet?" I asked incredulously.

"Yes," she said. "They smashed the glass in the office door and opened it. Then they took a screwdriver or something to the file cabinet. The letter's gone from the computer, too." Her voice went up a notch. Her control was slipping. "Miss Leeds is at the dentist again this morning. She'll kill me when she finds out. And Dr. Castle—Oh, that'll be worse. He'll fire me!" The last words were a wail.

She had called me because I knew about the letter. She had called for reassurance. I did what I could. "Of course he won't fire you, Rose. And Miss Leeds won't kill you, either. You didn't steal that letter. You did everything you could to keep it safe." I paused. "Was the file drawer the only one broken into?"

She sounded calmer. "It was the only one that was locked. But the others were opened and searched."

"Who knew about the letter?"

"Just you. And Miss Leeds and Dr. Castle, of course. Miss Leeds told him when he called in for his messages yesterday morning. He was very upset. The idea that one of our employees—" She paused. "Do you think maybe Kevin was the one who broke in?" Then she answered her own question. "No, he couldn't have. He didn't know that the letter had been found."

Then it hit me, blundering idiot that I was. Of course Kevin knew. I had told Amy yesterday. Kevin could have broken into the office, gone through all the drawers until he located what he was after, and erased the file from the hard disk. There was no way he could know that I had copied the letter into my notebook. Not even Rose knew that.

"Have you called Campus Security about the break-in?" I asked.

"Not yet," she said. "I have to wait for Miss Leeds. She'd be upset if I took it on myself to—" She gasped, surprised. "Dr. Castle! We didn't expect you back until tomorrow." She returned hurriedly to me. "Excuse me. I have to go. Dr. Castle's back."

I hung up, imagining the scene on the other end of the line. No doubt Castle had returned early with the intention of seeing the letter for himself, and now it was gone. I sat staring at the phone, cursing myself for an utter fool. If I hadn't been so intent on shaking Kevin loose, I might have foreseen the consequences of telling Amy about the letter. But it was too late for second thoughts. I had to locate Kevin.

The yellow Camaro was parked in Kevin's driveway, still sporting its bashed-in fender. But it wasn't Kevin who answered the doorbell. It was a young man in his late teens or early twenties. His name, he said, was Lou Keller. He was dark haired and so tall that I had to crane my neck upward to ask him about Kevin.

"Sorry," he said. "He ain't here." His beard was a dark shadow along his jaw, and his T-shirt was half in, half out of his jeans, his belt unbuckled.

"When can I catch him?" I asked. "It's important."

Lou rubbed his jaw. All he lacked was a cigarette in one corner of his full lips and he'd pass for Elvis. Except for the height, of course. He was too tall, too slender.

"Dunno," he said. "Like he wasn't here last night, either."

It made sense. If Kevin had stolen the letter and the computer disk, he was probably on the run. "Is he in the habit of not coming home at night?" I asked.

Lou grinned and an Elvis-dimple appeared in his unshaven cheek. "Lately he doesn't much. He's got a new girl."

It wasn't news to me about Amy, although I still found their relationship a little surprising. She was several years older than Kevin, at a time when age matters a lot, and much more self-assured. But maybe she needed somebody to need her. Kevin certainly seemed needy enough.

"You think I can catch him at her house?"

"Maybe," Lou allowed. He looked at his watch and corrected himself. "Like maybe if you hurry. He's got class in an hour."

"You wouldn't happen to know where she lives, would you?" I was already kicking myself for not finding out that crucial information from Amy herself.

He frowned. "I think her address is around here somewhere," he said. "Like, well, lemme see." When he came back he was carrying a junk-mail envelope with something scrawled on it. "First place I looked," he said, pleased with himself. "Which was the wall by the phone. I copied it for you."

I took the envelope. "Thanks," I said. I turned to go. "Oh, by the way, is that Kevin's Camaro? I saw him driving it last week."

"Nope," he said. "Mine. Like his car's been in the shop and I been lettin' him drive it." He frowned. "Hey, you see him, you tell him the rent was due like yesterday, huh?"

"I'll tell him," I said. "When I see him."

Which might be, like, well, never.

I located the address Lou gave me on a quiet street between the campus and downtown. It was a small, rectangular tract house sided with rusty red cedar shakes, with a dirty gray roof, peeling black shutters, and screens with ragged holes. The garage door was stuck halfway open. There was no doorbell, and nobody answered my knock. I went around to the back and opened the sagging gate. Amy's underpants and bra hung on a clothesline, still wet. I hadn't missed her and Kevin by much.

When I came back down the cracked concrete drive, I was nearly run over by a small girl of five or six on a pink-and-yellow plastic tractor. Her braids stuck out like fat yellow pencils, and her ripped red corduroys showed Shirley Temple knees.

"Beep beep," she said cheerfully.

I knelt down, putting myself at her level. "The person who lives there," I said, pointing to the house. "Do you know where she's gone?"

"Her'n' Kevin went somewhere," the little girl said. Her irises were light blue, ringed with a darker blue.

"You know Kevin?"

"Yeah, he's nice. He brings me gummy bears." She glanced speculatively at my pockets. "You got'ny gummy bears?"

"Sorry," I said. I stood up. "Fresh out of gummy bears."

"Beep beep," the little girl replied, and drove her tractor over my foot.

I had struck out in my effort to locate Kevin. My foot hurt. My heart hurt when I thought of what Amy's involvement in this business was going to mean to Ruby. I got in the car. I had already planned to see Kevin's parents this morning. Now that errand felt a lot more urgent.

I like a lot of things about San Antonio, but the freeway system is not one of them. The city is like a medieval town ringed with a wall—only the wall is a freeway, drawn in a circle around a piece of history: The Alamo, where Travis and Bowie and Crockett and a hundred and eighty-odd men held out against a Mexican army for thirteen days. After Santa Anna took the fort and shot everybody who was still alive, he marched east and massacred three hundred men at Goliad, then pushed on to San Jacinto, where he camped in a bend in the river—probably the only place within a hundred miles where he could be trapped and defeated. All this bloodshed led to independence from Mexico, then to statehood, the Confederacy, and finally the freeway system, stretches of which have been under construction for my lifetime.

Mesquite Drive was northwest, south of De Zavalla Road and not far from UTSA campus, a neighborhood of winding streets, wide lawns, and tidy two-story split-levels with brick facing and wrought-iron fancywork on the windows and doors. Mailboxes built to resemble ships or flower baskets or little houses studded the curbs, like rivals in a clever-mailbox contest. It had been a mild winter and the Saint Augustine was a thick green carpet, although I suspected it was pumped up with Chem-Lawn.

The property at 204 Mesquite sported a mailbox shaped like a red barn with a black and white cow painted on one side and a pink pig on the other, under a banner that read "The Scotts." The large live oak in the middle of the lawn was beginning to shed last year's leaves onto the clipped turf. In this part of Texas, live oak leaves hang tight until early spring, when they finally turn brown and are ejected by the new leaves, light green and shiny. In the morning sunshine, the tree glittered as if it were hung with bits of green foil.

As I got out of the car and started up the drive, a man in a yellow polo shirt, yellow-and-brown-checked polyester slacks, and yellow canvas shoes came out of the front door. He saw me at the foot of the drive and called, "Mind bringing the paper with you?"

I scooped up the *Express-News* and carried it to him. "I was sorry to see the old *Light* fold," he said, taking it. "Better to have two papers. That way, you get both sides." He sighed. "But these days, I guess two papers are more than anybody can hope for."

The man was probably in his mid-sixties, older than I had expected, given that Kevin was only nineteen or twenty. He had the look of a happily retired man on his way to a morning tee time. His white hair was thin on top, showing a freckled scalp, and his face was round and jolly, a summer Santa. I looked for a resemblance to thin, nervous Kevin and could see none.

"Charles Scott?" I asked.

"You got it," the man said cheerfully. He tucked the newspaper under his arm. "And you are . . . ?"

"China Bayles," I said, handing him Justine's card with my name and phone number written in the corner.

"Interesting name, China," he mused, looking at the card. "Don't believe I ever heard it before." His shrewd glance assessed my gray skirt, white blouse, navy blazer, low-heeled navy pumps. I wouldn't wow 'em on Fifth Avenue, but I looked professional. "You a lawyer?"

I nodded. I had already decided what I was going to tell him. "Ms. Wyzinski has asked me to do a background check on a former neighbor of yours, a Dr. Miles Harwick. I wonder if you could give me some information."

Charles Scott's jolly face darkened and spots of color appeared along his jaws. "Why are you asking?"

I gave him a level glance. I've done inquiries that called for an elaborate cover story, and those where I've come straight out with it. Instinct told me that this was a good time for the truth—some of it, anyway. I wanted to hold off mentioning Kevin as long as I could.

"Dr. Harwick was found hanging in his office at Central Texas State University last week," I said. "His death raises some questions. I'm hoping you might be able to help."

I was surprised by his reaction. He squeezed his eyes shut briefly, and when he opened them again, they held an unmistakable look of exaltation. He clenched his fist and punched the air with a jubilant gesture.

"Sonofabitch," he shouted. "Son-of-a-bitch!" He wheeled, strode to the front door, and smacked it open with the flat of his hand. "Annie," he yelled. "Annie! Get down here! You gotta hear this!" He turned to me, opening the door wide.

"Come on in, Ms. Bayles," he said cordially. "You just come on *in.*"

Perplexed, I followed Charles Scott down the hall toward the back of the house. He didn't exactly skip, but there was an almost gleeful jauntiness in his walk. The hall opened into a sunny family room that was divided by a counter from a generous kitchen, its ceiling hung with copper-bottomed pans, braids of garlic and ropes of peppers, and various cooking implements, most of them decorative, all of them expensive. There was a Cuisinart on the counter and a charcoal cooktop built into the Jenn-Air range, under the arch of a brick hearth that concealed an exhaust hood. He motioned me to a stool at the counter and headed for the coffee maker, which was recessed under a cupboard.

"Hold off on the details until my wife gets here," he instructed, with the air of a man who is used to giving orders. "Decaf okay?"

"Fine," I said, sitting down on the stool.

Anne Scott came in as I was taking my first sip. She was younger than her husband by perhaps ten years, a plump but attractive woman made more attractive with judicious makeup, her clear olive complexion and dark eyes set off by the red sweats she was wearing. I couldn't see any resemblance to Kevin there, either.

"Well?" She stood in the doorway, raised brows quizzical. Her dark curly hair was damp, as if she'd just showered. "What's all the shouting about? I thought you had a ten-thirty tee time, Charlie."

Scott went to his wife and put both arms around her. "Harwick's dead, Annie." Exuberance charged his voice. He might have been announcing that they had won the lottery. "Bastard hung himself."

"Oh!" Anne Scott gave a long, low cry—almost, I thought, a cry of triumph—and buried her face against her husband's shirt. They stood holding on to one another as if the earth were rocking under their feet. I stared at them. Whatever response I might have expected to the announcement of Harwick's death, this wasn't it. They reminded me of the way a victim's relatives sometimes act in the courtroom after the jury brings in a guilty verdict.

Charles Scott was the first to break the embrace. "Let's hear the story, huh?" he asked softly. He smoothed his wife's hair, kissed her forehead, stepped back. "I'll get you some coffee." Over his shoulder, he added, "This is China Bayles. She's with some lawyer's office here in town. She's the one who told me."

Anne Scott went into the family room and sat down in a black-and-white upholstered chair on one side of a brick fireplace. Following her, I carried my mug to the white sofa that faced the fireplace and sat down. The fireplace was hung with brass-plated fire implements; beside it a stack of cedar was ready for the next fire. The mantel was a gallery of family photos.

Anne Scott leaned forward eagerly. "He's *really* dead?" Her dark eyes glittered and her voice was hoarse. "This isn't some kind of joke?"

"He died last Wednesday evening, in his office at CTSU," I said.

"He hanged himself?" The intensity of her joy, juxtaposed to the starkness of her words, was startling. "He actually *hanged* himself?"

"He died by hanging," I said carefully. If Kevin's mother and father could be so openly, so unabashedly elated by Harwick's death, how had Kevin felt? "I'm here because I understand that he was once your neighbor."

"He lived next door, but he was no neighbor," Charles Scott said, making an emphatic distinction. He put two mugs of coffee on the coffee table and sat on the arm of his wife's chair, his left hand protectively on her shoulder.

"It's a good thing he moved," Anne Scott said thinly. She stopped talking and pressed her lips together tight. Her chin quivered while she struggled to get control of her voice. After a moment she swallowed and went on. "If he hadn't, if we'd had to look at him day after day, I really think Charlie would have killed him. Or I would have." She felt upward to her right shoulder for her husband's hand. "Or both of us. Without a shred of remorse."

Charles Scott sucked in a ragged breath. "You bet your ass I'd've killed him," he growled. "And hanging is exactly how I'd've done it, too. What I want to know is why it took the bastard so long to get around to it."

I put my cup down on the coffee table. "Mr. and Mrs. Scott," I said quietly, "it seems clear that Dr. Harwick was the source of some terrible unhappiness for you. Our discussion might be less painful if you would simply tell me if this is true and briefly describe what happened. I cannot promise to hold your information in confidence, but I can promise not to reveal it unless it becomes germane to the issues." I hadn't said what issues, but I honestly didn't think they cared.

I was right. Anne Scott threw back her head and laughed, showing several gold-crowned molars. It was not a pretty laugh. "Go ahead," she said fiercely. "Tell as many people as you like. Put it in the newspaper if you want. Tell the whole *world* what that sadist did!"

I stared at her. Sadist? That had been Amy's term.

Charles Scott squeezed his wife's hand once more, released it, then leaned forward to pick up his coffee. "It doesn't take long to tell," he said. His voice was carefully flat, expressionless, but the hand that held the coffee mug was shaking so hard that he spilled coffee on his yellow-and-brown plaid slacks. He didn't notice. "Miles Harwick was a child molester."

Anne Scott made a small, choked noise and turned her head to the left, covering her mouth with her left hand. Charles Scott gave up trying to drink his coffee and set the mug on the table, hard, the contents sloshing over.

"Harwick abused our youngest son, Tad," he said. "The boy was eight when it started, and it went on for about six months."

Anne Scott turned toward me again. Her eyes were blazing, her voice thick with outrage and pain. "The man was our friend. We invited him into our home. We even let Tad stay with him weekends when we were gone! We had no idea what kind of horrible person he was!"

Scott's face was a taut mask. "I was a civil engineer before I retired," he said in a low voice. "The last couple of years, I had a big job going on the West Coast. It seemed like a good time for Annie and me to get in some long weekends. The two other kids—our daughter and our son—were busy with their friends. Harwick was always around. He told us he'd like to have Tad stay with him."

Anne Scott was beginning to cry softly. "That's what made it so bad," she said, choking out the words. "If I'd just stayed home, if I'd paid more attention to what was going on—"

Her husband pulled her against him, resting his cheek against her hair. "Don't, Annie," he whispered. "It's been over for a long time. You can't keep on raking yourself over the coals." Still holding her, he said to me, "We didn't find out what was going on until a couple of weeks after Harwick moved. Tad told us."

"I see," I said.

"He was afraid Harwick would kill him if he told," Mrs. Scott broke out. "He was afraid *we* might be killed. The whole family!"

"Harwick was too yellow for that." Her husband's voice was disgusted. "But Tad was just a kid. He couldn't know that the bastard was full of bluff.''

I looked at them. "After Tad told you, what did you do?"

"We took the boy to a therapist," Charles Scott said. His mouth was twisted into a bitter smile, showing chalky teeth stained with nicotine. "Shrinks know everything, don't they? This one did. My fault. I shouldn't have listened. I should have trusted Tad. I should have done what was right and screw the rest of it.''

"No, Charlie," Anne Scott said, her voice softening. She put her hand on her husband's knee. "It wasn't your fault." She took up the story. "The therapist—Dr. Rupert—advised us not to press charges. He said it was Tad's word against Harwick's, and that the trial would be torture for Tad. For all of us. He thought it would be better to work out Tad's problems in therapy, rather than the courts." She shook her head. The tears were coming, unchecked. She was almost incoherent. "I think Dr. Rupert thought Tad was lying. He was always an imaginative boy, making up stories about everything. Anyway, Dr. Rupert kept saying he was getting better.''

Charlie Scott blinked and pressed his wife's shoulder, his mouth quivering. "But he wasn't. He was getting more and more depressed. His schoolwork went to pieces. He gave up his music, tennis, friends. A year after Harwick left, he committed suicide.''

My stomach tightened. "How?" I asked, but I already knew the answer.

Anne Scott turned her face into her husband's yellow shirt. "He hanged himself," she whispered. Her voice was raw anguish. "From the branch above his treehouse. Nine years ago last Wednesday, on his birthday.''

I pulled in my breath. Last Wednesday was the day Miles Harwick had died. "I'm . . . sorry," I said inadequately. "I'm so . . . terribly sorry.''

Charles Scott's round face was gray. "If we'd gone to court, maybe Tad would've felt better. Maybe he thought we didn't believe him.''

"It was so hard on the other children," Anne Scott said. Her voice broke. "Kevin especially. He was just a year older than Tad. The two boys were so close."

I started to speak, then sat back. There wasn't any point in asking about Kevin. I had heard more than enough to know why he would want to kill Miles Harwick, and why he had to break into the biology department and steal that incriminating blackmail letter. The only mystery left involved the clues pointing to Dottie—her hair and the rope. But Anne Scott was already on her feet.

"Let me show you their pictures," she said. She stepped to the fireplace and took down a silver frame, then another. She handed the first to me. "This was taken at Rockport on a fishing trip," she said. Her voice trembled slightly. "Just look at them. Aren't they a pair?"

The photo showed two boys standing on a dock in typical trophy pose. The smaller—a slight, dark-haired, dark-skinned boy with sharply tilted Oriental eyes and a proud smile—was holding up one end of a string of large brown flounders. The taller boy was holding the other end. The taller boy was Kevin. The photographer had caught the two boys looking at each other, rather than the camera. It was clear from their faces that they shared a special secret, a special love.

"Yes, I see," I said slowly, puzzled by the younger boy's obviously Oriental features.

"Kevin's a student at UT in Austin," Mrs. Scott said. "He's working on his biology degree." She held out the other photo. "And this is Tad with his sister, taken just before his piano recital. He was quite a musician, very talented." Her voice choked. "We were *all* proud of him."

I looked at the photo. Tad, wearing white shirt, tie, and dark suit, was standing beside a grand piano. Behind him, both hands on his shoulders, stood a teenage girl, quite tall, her head a mop of curly red hair, her smile achingly familiar.

Ruby's hair. Ruby's smile.

The girl was Amy.

CHAPTER 15

I stared at the photo, uncomprehending. "Amy Roth is your daughter?"

"You know our Amy?" Charles Scott asked, frowning.

I handed the photo back, keeping my face hidden. I had just realized that Amy's reason for wanting Harwick dead was exactly as powerful as Kevin's, and the knowledge was like an exploding missile in my stomach. "I've . . . met her," I said.

Anne Scott returned the photos to the mantel, arranging them affectionately. "You're probably wondering about the last names," she said. "Roth was my first husband's name, Ellis Roth. He and I adopted Amy when she was a tiny baby, a newborn, really. He died when she was eight. Charlie and I got married two years later, and we adopted the boys. Amy always felt close to Ellis and wanted to keep his name." She smiled slightly. "Amy's like that. She *cares*—passionately. A couple of years ago she decided to find her birth mother. I didn't think it was such a good idea, but she wanted to do it so badly that I had to support her. Anyway, when Amy decides to do something, there's absolutely no stopping her."

191

Charles Scott stood up. "I'm not sure I understand," he said. His voice had gone scratchy, like an antique thirty-three r.p.m. record, and his frown was colored with something— alarm? Apprehension? "How did you happen to meet our daughter, Ms. Bayles? She's not mixed up in this . . . in Harwick's . . . is she?" He stopped and started over. "How *did* you meet her?"

I looked at him, realizing that the same thing had occurred to him that had occurred to me. What he couldn't have guessed, and what I wasn't ready to tell him, was that Amy and her brother Kevin were both in this—together.

I extricated myself from the Scotts, got back in my Datsun, and headed for I-35. I had plenty to think about. The outline of events as I knew it, illuminated by what I had just learned from Kevin's and Amy's adoptive parents, seemed incontestably clear.

At some point in the past year, motivated by hatred and their desire to avenge their brother's suicide, Amy and Kevin had tracked Miles Harwick to CTSU. At the beginning of the spring semester, Kevin—allowing his parents to assume that he was still going to school in Austin—had gotten a job in Harwick's animal holding facility. Kevin or Amy or both must have planned all along to kill Harwick on Tad's birthday, which was also the anniversary of his death. In the meantime, their blackmail letter was an inspired way of putting him on notice, an exquisite means of drawing out his agony. And the demonstrations Amy organized in the mall—especially the signs, like "Hang Harwick Instead"—must have been meant as a constant torture, a continual reminder to him of their threat.

Had Harwick recognized Kevin and Amy as Tad's brother and sister? If he had, of course, there was very little he could do: to reveal their identities, to take their blackmail letter to the police, would only trigger their revelations of his culpability. He couldn't be criminally prosecuted because the only witness to his crime was dead. But he had plenty to lose if the story got into the newspapers. For the last several weeks of his life, he must have felt tortured, vulnerable, afraid—exactly like the animals in his experiments.

Had he been driven to suicide by his fears? Or had Kevin and Amy killed him? I was no closer to an answer to that central question, although the break-in at the biology office now made sense. Even if they had played no active role in Harwick's death, they would be afraid that the letter would implicate them. When I told Amy that the letter had been found where it was, they decided to steal it. The only thing I still couldn't account for, either way, was the presence of Dottie's hair in the noose and the hangman's rope in her garage.

I glanced at my watch. It was nearly eleven-thirty and Pecan Springs and lunch was only forty-five minutes away. But I needed to check in with Justine and Ruby, who was in New Braunfels looking for an elusive man with a greyhound who had something on Harwick. At the thought of Ruby and the pain that lay ahead for her, my stomach clenched like a fist. To lose a daughter for nearly twenty-five years, find her, and lose her again in this terrible way was too awful to even think about.

I took the Thousand Oaks exit, found a 7-Eleven, and bought a plastic-wrapped poor boy stuffed with something that was supposed to be turkey, swiss, and tomato. It tasted like damp Styrofoam seasoned with yellow paste. I used the public phone out front to call the shop, plugging one ear so I could hear over the din of the motorcycles and the eighteen-wheelers on the highway.

Laurel answered and gave me a quick run-down on the morning. Thyme and Seasons had been so busy that she had called her sister to handle the Cave. I was glad I could count on Laurel. I couldn't imagine a more capable person to handle the shop while I was pinning a murder on Ruby's daughter. The thought was like a bullet.

"Ruby called a couple of minutes ago," Laurel said. "She said to tell you that she's located the guy with the greyhound, whatever that means. She's supposed to meet him at his house, which is also his office or his business or something, at twelve-fifteen. She wants you to be there. She says she thinks the guy seriously wants to talk."

"I suppose I can make it," I said unenthusiastically. Wanting to talk could mean that the guy actually knew something. Or that he was lonely and had nothing better to do. Joining Ruby for a dead-end conversation would only delay my getting back to Pecan Springs and setting in motion the processes that would bring the case to its inevitable sad conclusion. On the other hand, I had assigned her to track the guy. There'd be heartache enough for her as this thing wound down—and for me, too. One hour more or less wouldn't make much difference in the grand scheme of things. "Did she give you an address?" I asked.

I took down the information Laurel gave me. "Any other calls?"

"Yes, two," Laurel said. "Somebody named Beulah Bracewell wants you to call her at work."

"Beulah?" I was curious. "What did she want?"

"Didn't say, but here's her number," Laurel said, and gave it to me. "And Mike called to tell you that he's got the lease and wants you to sign it. He'll bring it to dinner." She paused significantly. "You actually found a house?"

"Yeah," I said. "A big Victorian, off Limekiln Road." I was looking through my purse for Justine's phone number. She was next on my list of phone calls.

"Hell," Laurel said. "That means I just lost twenty dollars."

Having found Justine's card, I cleverly dropped it in a puddle from a spilled Coke can. "Twenty dollars?" I picked the card up by one corner and flapped it to get the Coke off it.

"Yeah. I bet Ruby twenty that you'd never say yes to Mike. I figured that the two of you were like Nancy Drew and Ned What's-his-name. You'd just go on forever, never getting close enough to do more than kiss."

"I didn't say yes to McQuaid," I said, irritable. "I said yes to a place to live so I can expand the shop so we won't fall all over one another trying to handle hordes of customers."

Laurel gave a short laugh. "China, you are so full of shit. What are you afraid of? And it's still going to cost me twenty dollars, whatever you said yes to."

"It's your own fault," I said heartlessly. "Didn't your mother ever tell you not to bet?"

"If you don't hurry," Laurel said, "you'll be late for lunch."

I came up empty on the other two phone calls. The Whiz was in a pretrial hearing and wouldn't be available until midafternoon. Beulah's line was busy. I wasn't in any mood to wait. I'd call her from New Braunfels.

Like Pecan Springs, New Braunfels was founded by Germans, about six thousand of them, in the eighteen-forties. The settlement beside the Comal Springs was established by Prince Carl zu Solms-Braunfels, who named the place after his hometown. The local Indians—Lipon, Tonkawa, Karankawa, and Waco—were not too pleased to see the first oxcart-load of settlers show up on Good Friday, 1845. They made things pretty miserable for a while, but the Germans persevered. Their tradition still dominates the community, as you can see from the newspaper (the *Herald-Zeitung*), the names of local establishments (the Faust Hotel, Krause's Cafe, and the Schlitterbahn, a made-up German word that means "slippery road" and refers to the seventeen waterslides and seven inner-tube chutes in the water park). And the food. Wursts of every kind abound, and sauerkraut and sauerbraten and strudel and schnapps.

The address I was looking for was off Seguin, on a street of shops and small businesses housed in remodeled, gentrified houses, some of which were also residences. The place turned out to be an office with a large wood-framed sign on the lawn that said "Jim Long Associates, MSA, CPA, CFE. Business * Individual * Tax Planning & Tax Returns * Accounting & Auditing."

Ruby's Honda was parked across the street, and Ruby was sitting in it. When she saw me pull up, she got out of her car and came to my window. She was wearing a thirties costume: narrow black skirt that came almost to her ankles, long-sleeved hip-length white blouse with several strands of pearls, and black floppy-brimmed straw hat with a huge orange rose on it. The hair that showed under the hat was such a vibrant copper that it looked as if she had put on her hat to snuff out a blazing fire.

I opened the door and got out, blinking. "What have you done to your hair?"

She jammed her hat down on her head. "Is something wrong with it?"

"It's *very* red." At the look on her face, I repented. "But on you, very red is good. Gives you a little extra whoomf." As if she needed it.

"I hennaed it last night," she said. "With paprika and cinnamon."

"You're kidding."

"Scout's honor." She held up three fingers.

I stood on tiptoes to sniff. "You're right. Definitely cinnamon. You smell like apple pie."

"Next time I'm going to try nutmeg and allspice." She

...rned to glance over her shoulder. "I'm glad you got here," ...he added. "He says he's got something important to say. But ...get the feeling he's afraid to incriminate himself. I think he ...ants us to help him cut a deal."

"He who?" Ruby has a way of beginning in the middle, ...aving me fishing for loose ends.

"Jim Long. He used to work in the grant accounting office ...t CTSU." She motioned with her head. "Come on. He knows ...e're here. I saw him peeking out the window a minute ago."

I locked the car. "Hold on a sec," I said. I've always hated ...oing into an interview blind. "Give me some background."

"I phoned my friend who knows about greyhounds," Ruby ...aid patiently. "When I mentioned New Braunfels, she knew ...ght away who I was looking for. The guy adopted two grey-...ounds through their placement program—dogs retired from ...e racetrack."

"Good work," I said. "V.I. Warshawski would be proud ...f you. So you phoned Jim Long."

She nodded. "I said I was working for Justine Wyzinski on ...ehalf of Dr. Dorothy Riddle, digging up background infor-...ation regarding the unfortunate demise of Dr. Miles Harwick ...lah blah. I said it had come to our attention that he and Dr. ...arwick had dealings some years ago blah blah and did he ...ave any ideas regarding Dr. Harwick's passing."

The blind at the front window twitched. Someone was look-...g out. "And Long said?"

"He said he'd been waiting for somebody to get in touch ...ith him and he didn't know why it hadn't happened sooner. ...e sounded like he had a cork in him and he was about ready ... pop." She looked down at me, squinting. Even in her flats, ...uby is head and shoulders above me. "But he said he ...ouldn't talk to us without getting something in return. Like ...aybe he was angling for immunity."

"Only the D.A. can give him that," I said. "Anyway, we

don't know whether he's actually got anything worth trading.'
I didn't want to tell her that we were beating a dead horse
that Harwick's murder had already been solved, and that he
long-lost daughter and her daughter's stepbrother were impli
cated. I straightened up. "But we won't know whether he'
got anything important or not until we've talked to him. Let'
go hear what he has to say."

The front door displayed a "Welcome—Come In" sign. I
opened onto a small reception area that was supposed to loo
like a garden room, with a white tile floor, green rugs, an
green-and-white bamboo wallcovering. The cushions on th
white wicker chairs and loveseat were covered with a match
ing bamboo print, and large potted plants were placed strate
gically in the corners and on the tables. A receptionist's des
was empty, but the wall behind it was crowded with frame
diplomas and numerous certificates attesting to the competenc
and professional training of James L. Long and two associate
I noticed that the business had earned a Chamber of Com
merce citation for assisting with the Christmas Fund Drive an
a Friends of the River certificate for picking up litter along th
Comal River. Jim Long was obviously an upstanding citize
of the New Braunfels community.

The door to my right was open, and I could see a man i
a brown sports jacket and white shirt hunched over a compute
printout. When he saw us, he stood up, straightened his ti
and came to the office door.

"Hi," he said, as if he were surprised. "Didn't see yo
come up the walk." He stepped forward and thrust out hi
hand with a heartiness that barely disguised the underlyin
anxiety. "Name's Jim Long. Something I can help you ladie
with?"

"I'm the one who called, Mr. Long," Ruby said. "Abo
Miles Harwick." She introduced herself and me.

"Oh, yeah, sure," he said. Studiedly casual, he went to th

front door, flipped the lock, and switched the sign to the "Closed for Lunch" side. "No point in being interrupted by walk-ins," he said, and led us into his office. "Have a seat." He gestured at two straight chairs in front of his desk and closed the office door, too. Whatever Jim Long had to say, he didn't want it overheard.

The waiting-area garden theme was only minimally extended to the small office we had entered: a faded jade plant sat on a stand in the corner, its leaves pale green and shriveled. The desk was empty except for the computer printout, an engraved citation from the Lion's Club for "Honesty and Integrity," and a gold-framed studio photograph of a blond, sweet-faced woman and three small girls in white dresses, triplets from the look of them, posed in front of a drape with a gold cross on it. Beside the desk was a computer and a calculator and a plaster-of-Paris plaque bearing the impression of three small hands. The file cabinet in the corner was topped with a papier-mâché sculpture painted in awful shades of grape and green, obviously the earnest work of the small hands in the plaque, and several children's drawings were taped to the wall. Jim Long was the most family-oriented accountant I'd ever met.

Long himself was neat and plain, with the exception of the tie. Burnt orange is a color that only Texas Exes wear without embarrassment. Given the rest of him, I guessed that Long wore it because it was good for business. His brown hair, clipped short above the ears and combed back with precision, matched his mustache, and his brown eyes were wary behind gold-framed glasses. His brown jacket concealed his slightness, but even so his shoulders were sloping and his chest concave. It was the shape of a man who hunched over numbers all day long and whose idea of exercise was a Saturday at the Schlitterbahn with the wife and kids. His pained expression— tight mouth, knotted jaw, furrowed forehead—suggested a

chronic distress somewhere in his innards. I knew I was right
when he opened a drawer, took out a role of antacid tablets,
and put one in his mouth. He leaned back carefully and put
his hands flat on the desk. He didn't relax.

"Ms. Wilcox and I are conducting an investigation," I said,
"on behalf of the woman who has been charged with the death
of Miles Harwick. Are you familiar with the circumstances?"

"I read about it in the *Herald-Zeitung*," he said. "But I
don't understand the connection between Harwick and the
Riddle woman. What did she have to do with it?"

Ruby looked at him from under the brim of her black hat.
"We don't believe she had anything to do with it," she said
firmly. "You have been mentioned, however, as having certain
information about Dr. Harwick. If that is the case, you might
be able to help us clear Dr. Riddle." She glanced pointedly
at the Lion's Club award for honesty and integrity. "I'm sure
a man of your standing wouldn't allow an innocent woman to
be convicted for a murder she didn't commit." *Zing*.

I gave Ruby an approving glance. I couldn't have put it
better myself.

Long shifted uncomfortably. "Well, I don't know about *information*, exactly," he said, speaking in the wary tone he
might have used if we were discussing an IRS audit. "There's
a slight problem. You see, I'm worried about . . . That is
we . . ." His tongue darted out and licked the lower edge of
his mustache. "Excuse me," he muttered, and got up and
opened the window behind him. Then he must have remembered that he wanted privacy. He closed it again.

When he sat down again, I felt I needed to help things
along. "If there is a problem with your speaking out," I said
delicately, "we might be able to intercede on your behalf with
the district attorney." I couldn't imagine what he was con-
cealing, but I was betting that it wasn't as immoral or as illegal
as he imagined.

"Well, I don't know if that's what I . . ." His forehead furrowed and he reached for another antacid. "But maybe I do," he said. "I've been thinking a lot, ever since I read in the paper about . . ." His voice trailed off.

I waited. After a minute I said, reassuringly, "I can't anticipate the prosecution's decision in this matter, of course, but I can tell you that crimes of lesser significance are often overlooked in order to resolve more heinous crimes." Lawyer's gobbledygook. I hate to talk that way, but some people feel a certain reassurance when they hear polysyllabic words and long sentences. It sounds as if there may indeed be order and justice in the land, and the speaker knows where to locate it.

"I think she's saying," Ruby translated helpfully, "that we might be able to help you cut a deal."

Long winced. "Well, I suppose I really ought to . . ." His glance went to the photograph on his desk and clung to it, as if it were a lifeline and he were a drowning man. "But I can't do that until I know that . . ."

Didn't *anybody* in this case finish their sentences? "Mr. Long," I said crisply, "I am afraid that it is not possible to assess the value of your information before we know what it is."

"She means," Ruby interpreted, "that nobody's going to make a deal until they hear what you have to offer."

It was the old one-two punch. But it was apparently what Long needed. He straightened his shoulders and firmed his jaw, as if he were preparing to finish almost all his sentences. "I guess I'd better explain the situation to you," he said. "But I *will* need your guarantee of confidentiality."

I shook my head. "I'm sorry," I said. "We are not in a position to give that guarantee. However, we will attempt to ensure that your interests are protected, insofar as we are able." Whatever he was hiding, it couldn't be *that* bad. He was an accountant—had he cheated Harwick out of some money? Had he and Harwick been involved in a scheme to cheat somebody else out of some money? Had there been some sort of tax fraud?

He pushed his glasses up on his forehead, rubbed his eyes, and pulled his glasses down again. His lips were pressed tight together.

"In other words," Ruby said gently, "you'll just have to trust us to do what we can for you." Her voice became softer, more persuasive. "You *do* need to get this matter resolved, Mr. Long. You said on the phone that you've been expecting someone to call. Hasn't this difficult situation gone on quite long enough? It must be very painful for you." Her eyes lingered on the photograph. "And for those you love. We found you. Others will, too. They might not be quite as sympathetic."

Long leaned on his elbows and lifted his clasped hands, making a prayerful tent of his fingers in front of his face and running his forefingers down his nose, his mouth, his chin, and back up again. After making that tour several times with his eyes shut, he opened them and said, "Okay. I'll come clean." He dropped his hands and sat back. "Harwick and I were involved in an embezzlement scheme."

"When?" I asked.

"Ten years ago," he said. "When I was at CTSU. I used my part of the money to set up this business."

"If embezzlement is all there is to it," I said, "I think the D.A. will be interested in a deal."

Ruby gave me an eyebrows-cocked look, and I gave it back. I'd tell her later that I could speak with such confidence because the statute of limitations had run out. The Code of Criminal Procedure lumps embezzlement with theft. If you are a public servant and you steal government property, they've got ten years to catch you. After that, according to Article 12.01, you're in the clear. Depending on the exact date of the crime,

Long was probably already home free. But even if he could still be prosecuted, the D.A. was likely to make a deal.

"That's all there is to it," Long said. "I had nothing to do with Harwick's death." His mouth quivered and his voice went up a notch. "You *do* believe me, don't you?"

"Yes," I said, and fielded another glance from Ruby. This time I didn't return it. I could believe Long because I knew who actually *did* kill Harwick.

"That's good," he said, obviously relieved. "I tell you, I'll be glad to get this off my chest. Ever since it happened, I've walked around knowing that there was a land mine out there and that someday it was going to blow up in my face. It would ruin my family." His glance went back to the photograph. "I wasn't even married at the time."

"I understand," I said, wondering what the hell we were talking about. "Can you be specific about the embezzlement?"

He picked up a pencil and began to tap it on the desk. "I was working in the accounting office. My job involved setting up grant accounts, establishing the appropriate procedures for monies to be moved in and out of the accounts, and monitoring the process until the monies were fully expended for the purpose for which they were granted."

Talk about gobbledygook. I guess every profession has its own brand.   •

Ruby looked confused. "This has something to do with Dr. Harwick?"

"Yes," Long said. He sat back and used the pencil to tap his teeth. "Dr. Harwick was hired in September of that year. He brought a grant with him from a San Antonio company called Cosmetech, not a large grant, more on the order of start-up money. He was doing animal experiments to measure the toxicity of cosmetics, something like that."

Once he got started on his story, Long kept at it in a well-organized fashion, explaining how the grant account was set up, how requests for expenditures—for equipment, supplies, and salaries—were made, and how the purchases were paid for. "It's all very orderly, you see," he said, still tapping. "A very good system."

"But any system can be manipulated," I remarked, "by a person who knows how to use it."

"Yeah." He tossed the pencil on the desk and sat up. "There wasn't any monkey business with the original grant. That went by the book. It was a grant that came the next spring. A gift, actually."

Something clicked. "For the lab?" I asked.

He looked at me. "You know about that?"

"I know that the company that sponsored Harwick's research promised to give the university a small amount to set up an animal research unit. But Revlon bought the company out, and Revlon had a research link with a different university. So the money went there instead."

Long shook his head. "No, it didn't. That was the story we floated. The money came to CTSU just *before* the buyout. And it wasn't a small amount, either. It was a quarter of a million dollars."

I long ago schooled myself not to be surprised by anything a client told me, but I'm out of practice, and anyway, Long wasn't a client. I whistled under my breath.

The orange rose on Ruby's hat bobbed excitedly. "A quarter of a million!" she exclaimed. "That kind of money ought to build a pretty nice lab."

"It didn't, though," I said, thoughtful. "It didn't build any lab at all. What happened?"

Long looked even more uncomfortable. He cleared his throat. "What happened," he said, "is that I set up an account and arranged the payout procedure as I normally would. But the money didn't go for expenses in the normal way. Over a period of eleven months, it went into the computerized bank deposit system.''

"Which is?" I prompted.

"Which is the direct-pay system normally used to deposit a paycheck into an employee's bank account. I'm sure they've changed the procedure by now because it was too easy to manipulate. But back then, once the thing was set up, it was practically invisible. The computer just kept on cutting checks until the money in the account was exhausted. And since I created the account after the fiscal year began and closed it out just before the fiscal year ended, it didn't show up in the normal end-of-year audit of deposit accounts.''

"Nobody in your office kept an eye on the system?"

"There was nobody between me and the computer—during the fiscal year, anyway. End of year, that was a different story. If the state auditors had happened to drop in during this time, of course, they might have stumbled onto it. But that was a slim chance. I could have cut off the deposits when I learned they were coming.''

I'd heard of some computer scams in my time, but this one sounded more creative—and less risky—than most. "Not a bad setup," I said.

He nodded. "The biggest problem was actually at the other end. Pecan Springs is a small town. If we used our bank accounts, somebody at the bank might question why the university was putting this money into our accounts, on top of our regular paychecks. So we set up a fictitious company—Blue Star Scientific Supply Company—with a P.O. box address in Houston. Naturally, we used a Houston bank.''

I did a quick calculation. "So you were dumping nearly twenty-three thousand a month into the Blue Star account." I looked at him. "From there, I presume, it came back to you?"

He colored swiftly and shook his head. "I didn't get the bulk of it. All I got was ten percent." The red spread along his jaw and his mouth took on a bitter twist. "Enough to incriminate me. Enough to buy my silence. Enough to allow me to start my own accounting office. But not enough to make it worth the risk." His eyes were pulled back to the photograph. "At least not now. I've got too much to lose. I'm afraid that if Claire found out, she'd leave me and take the kids."

Ruby frowned. "If the lab never got built, why didn't the company that gave the money make a fuss about it? Why didn't they ask whatever happened to this great project they funded?"

"That was the beauty of it," Long said. "Cosmetech's officers were sacked after the buyout, so the company lost its corporate memory. You know what happens to the internal accounting systems when a business changes hands—it's like Hurricane Andrew. Everything's wiped out. Nobody knows anything. Anyway, the grant to CTSU was small change, as far as Revlon was concerned. The officers who took over, if they ever heard about it, would naturally assume that the grant was an outright gift. No strings attached, no follow-up necessary."

"So you took your twenty-five thousand," I said, summing up, "and Harwick pocketed the rest." Two hundred twenty-five thousand. Not a bad piece of small change.

He shook his head. "No. The two-twenty-five got split fifty-fifty. Between the two of them."

"The *two* of them?" Ruby asked, confused. "Harwick and—who?"

He looked from one of us to the other. "Didn't I say? The third party to this transaction was the department chairman. Frank Castle."

I stared at him, nonplussed. "But I thought Castle was really gung-ho on his animal research unit, even back then. Why would he steal the money that was supposed to build the lab? And for that matter, why would Harwick do it?"

Long shook his head. "I can tell you why *I* did it and how it got done," he said. "But Castle will have to tell you the rest." He reached into his pocket for a handkerchief, folded it, and wiped his shiny forehead. "Harwick can't, of course."

"You were seen at Harwick's house," I said. "What was your continuing connection with him?"

He sighed. "Harwick and Castle controlled the Blue Star account. We agreed that we'd leave the money there and take it out a little at a time, rather than calling attention to ourselves with a sudden windfall. I had to push Harwick to get my share. I haven't seen Castle since we set up the original plan. But I heard from him just a few days ago. He phoned me."

My antennae went up. "What did he say?"

Long took off his glasses again and wearily rubbed his eyes. "He was terribly nervous. It had something to do with a letter, although he wasn't clear on the details." The corner of his eyelid twitched. "It was a . . . well, a blackmail letter. Harwick apparently received it, but not Castle. He wanted to know if I had gotten one. I told him no."

I leaned forward. "What did the letter say?"

"I didn't see it. But Castle said that somebody had found out about the embezzlement. He said the letter threatened to take the story to the newspaper if Harwick didn't lay off some experiment he was doing." He put his glasses back on and pushed them up on the bridge of his nose. His eyelid was still twitching.

"I see," I said. When Harwick got the blackmail letter, he must have thought first of the embezzlement—not of Tad. He had gone running to Castle with the letter. At the time, neither Harwick or Castle apparently had any idea who wrote it. But Castle must know *now* that it had come from Kevin. Cynthia Leeds had told him yesterday, while he was still in Boston.

"You must have been pretty shocked," Ruby said understandingly. I glanced at her, remembering that I hadn't told her about the letter. And of course, she had no idea who had written it, or why.

"Shocked is right," Long said. "I was totally freaked. I told Castle I hadn't received any threats. He said the blackmailer must think Harwick was the only one involved in the scheme, and I should forget he had called. That was the end of it. That is, until I read that Harwick was dead. Then all I could think of was the way Castle had sounded over the phone." His eyes went to the picture and the sweat stood out in beads on his forehead. "I don't want to end up dead, too," he said, in such a low voice I could hardly hear him.

Suddenly I understood. Yes, Long was afraid of the law, afraid of being called to account for what he had done ten years ago, afraid of losing his wife and kids.

But he was even more afraid of the man he thought had killed Harwick.

He was afraid of Frank Castle.

CHAPTER 16

"Well!" Ruby said breathlessly. "*That* puts a different face on things, doesn't it?"

"It sure does," I said, getting into my car. I didn't want to tell her whose face the killer had worn just the hour before, or what color hair she had. Of course, it was still possible that Amy and Kevin had killed Harwick. But they were no longer the only suspects.

"Shall we meet back at the shops?" Ruby asked.

"Yeah." I closed the car door and rolled down my window. "Congratulations, Ruby," I said with total sincerity. "Your detective work has helped to clear an innocent woman." Possibly two innocent women. And one innocent young man. *If* Kevin and Amy were innocent. Were they?

"Thanks," Ruby said, looking modest under the brim of her floppy black hat. "I didn't do anything Harriet Vane wouldn't have done."

I had to smile. Suddenly her costume made sense. "I doubt that Harriet Vane ever thought of putting paprika in her henna." I started my car, wondering how Dorothy Sayers would resolve this. What would Lord Peter say if he sauntered onto the scene right now? Would he put his finger on Amy and Kevin, or on Frank Castle?

Ruby got back to Pecan Springs quicker than I did, partly because she pushes her Honda to the limit while I baby my decrepit Datsun, and partly because I stopped at the Shamrock station on the way out of New Braunfels to call Beulah Bracewell. Her line was busy again, which wasn't surprising. There's a lot of phone traffic in Personnel. I also tried to reach The Whiz, but she was still out of the office. I was just as glad. The half hour it would take to get home would give me time to chew on the facts of the case before I reported to her.

Chew on them I did, although by the time I pulled up in front of Thyme and Seasons I still wasn't clear about several important things. I was seeing the situation from Long's point of view, which gave it an entirely new slant. I could understand why Long was afraid of Frank Castle. But there was a problem in timing. The embezzlement had taken place so long ago that the statute of limitations had run out, for Castle and Harwick as well as Long. If Castle had wanted to get rid of Harwick, he could have done so at any time. Why now?

I had hardly framed the question when I began to turn up possible answers. What if Castle and Harwick had jointly invested the money in some nefarious scheme and had a falling out? Thieves do. Or what if Harwick had repented of his thievery, decided to turn himself in, and pressured Castle to join him? Long hadn't known about the statute of limitations; Harwick and Castle probably didn't, either.

Or what if the lab grant wasn't the *only* cooking of the books that Castle and Harwick had been involved in? What if they had continued to dip into other grants Harwick brought into the department? That might mean that they weren't protected by the statute. And in any event, the statute didn't protect them from the dark frown of academic censure. Tenure or no tenure, when CTSU found out what they had done, both of them would be out of a job before you could say "misappropriation of funds."

But a gut feeling told me that the best answer was none of the above. It was the blackmail letter, which accused Harwick of an unspecified crime that had taken place ten years before. *I* knew that the writer or writers—Kevin or Amy or both— were referring to Harwick's criminal abuse of their brother. But when he showed the letter to Castle, Harwick had assumed that it referred to the embezzlement. Castle, who didn't know about Tad Scott, shared that assumption—that's why he called Jim Long. And when he found out that Long hadn't gotten a letter, Castle figured that the blackmailer knew about only *one* embezzler: Miles Harwick. With that information, Castle's next step was clear: Do away with Harwick and leave the blackmailer holding an empty threat.

Working on those assumptions, it wasn't hard to reconstruct the crime. Castle knew Harwick's work habits. He expected his victim to be in the office on Wednesday evening, so he came equipped with what he needed for the job. He knocked at Harwick's door, Harwick admitted him, and the two talked and drank coffee until Harwick was groggy—too groggy to protest when Castle strung him up and caught a plane for Boston the next morning. It was spring break, and Castle might have counted on the body not being discovered for several days at least. Suddenly I recalled the ashes in Harwick's ashtray. Castle might have burned the blackmail letter on the spot. And then I thought of something else. When Castle learned that Rose had discovered the backup copy on the computer, he could have gone immediately to the Boston airport and got a flight home in plenty of time to fake a break-in of the biology office.

And the clues to Dottie's guilt—her hair, and the rope? I hadn't been able to come up with a reason for Kevin and Amy to frame Dottie, but I could certainly see why Castle would want to implicate her. She had been in his way since the beginning, first opposing his chairmanship, then his plan for an animal research unit, and finally his hope for a state-of-the-art lab. She had been a thorn in the royal side for ten years, a pain in the royal ass. If she were convicted of Harwick's murder, she'd be out of his face for good.

But where had he gotten Dottie's hair? Well, even that wasn't too difficult. Dottie's house was isolated. He could have gone there when he knew she was in class, climbed in through a window, and found her hairbrush in the bathroom. That's when he could have planted the rope in the garage, too.

It all fit, and I had to admit to a great sense of relief as the last piece slipped into place. The way things were shaping up, if Ruby's daughter was guilty of anything, it was threat, which was a Class B misdemeanor. Under the circumstances, she wasn't likely to be prosecuted. If Castle was the man we were looking for, I could face Ruby with a clear conscience.

But what to do about Castle? I felt confident that I could uncover the facts that would confirm Long's story about the chairman's role in the embezzlement. But unfortunately, as far as the murder was concerned, all I had was a theory. The evidence to support it was only circumstantial. It certainly wasn't sufficiently compelling to force either Bubba or the D.A. to give up the perfectly good suspect they had already booked and were planning to bring before the grand jury. To make *that* happen, I would need something more substantial, more dramatic. A confession before witnesses, preferably. To get that, somebody had to confront Castle. Somebody who already knew enough about the situation to buy my version of it. Somebody credible. Somebody with an authority he would have to respect.

I smiled. I knew just the woman for the job.

Smart Cookie.

*   *   *

When I got back to the shop, Laurel was waiting on two customers at once—Rosemary Robbins, who does taxes for Ruby and me, and Fannie Couch, who at the advanced age of seventy-eight has become a local celebrity. Fannie does a talk show on KPST Radio every weekday. She knows even more about what goes on in Pecan Springs than Constance Letterman, the gossip columnist at the newspaper.

"You got to listen to the show next Monday," Fannie told me as Laurel rang up the herbal soap she'd bought. "I've got a special guest."

"Who?" Laurel asked.

"The Guv," Rosemary said. "Fannie's going big time."

"No kidding?" Laurel sounded impressed. I was, too.

"No kidding," Fannie said. She turned to Rosemary. "Claude said to tell you he'll have our tax stuff ready in a few days. If he can get up off the couch, that is." Fannie's always making jokes about her husband being a couch potato.

"That's fine," Rosemary said. Rosemary is short and petite, with a look of permanent anxiety that no doubt comes of sharing the tax secrets of dozens of people. She glanced at me. "How about you, China?"

"I don't want to think about taxes," I said. To Laurel, I said, "I've got a couple of phone calls to make and some errands to run. Don't count on me for the rest of the afternoon. Okay?"

"Okay," Laurel said. "Make one of your phone calls to Beulah Bracewell. She's called twice."

"Beulah?" Fannie dropped her change into her coin purse. "Tell her that Florence Tuttle phoned in that recipe for black bean soup she was looking for. The one with peppers."

Laurel closed the cash register. "My mother's got a great recipe for bean soup with peppers. You take a couple of good-size dried chiles, roast them—"

"Will somebody tell me," Rosemary said, "exactly how to roast a pepper?"

I left them to their discussion of the fine art of roasting chiles and went around to the kitchen, where I put on the kettle for tea and dialed Beulah's number. This time I got through. Beulah jumped right in without any preamble.

"I told you the truth when I said that Sheila Dawson took Dr. Harwick's personnel file," she said. "But after you left, just out of curiosity, I brought up the computer log we keep of personnel transactions and made a hard copy of it."

"I saw the log in Harwick's file," I said. "Sheila Dawson made a copy before she gave it to Chief Harris."

"Did you notice the changes in Dr. Harwick's insurance beneficiary and in the amount of his policy?" Beulah asked.

"He removed his mother as beneficiary, didn't he, and left the money to the university? It was quite a sum, as I recall—a million dollars."

"That's right," Beulah said. "The changes were made about a year ago, shortly after Dr. Harwick's mother died. After I thought about it, I got curious. So I went to the insurance section and pulled the paperwork." Her voice grew tense. "Between the two of us, China, I don't think Dr. Harwick signed either the Change of Beneficiary or the Change of Coverage forms. Graphology is a hobby of mine, you see. I took a course last year from the American Association of Handwriting Analysts. Dr. Harwick's signature doesn't look right to me."

My skin prickled. "Are you saying that somebody *forged* Harwick's insurance application?"

"I'd certainly hate to think so," she said, "but I don't see any other explanation. Both documents are dated last July, the fifteenth, to be exact. I distinctly recall that last July Dr. Harwick was in Hamburg, Germany, attending an international biology symposium. I know, because I processed his Request for Foreign Travel. That's the form you have to submit to get permission for travel abroad. He left in June and didn't return until early August.''

"Beulah," I said, "is there *anything* a faculty member can do without asking your permission?"

"Somebody killed Dr. Harwick without my permission, didn't they?" Beulah's voice was acerbic.

I atoned for my facetious question with a serious one. "There must have been a pretty steep increase in the monthly insurance premium. If Harwick didn't sign off on the increase, why didn't he complain when his premiums went up?''

"Because he might not have noticed," Beulah said. "Dr. Harwick's Change of Beneficiary and Change of Coverage forms came through with the RBAs that are processed at the beginning of each fiscal year.''

"The RBAs?" I was rapidly losing track, but Beulah was patient.

"Request for Budget Adjustment. The paperwork that authorizes any kind of payment, including changes in salary. A salary RBA originates in the department, is signed by the dean and the vice president, then comes here, where it gets plugged into the payroll system.''

"So Harwick got a raise at the same time his insurance premiums went up?"

"Exactly. But since his payroll check was deposited directly into his bank account, it's possible that he didn't even notice the increase. His raise covered it, as well as the additional IRS withholding, with some left over." Beulah's tone was crisp. "Anyway, Dr. Harwick might not have kept very good track of the deposits into his account. I've had plenty of people tell me that they never look at the pay stubs the bank sends with their canceled checks. I wonder if they even look at the canceled checks themselves.''

I'm one of those who save my canceled checks for a rainy

afternoon. Unfortunately, it doesn't rain all that often in Pecan Springs, and when it does, there are other interesting things to do. I pushed that embarrassing thought aside and went back over what Beulah had said. The RBA and the fraudulent insurance documents had all originated in the department. And the beneficiary, as I remembered, was—

"Hold on a minute, Beulah," I said. "I want to check something." I put down the phone, fished my notebook out of my purse, and began to riffle pages. It took only a minute to find what I was looking for: "bio. exper. acct." Biology experiments account.

The million-dollar payout from Miles Harwick's insurance company would end up in the hands of the biology chairman.

I picked up the phone again. "Beulah," I said, "if you had to hazard a guess as to who was in a position to have dreamed up a scheme like this and pulled it off, what would you say?"

"It's not something I would like to guess about," Beulah replied tersely. "Falsification of university records is a serious offense. And when there's this much money involved—"

"I appreciate the seriousness of it. That's why it's important to understand what might have happened."

There was a silence. "Well, then," she said cautiously, "I suppose it would have to be somebody in the biology department office."

"The chairman?" I asked, remembering that Frank Castle was the one who had asked the dean to move Beulah to another job.

Another silence. "Possibly." Was there a slight satisfaction in the word?

"Would you be willing to show me those signatures? And can you dig up something that you're sure Harwick signed so we can compare them?"

"How soon will you be here?"

"As soon as I can. Oh, by the way, Fannie Couch says to

tell you that Florence Tuttle phoned in the recipe you wanted. The one for bean soup with peppers."

"Florence Tuttle?" There was a frown in Beulah's voice. "I worked with her once on a fund-raiser for the Garden Club. That woman never gets anything right. I wouldn't trust a recipe of hers even if she copied it straight out of *Better Homes and Gardens*. Which she probably did."

I had to smile. "Then you might call the shop and ask Laurel about her mother's recipe. I heard her telling Fannie that you start out by roasting a couple of chiles."

"Now, that's more like it," Beulah said.

Two phone calls, a trip to Personnel, and one hour later McQuaid and I were standing in front of Smart Cookie's office. "You're a hundred percent sure about this?" McQuaid asked, frowning as I knocked.

"Of course not," I said. "I'm never a hundred percent sure about *anything*. Do you have another conclusion to offer?"

"Not offhand," McQuaid admitted. "But it sure is one hell of a complicated—"

The office door opened. "What took you so long?" Sheila was very pretty and feminine in a pink suit with close-fitting jacket, white shell, and pearls. I haven't worn pink for years.

"I couldn't find a parking place," I said. "This place is bloody hell in the afternoons. Why don't you build a parking garage or something?" That's a joke. The parking garage has been on CTSU's agenda ever since I moved to Pecan Springs. The idea is debated in the newspaper at least twice a year, but nothing ever gets done. In the meantime, people who live around the campus complain endlessly about cars blocking their driveways.

Sheila went to her desk and motioned us to chairs. "Sit down," she said. "I'd like to hear this story top to bottom."

"You'll have to take notes," McQuaid said. "This ain't easy."

"I don't get paid to listen to the easy ones," she said. "What have you got, China?"

Ah, Smart Cookie. I was beginning to like this woman. I started my story, making it as concise as I could, limiting my description of Amy's and Kevin's roles to the threatening letter and eliminating altogether Amy's relationship to Ruby, which didn't figure in the plot. The narrative took all of ten minutes. I hoped I'd gotten everything straight.

When I was finished, Sheila pulled the computer printout from Harwick's personnel file and spread it out on her desk.

"That's it," I said, pointing to the relevant insurance transactions. "Right there."

"You're *sure* Harwick didn't sign off on these changes?" Sheila asked.

McQuaid spoke up. "China and I just came from Personnel. I looked at the original signatures and compared them to a midterm grade report that Harwick turned in the week before he died. Beulah Bracewell is right. He didn't sign those insurance documents."

"So where does that leave us?" Sheila asked.

"With insurance fraud, for starters," I said. "And Castle is the logical suspect. Those documents could only have been prepared in the biology department."

"Embezzlement, too, of course," McQuaid added, "if this Jim Long character is telling the truth."

"I think we can assume he is," I put in. "Long was in a position to do what he said he did. He knows that his story can be checked out. And it's hard to see what he'd gain by incriminating himself."

"I'd suggest that Internal Audit take a good hard look at the Cosmetech gift—and at more recent biology grant accounts," McQuaid said. "It sounds like Castle and Harwick successfully pulled off one scam. They may have tried others.''

''I agree,'' Sheila said, making a note. There was a silence. I cleared my throat. ''Hey,'' I said, ''Aren't you guys ignoring the obvious? If all this is true, Castle had an excellent motive for murder.''

McQuaid and Sheila traded cop glances. I understood. The campus police had authority to initiate an investigation into allegations of insurance fraud and embezzlement. The murder investigation was a different matter. It had already been turned over to Bubba Harris and the Pecan Springs PD.

''Well?'' I asked. ''What about it?''

''Is she always this subtle?'' Sheila asked McQuaid.

''She has a devious mind,'' McQuaid said. ''She thinks like a defense attorney, and we know about *them*.''

I started to say something and thought better of it. Let them have their little cop joke, if it made them happy.

''Harwick's death aside,'' Sheila said cautiously, ''I think we've got enough to talk to Castle.''

''You could start off with the embezzlement,'' McQuaid said, thinking out loud, ''then get into the insurance fraud.''

''I could,'' Sheila said, picking up the phone. She looked at McQuaid. ''But I'd feel a lot more comfortable if you were in on this too.'' She grinned at me. ''I'm chicken. I always like to have a big guy hanging out close by when there's a possibility of trouble.'' She began to punch in a number. ''Let me call my assistant and have him get the ball rolling with the auditor.''

''What about me?'' I asked. ''I want to be in on this thing with Castle.''

''You're already in,'' Sheila said. ''You're doing a separate investigation, and you just happened to turn up these allegations, which you quite properly brought to my attention. I need you to identify any discrepencies in his response. The two of us will talk to him, while Mike hangs out in the hall.'' Somebody answered on the other end of the line. ''Carl, I'd like you to arrange for the director of Internal Audit to be in my office first thing in the morning.'' She paused. ''No, I think seven-thirty. Yes, that *is* early, isn't it? Tell you what, why don't you come at seven-fifteen, and bring doughnuts and coffee. We can at least give him breakfast. Oh, yes, ask him to bring a list of the current grant accounts managed by the biology department. He should also check back through the accounts for ten years ago. Ask him to look for a record of payouts to Blue Star Scientific Supply Company of Houston. We'll want the bank and the account number. He probably won't be able to get the names on that bank account by tomorrow morning, but tell him that will be his next step. He'll want to put a priority on this one.'' She put the phone down and stood up, looking from one of us to the other. ''Well, what are we waiting for? Let's go see what Frank Castle has to say for himself.''

''Hang on a minute,'' McQuaid said. ''What's our objective here? Are we trying to scare the guy? Wring a confession out of him? What?''

''I've been thinking about that,'' Sheila said. It only took a minute for her to let us in on her game plan. When we were finished, we went across the quad toward the science building. On the way, McQuaid turned to me. ''I've got that lease in my office,'' he said. ''Before you leave this afternoon, would you sign it?''

''So you two are actually moving in together?'' Sheila asked.

''That's what it looks like,'' I said, guarded.

She eyed me. ''You mean there's some question?''

McQuaid reached for my hand. ''No,'' he said firmly. ''No question at all.''

*   *   *

Sheila and I went into the biology department office. The broken door window had been replaced, but the bottom drawer of the file cabinet still bore signs of forced entry. It was nearly five. Rose's chair was pushed against the desk, her typewriter was covered, and her work station had the tidy look of jobs done for the day. But Cynthia Leeds was still at her typewriter, her back straight, the shoulder pads of her green suit jacket giving her the appearance of emphatic authority. Her no-nonsense gray hair was cut crisp and short. Black plastic-framed reading glasses were perched on the tip of her nose. Her dark eyes had the look of someone who never missed a detail. Remembering Beulah, I thought again how important such women were in organizations that depended on paper-work.

Cynthia gave me a curt nod of recognition and turned to Sheila. "I'm sorry, Chief Dawson, but Dr. Castle is *never* available for unscheduled meetings in the late afternoon. I'll be glad to make an appointment for you in the morning, however." She picked up a large calendar book from her desk. "He's free between nine-thirty and eleven. Do you think a half hour will be long enough?"

Sheila glanced toward the partly open door to Castle's office. "He's here now, isn't he?"

"Yes." Cynthia took off her reading glasses. "But he's just gotten back from a trip, and he has a great deal to—"

"I am sure," Sheila interrupted in a clipped tone, "that Dr. Castle will want to speak with us. We are here on official university business, to discuss certain irregular transactions that have taken place in this office over the past few years."

There was a nearly imperceptible flicker in Cynthia's expression, but her spoken response was calm. "If there's a problem with our office procedures, it won't be necessary to disturb Dr. Castle. I can help you."

Sheila turned toward the door. "If you will excuse us," she

said, "I believe we can find our way in."

Frank Castle's navy suit jacket and maroon tie were hanging on the open closet door. He was behind his desk, signing his name with a slim gold pen to a stack of letters, the collar of his blue pin-striped shirt unbuttoned, the sleeves rolled up. He looked up sharply as Sheila and I came in.

"Didn't Miss Leeds tell you that I don't see people at this hour?" With a start, he recognized me. His glance, questioning, swiveled to Sheila.

Cynthia was at the door behind us. "I told them, Dr. Castle," she said, her dark eyes snapping angrily, "but they insisted. They—"

Sheila interrupted her. "My name is Sheila Dawson, Dr. Castle," she said pleasantly, holding out her hand. Automatically, Castle rose and shook it. "I am chief of Campus Security," she went on. "You already know Ms. Bayles, I believe. I'm sorry to interrupt you. But our business *is* important."

Behind us, Cynthia moved. I turned to look. Her eyes were slitted, wary. "Dr. Castle, would you like me to call Campus Security?" She stopped, remembering that we *were* Campus Security.

Castle ran a hand through his salt-and-pepper hair, smoothing it back. "Since they're here, Cynthia, I might as well see them."

Cynthia frowned. "But Dr. Castle, don't you think it would be better to—"

Castle's look silenced her. As she left the room, I noticed that she didn't quite shut the door behind her. I wasn't surprised. Women who keep the organization running also make it a practice to know all its secrets.

CHAPTER 17

Castle sat down in his swivel chair, realized he still had his pen in his hand, and laid it on the desk. "I hope this won't take long," he said. He gave us a disarming smile and put his hand on the stack of papers. "If these RBAs don't get signed tonight, the bills won't get paid on time. You know how people feel about that."

"Of course," Sheila said. "We'll be as quick as we can." She frowned slightly. "I wonder, though. It's a formality, of course, but some of these questions . . . Maybe you'd be more comfortable with your attorney present."

Castle looked at her and laughed a little, patronizingly. I had the feeling that he wasn't taking her seriously. With her corn-silk hair falling against her cheeks, her close-fitting pink suit and pearls, she looked very feminine, almost fragile. I couldn't blame him for being fooled. "My attorney?" he asked lightly. "I can't imagine why that would be necessary. Sit down."

We took chairs. I sat where I could see the door out of the corner of my eye. It was open about three inches. As I watched, it eased open another inch.

Sheila crossed her legs, showing a seductive stretch of thigh below the hem of her pink skirt. Her smile was a fascinating blend of deference and apology and when she spoke, her clipped voice was softened by a southern accent I hadn't heard before.

"I decided we should talk, Dr. Castle, after Ms. Bayles brought one or two little things to my attention this afternoon. Maybe you know," she added helpfully, "that she's working with Dr. Riddle's attorney?"

Both of her sentences ended with the interrogative upswing that turns statements into tentative questions—a speech style that belongs almost exclusively to women. The habit tends, I have always thought, to make the speaker sound ingenuous and vulnerable—the voice of "just li'l ol' me." Smart Cookie was using all her resources.

Castle glanced at me. "I'm glad to hear Dottie has obtained competent counsel." His tone belied his words.

Sheila cleared her throat and ducked her head, managing to look even more deferential. "Ms. Bayles had a little talk today with a man by the name of Jim Long. Maybe you remember him? He worked in the grant accounting office nine, maybe ten years ago."

There was, I thought, a subtle reaction, a slight hardening of Castle's gaze. But if I had been hoping for something more noticeable, I was disappointed.

"Long?" Castle appeared to search his memory. "Afraid not," he said. "I don't remember anybody named Long. Actually," he added, "I've learned over the years that it's best to have as few dealings with the accounting office as possible." He smiled. "All they do over there is think up new hoops for the rest of us to jump through."

Sheila smiled to show that she appreciated his humor. "The thing is, sir," she said with great reluctance, "Mr. Long remembers *you* quite well. He gave Ms. Bayles a fairly detailed sketch of a certain financial transaction that he claims you, he, and Miles Harwick were involved in some years ago. Ten years ago, to be exact.''

That did get a response, but not a revealing one. Castle leaned back in his chair, slowly and carefully, his face impassive. At the same time, I was aware of movement outside the door. Cynthia was standing close, listening, her broad shoulders casting a bulky shadow on the frosted glass. It passed through my mind that it might have been just as well to have her in on this conversation so we could see her reactions too, but it was too late for that now.

''A financial transaction?'' Castle said. He took off his gold-rimmed glasses and inspected them for dust. ''I'm afraid I don't know what you're talking about.'' He reached in the drawer, took out a packet of lens cleaners, and polished the lenses.

Sheila's smile was relieved. ''I am mighty glad to hear that,'' she said. Her southern accent was just a little bit broader. ''It does ease my mind a good bit, because if what Mr. Long says is true—well, I was afraid it might present a bit of a problem.'' She waved her hand. ''But if there's nothin' to it, Internal Audit will have the whole matter cleared up in a shake. The director is in the process of checking things out right now.''

Castle put his glasses back on. ''Internal . . . Audit?'' He was visibly paler.

Sheila nodded. ''As long as you've been in this position and as much respect as people have for you in this university, I *knew* you'd want to have things straightened out as soon as possible. That's why I went ahead and requested the audit.'' She smiled. ''But I was of two minds about it. Even if it turned out there was a little something to Mr. Long's charges, the university would probably think it wasn't worth pursuing—

given your outstanding record. And given the fact that the statute of limitations has expired."

Castle looked down, but not before I saw the obvious relief in his eyes. "The statute of limitations?"

"Ten years." She became rueful. "Actually, I wouldn't have bothered you with this at all—if Ms. Bayles hadn't turned up something else I thought I should ask about."

"I . . . see." Castle shot me a glance. I was to blame for *all* of this. He sat up straight, his posture suggesting renewed confidence in his authority. "Perhaps you'll tell me what this 'something else' is, and then leave me to my work. I really don't want to be here all evening."

Sheila leaned forward, the very picture of concerned respect, earnestly eager to do the right thing. "Well, to be totally honest, sir, this is what worries me the most. What Ms. Bayles stumbled across, you see, was an insurance transaction involving a change in the beneficiary and the amount of Dr. Harwick's life insurance. It is clear that Dr. Harwick himself did not sign the documents. Someone forged his name."

I was so engrossed in the drama being played out in front of me that the movement on the other side of the door almost didn't register. Half smiling, faintly amused at Sheila's innocence, Castle shook his head.

"It's obvious you haven't been around this university very long, Chief Dawson." He said the word "chief" almost playfully.

"Not very long, sir," she said. Her smile was alluring. "I'm still learning the ropes, so to speak."

He tilted his chair back, his confidence growing. "Well, my dear, I'll let you in on a little secret. The paperwork system doesn't always work the way it's supposed to. People don't always fill in the forms right. Sometimes they don't even sign them. Rather than hold things up, somebody in the departmental office fills in any blanks."

Sheila looked surprised. "No kiddin'?"

"I know," Castle said, "it sounds irregular. But after you've learned the ropes, as you so originally put it, you'll see that we all cooperate to keep the paper flowing. What it boils down to is that we trust one another's good intentions." He cocked his head and narrowed his eyes, concentrating. "Sure, now I remember. Of course. This instance you're asking about—it was after Miles' mother died, as I recollect. She had been the beneficiary of his life insurance. He had no other relatives, so after she was gone, he decided to make the university his beneficiary."

"I had a question about that, too," Sheila said. "Isn't it just a teeny bit unusual for a faculty member to leave such a large bequest to the university?" She took a small notebook out of her purse, opened it, and consulted a page. "Three quarters of a million dollars, I think it was."

"A million," he corrected her.

Her gorgeous eyes widened. "My goodness. Whyever would he *do* such a thing?"

"I suppose," Castle said, "that he wanted to ensure the continuation of his work, if he were no longer here to carry it out himself. A million dollars is enough to fund a chair in his memory. That, in fact, is the purpose to which the money will be put."

"Leaving this money—it wasn't something he had discussed with you?"

"No, it was a total surprise. I didn't know he was doing it until the paperwork crossed my desk."

She smiled, respectful. "I can just imagine how shocked you must have been, coming across something like that, so completely out of the blue."

Castle was relaxed now, enjoying himself. "You *bet* I was shocked. I looked at the form, and when I saw the amount and the beneficiary, I did a double take. Then I noticed that Miles had neglected to sign it. So I picked up the phone, got his okay, and forged his signature.'' He grinned and held up both hands in a gently self-deprecating gesture. ''Yes, mea culpa. It was a little irregular, maybe, especially given the amount of money involved. But I'm sure you understand. You'll reduce my punishment to twenty lashes?'' It was clear from his look how he'd like to have those lashes.

Sheila smiled. ''You recall his telephone authorization, then? I suppose that would have been—'' She turned a page of her notebook. ''The fifteenth of July? Does that ring a bell?''

''That's right,'' Castle said triumphantly. ''The fifteenth of July. I remember, because it's my birthday.''

Sheila was beaming, obviously relieved that he had such a satisfactory explanation. ''Then perhaps you'll also recall, Dr. Castle, where you called Dr. Harwick from, and where you reached him?''

Castle concentrated. ''Well, I called from this office, of course. And I reached him . . .'' His forehead furrowed. ''Oh, gosh. I don't remember whether he was at home or in his office.'' He tilted his head and gave her a sexy smile. ''Does it really matter?'' He looked at his watch. ''Say, it's getting late. How about adjourning for happy hour? We could continue this over a drink.''

Sheila frowned slightly. ''You're sure that you called from this office?''

He nodded emphatically. ''Oh, yes,'' he said. ''Of that, I'm positive.''

Sheila put her notebook back in her purse. ''Then you should be able to supply the International Telephone Call Authorization form you filled out, stating the purpose of your call,'' she said, ''as well as the billing to Hamburg, Germany.''

Castle stared at her. ''Ham . . . burg?''

"That's right," Sheila said. "On July fifteenth last year, Dr. Harwick was neither in his office *nor* at home. He was in Hamburg, attending a professional meeting."

Castle looked down. When he looked up, his face was set. He'd forgotten all about happy hour. "I've said all I have to say on this matter."

Sheila's voice was firm and her southern accent had all but disappeared. "I have another question, Dr. Castle. I need to know where you were last Wednesday evening."

He stared at her. "Wednesday evening?"

"That's right," she said. "The night Miles Harwick died."

With a jerk, Castle's chair came upright. "Are you implying that I was involved in Dr. Harwick's death?"

"Well, sir," she said, "you can see why I have to ask. I've been given to understand that you and Dr. Harwick stole a substantial sum from the university, and that you forged his signature to insurance documents leaving an even more substantial sum to the department—under your direct control." She paused, letting that percolate. "And then there's the matter of the blackmail letter Dr. Harwick received, which was stolen from this office last night. It's very fortunate, of course, that Ms. Bayles made a copy."

"A copy?" His nostrils flared as he turned to look at me. "You made a *copy*?"

I cleared my throat and spoke for the first time. "That's right," I said. "Perhaps it would help if I review our reconstruction of the events with you. Dr. Harwick showed you the letter right after he received it. Both of you feared that his role in the embezzlement scheme was about to become public knowledge. Your part in it would inevitably be known as well, and your career ruined, even though you might be protected from prosecution by the statute of limitations. But the blackmailer did not appear to know about you, or about Jim Long, with whom you also checked. If Harwick were to die, you

thought, that would be the end of it. The blackmailer woul
be stymied, and Harwick could no longer implicate you."

"You can see," Sheila said reasonably, "how easy it woul
be for someone to think *you* were the one who murdered Mile
Harwick."

Castle's face had turned ashen. "I think," he said in a lov
voice, "that I'd better not say anything more until I call m
lawyer."

The door clicked shut.

"Excuse me," I said abruptly, and stood up. I hated to leav
when the conversation was getting interesting, but I had t
know what was going on with Cynthia. Was she simply bein
nosy? Or was she—

The outer office was empty.

I crossed swiftly to the door just as McQuaid opened i
"Hey," he said, "who the devil was that woman? She cam
barreling out of the office like a bat out of hell. Almo
knocked me down."

"Where'd she go?"

"The parking lot exit." He took three paces to the windov
"There she is," he said, pointing to a gray Plymouth.

Cynthia was scrabbling in her purse for her car keys. Whe
was she going? And why was she in such a hurry?

I turned to McQuaid. "You'd better get in there with Sheil
I'm going after Cynthia."

"Did you get a confession?"

"Not yet," I said, halfway to the door. "He's phoning f
his lawyer. Go on, get in there."

"But I thought the plan was for me to—"

"The plan's changed," I said over my shoulder. "Sheila
one smart lady, but Castle's a crook. I don't trust him fro
here to the water cooler."

                    *   *   *

If the parking lot exit gate hadn't jammed, I might have lost
Cynthia. She inserted her card twice, but nothing happened.
She sat there, stuck, while I dashed for my car, climbed in,
and drove one aisle past the exit, where I could see what was
going on. A man walking through the lot spotted her dilemma,
came over and pounded on the contraption. It opened and she
drove through. So did the car behind her. Crossing my fingers,
I drove up to the gate, inserted my good-for-one-visit temporary card, and went through, too. Ruby would say that the
goddess had smiled.

The after-class rush to get off the campus was over, but
there was still plenty of pedestrian traffic, mostly undergrad-
uates on their way back to their dorms or to the video-game
hangouts. Dodging gangs of them—why do students always
seem to walk in multiples of five?—I got to the corner in time
to see Cynthia's Plymouth turn left on Hawkins Boulevard,
heading west.

I turned too, staying back a long block. Subterfuge was
probably unnecessary, since she didn't act as if she knew she
was being followed. But I did it anyway, to be on the safe
side, for the next couple of miles. That's why, when I came
around the blind corner at the Immanuel Lutheran Church and
saw that the street was empty for three blocks ahead, I almost
panicked. But when I looked up and noticed where I was, I
hooked an abrupt right. It was the Falls Creek blacktop. And
ahead of me was the Plymouth, heading north, fast.

Falls Creek? I frowned as I pushed the accelerator to the
floor. Did Cynthia live out this way? Maybe she'd forgotten
something she was supposed to do this evening and was hur-
rying home to do it. But by the time she turned left onto San
Gabriel, I began to suspect that this was something more than
a forgotten errand or an afternoon visit with a sick friend.
When she made another left on Sycamore, I was sure of it.

Three blocks later, she was pulling to a stop in front of a long
low, brown-shingled ranch, almost out of sight behind a screen
of yaupon holly and cedar.

Dottie Riddle's house. And Dottie's Blazer was in the drive

CHAPTER 18

Cynthia was out of her Plymouth and halfway up the walk
when I whipped a quick U-turn at the corner. I parked on the
far side of the vacant lot, angled through the weeds at a lope
and came up on Dottie's backyard. It was empty, and there
was no one in the cattery except a hundred and fifty-some cats
and God only knew how many guinea pigs. I looked in the
garage and the treatment room. There was no sign of Dottie.
She—and Cynthia—must be inside.

I went to the back door, put my ear to it and my hand on
the knob, and listened. Hearing nothing, I turned it soundlessly
and stepped inside, hesitating in the semidark of the kitchen
entry. Ariella brushed up against my leg like a vagrant ghost,
startling me. I stifled my squawk just in time. But I don't think
I would have been heard, because from the sound of the voices
down the hall, Dottie and Cynthia were in the living room. I
crept down the hall to the living room doorway, looked in,
and quickly ducked back.

Cynthia Leeds, both feet planted firmly on the floor and her
purse in her lap, was sitting at one end of the sofa, at right

233

angles to the doorway. Dottie was in the overstuffed chair to her right, her back to me. There was no way to get Dottie's attention, but Cynthia was in a position to see me unless I was very careful. I flattened myself against the wall.

"I still don't understand," Dottie was saying, "why you've come all the way out here for a United Way contribution, Cynthia. The fund drive was over two weeks ago."

I heard a rustle and the zip of a purse opening and took the risk of another look. "You're right," Cynthia was saying, as she pulled something out of her purse. "It is over. *All* over." She rested her right hand on the arm of the sofa. In it was a handgun. It was small and silvery but very businesslike. "I'm here about Miles Harwick's murder."

"What are you doing with that thing?" Dottie demanded irritably. "Put it away!"

"No," Cynthia said crisply, "I don't think so. I'm very sorry it has to come to this, Dr. Riddle, but I'm here to kill you."

Dottie laughed.

Cynthia's hand tightened on the gun. "That's just fine," she said bitterly. "Laugh if you want to. Don't take me seriously. But it won't help. You're going to pay anyway."

"But I didn't kill Miles!" Dottie exclaimed, misunderstanding.

"I know you didn't," Cynthia said. "I did."

Maybe I shouldn't have been surprised. Maybe I should have guessed. But I had put so much faith in the rational process. Kevin and Amy, intent on revenge for a dead brother's suicide, logically *could* have killed Harwick. Frank Castle could have done it too, for Harwick was a threat to his continued prosperity. That it might have been Cynthia Leeds had never even occurred to me.

Nor to Dottie. "You're kidding." She was incredulous. "*You?*"

"Why is that so hard to believe?" Cynthia asked, nettled. "What makes you think I couldn't kill somebody? Really, Dr. Riddle, you're every bit as bad as the men. Thinking that a woman—a mere secretary among all the glorious beings of the biology department—can't do something really big and important."

"No," Dottie said lamely. "I don't think that." For once, she seemed almost at a loss, and I was, too. Had I overlooked Cynthia as a suspect because it hadn't occurred to me that a mere secretary might be capable of planning and executing a murder? Was I as guilty as the males in Cynthia's department of failing to accept her as a real person, with real feelings and therefore a real motive for murder?

"But I don't understand, Cynthia," Dottie said. "*Why* did you kill Miles? What did he do to you?"

Cynthia's laugh was short and harsh. "You worked with the man for ten years. Didn't you ever want to kill him?"

"Well, sure," Dottie said. "At least twice a day. But I didn't. Why did *you*?"

"Because," Cynthia said heatedly, "he was an absolutely terrible man, a tyrant. He was nasty to the staff and the faculty, and even worse to students. Every week we got a complaint. His grading was unfair, he didn't hand back quizzes, he didn't read what the students handed in. And his research—" She made a distasteful mouth. "You weren't the only one criticizing him, you know. Several of the other full professors went to see him. They asked him to drop that research project and choose something that was less . . . well, flammable. Something with more scientific credibility. Less damaging to the department's reputation. The week before he died, he even got a letter from the funding agency asking for a more detailed protocol so they could review it. They'd gotten complaints, too."

Dottie laughed shortly. "No kidding. And I thought I was

the only one who cared that he was making a fool out of the department." She shook her head. "You're right about Harwick's shortcomings. But I still don't see why you killed him."

Cynthia's voice was level. "I suppose I wouldn't have, if it hadn't been for Dr. Castle. I felt so sorry for him. He was always having to soothe irate students and explain to people why Dr. Harwick had done this or that horrible thing. Last year, after a fuss about one of Harwick's finals, several of the other full professors even told him they wanted to hold a hearing and revoke Harwick's tenure. That would have been *so* embarrassing."

"Amazing," Dottie said. "All this shit was coming down and nobody ever told me?"

"Frankly, Dr. Riddle," Cynthia said, in the voice of a friend telling a friend she has denture breath, "you'd be the last to know. *You* aren't very well liked, either. You're always challenging, questioning, making things difficult. What do you expect?"

"*And* I'm the only woman."

"Well, that, too." Cynthia shook her head. "Sometimes I felt sorry for you, because you were so out of touch with what was going on. But the one I really suffered for was Dr. Castle. He didn't like Dr. Harwick any more than anybody else did. But he had hired him, and he was determined to be loyal if it killed him."

I was beginning to get a cramp in my leg from crouching down, but I couldn't move. Of course, it wasn't loyalty that drove Frank Castle to defend Miles Harwick. It was their earlier collusion, from which Castle could never extricate himself. A Latin phrase popped into my mind from one of my old law books. *Facinus quos inquinat aequat.* Villainy makes equals of all those whom it links. Once yoked with the devil, Castle could never cut the tie that bound them together.

"I still don't understand—" Dottie began, but Cynthia was going on with her story.

"And of course there were the bomb threats, which put everybody on edge, and all those animal rights protesters, marching around, chanting and yelling and carrying those awful signs. And the phone ringing for simply hours on end. It was impossible to get any work done. But the final straw was two weeks ago, when I found the blackmail letter in the computer."

"What blackmail letter?"

I started. *Cynthia* had found the letter Kevin and/or Amy had written? Even before Rose ran across it?

Cynthia spoke with the air of an informed insider. "I don't know the details, of course, and I couldn't tell who wrote it. Anybody could have gotten on the computer. But it seems that Dr. Harwick did something ten years ago, and somebody found out about it and was threatening to make it public. When I read it, I knew I had to tell Dr. Castle. It upset him terribly. He went to talk to Dr. Harwick, and when he came back, he was absolutely shaking. I'd never seen him in such a state. It was about that time that we got another bomb threat. I knew I needed to do something, immediately. Dr. Harwick was making a mess out of everyone's lives."

So I'd been wrong. It wasn't Harwick who had told Castle about the blackmail letter. It had been Cynthia. *She* had started this whole thing.

Dottie made a noise, half sympathetic, and Cynthia looked gratified.

"I'm glad you understand," she said. "The hard part, of course, was deciding to do it. But I'm a fairly logical person, and once I'd decided that it was the only way to save Dr. Castle—the whole department, really—I just went through it, step by step. It wasn't difficult. And I didn't think I'd be found out. After all, secretaries *are* invisible." The bitterness again.

"Why hanging, though?" Dottie shuddered. "It seems pretty grisly."

"Poetic justice," Cynthia said. "All those poor guinea pigs, you know. And I thought hanging might make it look more like a suicide, which would take everybody off the hook." She paused. "But then I happened to find your hairbrush—"

"My hairbrush?"

"You left it in the ladies' restroom one afternoon when we were both in there. I saw it lying on the counter, and it gave me an idea. I knew *you* had good reason to want Dr. Harwick dead. He was writing you those nasty little notes about your cats—"

"You knew about those?"

Cynthia pulled herself up. "Of course. He was using the computer, wasn't he? Really, Dr. Riddle. You underestimate me. Anyway, I knew there was bad blood between you. If you weren't around, life would be a lot easier for Dr. Castle. So I took some hair out of your brush, and then used the master key to return the brush to your office. I'm sure you didn't even miss it."

"I didn't," Dottie said ruefully. She shook her head. "I can't believe you killed him and framed *me*."

Cynthia sounded apologetic. "Well, I didn't actually think of it as *framing* you. I just thought that if for some reason the police didn't believe it was suicide, they'd want to suspect somebody, and I certainly didn't want that somebody to be me. But I got to worrying that the hair might not be enough, so I stopped by your house when you weren't there and left a length of the rope I planned to use on the shelf in your garage. And then I decided to use that euthanatizing drug you give your sick cats . . ." She paused. "From your point of view, I can see how you'd think I was framing you."

"It sounds like a good plan," Dottie said, "but carrying it out—"

"It wasn't easy," Cynthia admitted. "The hardest part was getting him up on the desk and into the noose. Believe me, I was glad he was such a little man." Her laugh was self-deprecating. "That's why I'm using a gun this time. I'm not fool enough to think I could get *you* into a noose, even though it'd be more convincing that way."

"But don't you see how crazy this is?" Dottie asked. "The police fell for your frame-up. They've already charged *me* with the murder. Why don't you just let me take my chances with the jury?"

There was a sudden movement against my ankles, and I looked down, trying not to move my head. It was Ariella, rubbing. I pressed myself backward as far as I could, praying that the cat's movement wouldn't attract Cynthia's attention.

Cynthia's face had grown hard. "Unfortunately, that won't work," she said. "That drop-out friend of yours—the one who used to be a lawyer—found out about the insurance papers. She and the Campus Security chief came over to see Dr. Castle."

I breathed a sigh of relief as Ariella abandoned my leg and walked into the living room, the white tip of her orange tail waving like a pennant. I lost sight of her as she went behind Dottie's chair.

"What insurance papers?" Dottie sounded irritated. "Really, Cynthia, you're making this *so* complicated!"

"It doesn't matter. You don't have to know all the details. To make a long story short, China Bayles and Chief Dawson have come up with some very good reasons why Dr. Castle might have murdered Dr. Harwick. I'm afraid they'll get you off the hook, and I couldn't bear it if *he* were charged with Dr. Harwick's murder. So you're going to type a note confessing to Dr. Harwick's death and saying that you're killing yourself because you don't want to stand trial. That way, peo-

ple will forget about pursuing Dr. Castle and that silly insurance—Yeiii!''

All hell suddenly broke loose.

But it wasn't the devil, it was Ariella, who had jumped onto
Cynthia's lap. It was a friendly move, but Cynthia didn't know
that. She wasn't expecting a furry creature the size of a lion
cub to suddenly catapult into her lap. Startled, she shoved
Ariella onto the floor. Ariella hissed and bared her fangs. Cynthia pointed the gun at her. Her finger tightened as she took
aim.

''No!'' Dottie yelled. With her hammer-throwing arm, she
grabbed a heavy glass ashtray off the table beside her chair
and coldcocked Cynthia.

And that was the end of it. Cynthia fell sideways on the
sofa, stunned, a sizable cut opened up at the hairline. Dottie
scrambled to pick up Ariella and made crooning noises into
her orange fur. I kicked the gun under the sofa, safely out of
reach.

Seeing me, Dottie's eyes widened, then narrowed. ''How
long have you been here?'' she demanded.

Cynthia moaned and put her hand to her head.

''Long enough to hear her full confession,'' I said.

Dottie was irate. ''Really, China, you could've let me know
you were there. I sat in that chair for a whole goddamned hour
with a gun trained on me, thinking she was going to kill me!
And she would've shot Ariella if I hadn't stopped her.''

''I had to let her go through the whole thing, didn't I?'' I
asked defensively. ''Anyway, it wasn't an hour, it was only
ten minutes. Less than that, maybe. And Ariella isn't hurt.''

Cynthia moaned again and put her hand to her forehead.
Dottie turned on her. ''And you've got *your* nerve,'' she
scolded. ''Trying to make it look like *I* was the one who killed
Miles. Honestly, Cynthia, if I weren't a law-abiding citizen,
I'd—''

"Dottie," I said, "just call the sheriff, okay?"

Dottie turned to look at me. "The sheriff? Shouldn't I call Chief Harris? He's the one who arrested me."

"No," I said firmly, "call the sheriff."

Somehow I thought it might be easier to explain all this to Blackie. It was his jurisdiction, anyway.

CHAPTER 19

"Have another piece," I said, passing the plate. "There's plenty."

"What *is* it?" The Whiz asked, helping herself to a slice of the sweet tortelike cake. "Tastes pretty good."

"Castagnaccio," I said. "It's supposed to be made with chestnut flour and rosemary. But chestnuts don't grow around here and chestnut flour costs *mucho dinero*. I used ground pecans."

Ruby took a slice of pecan castagnaccio and handed the plate to Sheila. "China can give you the recipe," she told Justine.

The Whiz shuddered. For her, cooking is a fate worse than death. "No, thanks. I'll stick with Sara Lee." She frowned. "If you ask me, this Dottie business turned into a *very* complicated case."

"A Riddle inside an enigma, you might say," Ruby remarked brightly. In unison, we gave an exaggerated groan.

"What I want to know," Sheila said, taking a slice of castagnaccio and passing the plate to me, "is exactly what Bubba

242

Harris said when Sheriff Blackwell took Cynthia Leeds in.''

I grinned. "No, you don't," I said. "It would blister your pretty shell-like ears." Sheila was wearing a yellow suit this afternoon (the day after Ariella jumped into Cynthia's lap), with a yellow-and-white polka-dotted blouse. I always thought blondes couldn't wear yellow. I was wrong. "As far as Dottie was concerned," I added, "the operational words were 'charges dismissed.' Dottie's home with her cats to stay."

"And another seventeen guinea pigs," Ruby said. "As of this morning."

A look of distaste passed across The Whiz's face. "How many does that make?"

"God knows," I said. "Why are you asking? Would you like to adopt a hundred or so?" I put a piece of castagnaccio in my mouth. It *was* good. Maybe I had invented a new dish.

"A hundred guinea pigs? *Me*?" The Whiz hastily poured herself another dry sherry—not exactly the drink to accompany an Italian sweet, but who cares?

Ruby turned to Sheila. "Now that the murder's cleared up, what's going to happen to Frank Castle? Will the university throw the book at him?"

Sheila leaned back, kicked off her dyed-to-match yellow pumps, and propped her pretty, pedicured feet up on my antique milking stool. Some women would kill for toenails like that.

"The whole thing's under discussion at the highest echelons," she said, "and probably will be for some time. Internal Audit confirmed that the embezzlement itself took place just over ten years ago. That's when Harwick talked Castle into the scheme."

"Says who?" The Whiz asked skeptically. "Says Castle, I'll bet. Good thing for him his partner isn't around to contradict him."

Sheila shrugged. "I talked to Long this morning. It was his

impression that Harwick was the prime mover. Castle wasn't opposed, of course. Anyway, ten years ago is when they got Long to move the money out of the grant account.''

"So it's outside the statute," I said. Khat came out of the bathroom, where he had been sitting on the counter, admiring himself in the mirror, and asked for dinner. It was five-thirty, so I got up and went to the refrigerator to look for his chicken liver.

"Maybe not," Sheila said. "They left the money in the Houston bank account for eighteen months or so, under the name of Blue Star Scientific Supply. The university attorney says, technically speaking, that the crime itself wasn't committed until they transferred the Blue Star money into their own accounts. Which means that it's still within the statute. If so, the university will prosecute Castle.''

"Will they?" The Whiz asked with heavy irony. "Are you sure?''

Sheila shrugged. "Who knows? Maybe they will, maybe they won't.''

"Maybe they'll take a plea," I said, still searching for Khat's chicken liver. There wasn't any. "Sorry, Khat," I said. "You'll have to settle for canned food.''

The Whiz snorted. "*Might* take a plea? Bet your boobs they'll take a plea. They'll never wash that dirty linen in open court. They'll seize as much of the money as they can get their hands on, revoke Castle's tenure, fire his ass, and sweep the whole mess under the nearest executive carpet. Then they'll give him his four stars and tell the world he retired early.'' She frowned. "What about Long?''

"He's offered to pay restitution," I said, putting the cat food—tuna and shrimp Gourmet Goodie—in front of Khat. "He doesn't want to be hauled up before his professional ethics committee.''

"What about the fraudulent insurance papers?" Ruby

asked. "What's the story there?"

Sheila sipped her sherry. "Apparently, Cynthia Leeds wasn't the only one who felt the need to cash Harwick out. Castle seems to have entertained the possibility of disposing of his troublesome partner—ex-partner—since last July, at least. Harwick really *was* an embarrassment to the department, not to mention a serious threat to Castle. He thought he could call the shots, push everybody around, and Castle would protect him. But Castle was getting fed up. It must have seemed to him that if Harwick had to die, he might as well leave something useful behind."

"But Castle switched the insurance almost a year ago," I said. "Why didn't he kill Harwick right away?" I looked down. Khat was sitting in front of his Gourmet Goodie, staring at it, sulking. "That's all there is, Khat. Eat it or starve."

"He must have been waiting until the regents approved the animal lab," Sheila said. "And the university's insurance carrier won't pay the death benefit on a suicide unless the policy is over two years old. But Cynthia had no reason to wait. She didn't find out about the life insurance until she heard me tell Castle that *we* knew. That's when she learned about the original skulduggery, too. The embezzlement, I mean."

I pushed the saucer with my foot. "I know of a whole bunch of homeless kitties who would give their last whiskers for tuna and shrimp," I told Khat. He looked up at me, looked back down at his saucer, and leaned over to sniff, delicately. Deciding that he preferred Gourmet Goodie to starvation, he settled down to serious eating, with only occasional glances over his shoulder to let me know that he *did* bear a grudge. I went back to the table and poured myself the last of the sherry.

The Whiz propped her elbows on the table. "You know, it's that original theft that still puzzles me," she said thoughtfully. "Cosmetech gave that money to be used for an animal lab. The way I hear it, Castle and Harwick both wanted an animal lab in order to build their reputations. Why did they steal the money?"

"Dottie explained that to me," I said. "A quarter of a million dollars sounds like a lot of money, but it really isn't—at least, not as far as animal labs go. The money was enough to build a *small* lab, nothing like what Harwick and Castle wanted."

"For that," Ruby remarked, "they probably had to have a *lot* of money."

I nodded. "It looked like they'd get it, too, when the regents approved the plans for the new science complex. They apparently thought that if the university had the money for a small lab, that's all they'd ever get. You can understand their reasoning."

"Sure," Sheila said. "If that money went away, there'd be more. Very logical."

"Exactly," I said. "So they stole the money and waited for the regents to pony up—using their loot to make their waiting a little less tedious, of course. Castle found a new wife, and Harwick bought a house and dropped some money into a couple of small business deals."

"Ah," Ruby said, nodding. "Yes, that makes sense." She looked at her watch. "Oops, sorry, you guys, I've gotta run. China, that was marvelous casta-whatever. Make it again sometime."

The Whiz eyed her. "Heavy date, huh? Who is it? That guy from Wimberley? Max whazzit?"

"No," Ruby said regretfully. "I went out with him last night. I didn't like him all that much."

"You didn't?" I asked. "But I thought—"

"I know," Ruby sighed. "So did I. Sometimes these things work out, sometimes they don't." She stood up. "No, tonight is just an intimate family affair. I'm taking Amy and Kevin to dinner in Austin."

I was glad to see that Ruby and Amy were on speaking terms again. They had spent some time together that afternoon. Amy, Ruby told me, had explained that her chief reason for being so nasty was that she didn't want to involve her mother in the Harwick matter. I wasn't exactly sure about that, but I was willing to give Amy the benefit of the doubt, especially after meeting her adoptive parents and hearing the story about Tad.

"Amy's a nice young woman," The Whiz said approvingly. "Looks like her mother." She sighed and turned her sherry glass in her hand. "Sometimes I wish I'd had children. But it's too late now. The biological clock says it's way past eleven. And I haven't identified a suitable male."

"Hey," Sheila said, "it's never too late. A friend of mine had her first at forty-five. Or you could adopt. You don't need a man for that."

"Let's not be rash," The Whiz said. "A guinea pig would be easier."

Ruby was at the door, but she turned around. "China, that letter Amy and Kevin wrote to Harwick—it won't get them into trouble, will it? And what about the break-in?"

"On the letter, I doubt it," I said. "To prosecute them would take more work than it's worth. But the break-in is a different matter." Amy and Kevin *had* broken into the department. When Amy learned from me about the existence of the incriminating computer backup copy, they knew they had to steal it.

"I've advised them to plead and pay for the damages," Justine said. "They'll probably get off lightly. But I must say, they had quite a plan. It's just as well Cynthia Leeds got to Harwick first."

"It *was* quite a plan," I said. "Kevin got himself hired in Harwick's lab in order to dig up evidence of animal abuse, while Amy plugged into the local PETA to organize the protests. They were obviously out to destroy the man's reputation as a scientist, and to make a point about how the powerful victimize the powerless.''

"She's her mother's daughter," Ruby said. "If Harwick had abused my brother, I'd have done some of the same things she did." She looked at me. "I'm glad you figured out who it really was, China. Amy and Kevin could really be in trouble.''

"You know, Hot Shot," The Whiz said pensively, "you've got a lot on the ball. If you ever want to get back into practice, you could come in with me. And bring Ruby as an investigator.''

"No kidding?" Ruby asked eagerly.

"Forget it, Ruby," I said. "I'm sticking to herbs. They don't carry guns. Anyway, I didn't figure it out. I was as surprised as anybody when the killer turned out to be Cynthia.''

Sheila looked at Ruby, standing by the door with her hand on the knob. "How come you're going all the way to Austin for dinner, Ruby? There are half a dozen perfectly good places here in Pecan Springs.''

"None of them are vegetarian," Ruby said. "Amy and Kevin don't eat animals.''

"Amy has a T-shirt," I told them. "It says 'Cows Cry Louder Than Cabbages.' ''

"Cute," The Whiz said. She took her fork and cut the last piece of castagnaccio in half. "Louder than pecans, too, I'll bet.''

"What *are* you doing, China?" McQuaid said, making his third turn around my living room. "Why don't you just sign the damn thing and be done with it?''

"I'm reading the fine print," I said. "I never sign a legal

document without reading it first.'' I picked up the pen. ''Why are you pacing like that?''

''I'm estimating,'' McQuaid said. He sat down beside me on the sofa. ''I'm trying to figure out whether we can move all this stuff in my pickup, or whether we'll have to rent a U-Haul.''

I sighed. ''What happens if this doesn't work out? What if Brian hates living with me? What if Khat detests Howard Cosell? What if it turns out that you and I can't get along?''

McQuaid put his arm around me. ''We've got five bedrooms, haven't we?''

References

Readers who are interested in pursuing the fascinating mysteries of herbs have hundreds of wonderful books from which to choose. Some are listed at the end of *Witches' Bane*, the second book in this series. Here are the titles and authors of several other interesting and useful books. They demonstrate the current range of interest in herbs and herb products in the general area of this book.

The Healing Herbs, by Michael Castleman. Descriptions of traditional herbal remedies, with up-to-date research backgrounds, of 100 herbs. This book gave me the information about catnip that led to the title of Hangman's Root. (No, I didn't make it up! It is true that American colonists believed that tea made from catnip root made the drinker angry. If you want the full story on catnip, this is a book to consult.)

Cats Naturally: Natural Rearing for Healthier Cats, by Juliete de Bairachi Levy. A complete guide to the use of herbs for your cat (in addition to catnip), along with herbal treatments for feline ailments, written by a witty and affectionate cat lover. The author says that catnip (called *catmint* in England) is a "skin vermin deterrent and also an herb tonic."

Natural Insect Repellents for Pets, People, and Plants, by

Janette Grainger and Connie Moore. An excellent self-published review of herbal repellents, including catnip. The authors suggest that if you want to keep cats away from your catnip, you should plant a border of rue. Available from The Herb Bar, 200 West Mary, Austin, Texas, 78704.

Using Herbs in the Landscape: How to Design and Grow Gardens of Herbal Annuals, Perennials, Shrubs and Trees, by Debra Kirkpatrick. This book offers detailed information on garden styles, designs, and themes, along with planting, maintenance, and requirements. Catnip's gray-green color and compact growing habit makes it a lovely border plant.

An Elders' Herbal: Natural Techniques for Promoting Health and Vitality, by David Hoffman. Explains why herbs are effective healing agents, details common conditions, and suggests herbal therapies for older readers. According to Hoffman, catnip's volatile oils include citronellol, geraniol, and citra. "A traditional cold and flu remedy," he writes. Also for stomach upsets and diarrhea. Elders (and anyone else!) might try catnip tea as a mild sedative before bedtime: pour one cup of boiling water over 2 teaspoonfuls of dried herb; infuse for ten to fifteen minutes.

Herbal Treasures, by Phyllis Shaudys. Wonderful things to do with herbs. If your cat is one of those genetically disinclined to indulge, or if you don't have a cat, try the recipe for Candied Catnip Leaves.

The Herb Companion is a bimonthly magazine brimming with herbal information. That's where Ruby found out how to henna her hair with cinnamon and paprika. The article she read is called "Herbal Hair Care," by Kathleen Halloran (in the August/September 1993 issue).

China's Garden is an herbal newsletter published four times a year by China Bayles and her friends. In it you'll find sage lore, thymely tips, savory recipes, and a potpourri of information about herbs and gardening. For a sample copy, send two dollars and your name and address to *China's Garden*, P.O. Drawer M, Bertram, Texas 78605.

Here's a special excerpt from the next
China Bayles Mystery by Susan Wittig Albert . . .

ROSEMARY REMEMBERED

It was still early, but the heat was waiting outside like a ferocious tiger ready to pounce. Parked in the sun, my twelve-year-old Datsun was an oven, the seat scorching, the steering wheel too hot to grip. The air conditioner tried, but the air it blew on my face was a dry blast off the Sahara. I opened the window and the humidity rolled in. Texas in July. How did people survive here between the time the settlers built their log cabins and the first air-conditioning salesman knocked on the door? Especially the women, swaddled in long skirts and crinolines, buttoned into bodices so tight they could hardly breathe. It would be sheer torture being confined like that.

Just so I could tell McQuaid I'd been careful, I cast a cursory glance around. No sign of a six-feet three-inches black-mustached ex-con with a knife scar and a snake tattoo. Shaking my head at McQuaid's paranoia (once a cop, always a cop, always on guard against something), I pulled out onto Crockett, made a left, and drove a block to the courthouse square.

The tourists flock to the century-old stone-and-timber buildings in the center of Pecan Springs like pigeons to a roost. (In fact, the City Council recently built a public potty behind the library to meet their basic needs, a move which is said to have been instigated by Henry Hoffmeister of Hoffmeister's Clothing & Dry Goods. Henry said he got tired of spending two-fifty a week to provide toilet paper and a flush for the masses.) They come to Pecan Springs not just for scenic beauty but for a nostalgic taste of small-town Texas, which the merchants ladle out liberally. The square is decorated with flags, red-white-and-blue bunting, and posters announcing that the streets will be roped off on Saturday evening for the square-dance competition.

This morning, a small group of silver-haired ladies in summery dresses and white shoes were standing on the corner listening to Vera Hooper, the town docent. Wearing a denim skirt and yellow T-shirt handpainted with green cacti, Vera was extolling the architectural wonders of the Adams County Courthouse, which was constructed a hundred years ago of 160 flatcar loads of pink granite, hauled in from Burnet County by rail. As I passed, Vera pointed across the street to the Sophie Briggs Historical Museum, which features (among other enticements) a dollhouse that once belonged to Lila Trumm, Miss Pecan Springs of 1936, as well as Sophie Briggs's collection of ceramic frogs. The Sophie Briggs Museum is a big draw in our town. It's amazing the affection some people can feel toward ceramic frogs.

The square is the first stop on the Gingerbread Trail. After the ladies have admired the courthouse and availed themselves of the new public potty, they'll board an air-conditioned minibus ("The Armadillo Special") and tootle south on Anderson Avenue to stare at the fine old Victorian houses that line both sides of the street. Pecan Springs was settled by German immigrants in the 1840s, but the big building boom didn't come until the 1890s. That's when the arrival of the railroad brought a boom, during which the courthouse, the gingerbread Victorians, The Grande Theater, and The Springs Hotel were built. An opulent era, but I'll bet the residents would have traded it all for central air-conditioning. I'll further bet that Vera Hooper's ladies wouldn't have been so enthusiastic about the Gingerbread Trail if they were required to hoof it, rather than riding the air-conditioned Armadillo Special.

I waved at Vera and headed down Anderson to Chisos Trail and made a right. A few blocks west, I drove into Pecan Park, a recently built development of expensive homes surrounded by synthetic green lawns, unnatural rock terraces, and landscaped garden pools. Pecan Park isn't at all like the rest of Pecan Springs. As I drove along I was reminded of the Houston suburb where I used to live—green, serene, and empty. In fact, I'd be willing to bet that very few of the residents were around this morning to enjoy their upscale homes. Most of them probably had to work from before dawn to past dark to make enough money to pay their mortgages.

Rosemary Robbins lived on a winding street a couple of blocks off Chisos Trail. Her house was set back from the road behind a screen of cedar and yaupon holly, with a carefully arranged clump of purple crepe myrtle and plumy pampas grass surrounded by a bed of flaming red salvia—all heavily mulched with bark chips and without a single weed. A cement drive looped behind the streetside clump of oaks and onto the street again. Through the trees, I could see McQuaid's Blue Beast, sitting sheepishly behind Rosemary's stylish gray Mazda. This was not the neighborhood where a battered old truck might feel at home—or a twelve-year-old Datsun.

I swung into the drive, parked far enough behind The Beast to give myself maneuvering room, and got out. McQuaid had asked Rosemary to lock the truck and leave the key in the magnetic box under the fender. I wouldn't bother to knock on her door. I'd just get in the truck and drive off. McQuaid could come with me to pick up my Datsun this evening.

As I stepped out into the heat, the cicadas began a loud metallic drone. Their high-pitched crescendo was counterpointed by the sardonic clucking of a yellow-billed cuckoo, the bird that Leatha, my mother, called a "rain crow." When I hear that sinister clucking, I remember summer afternoons when I was ten, eleven, twelve, reading a book in my favorite tree, Leatha on a chaise lounge beneath me, her gin glass within easy reach. The rain crow is a bad-luck bird, Leatha always said, in her soft Southern drawl. When you hear it, watch out. Warnings like that were her defense against the random perils of a world over which she had little control. Look for cars. Keep your hand on your purse. Lock the car doors. Don't let him touch you.

Perversely, I left the Datsun unlocked. I walked toward The Beast, wanting not to think of Leatha's warnings—or of McQuaid's. Sure, Jacoby was a bad actor, and what he had done to his wife and mother-in-law was enough to curl anyone's hair. But Jacoby could be anywhere, Dallas or Houston or El Paso. Anyway, I reminded myself—or rather, the independent China reminded *me*—Jacoby wasn't the real issue. I slipped my hand under the fender and took out the magnetic key box. The real issue was a power issue. The real issue was—

No key. Well, no problem. Rosemary had probably left it under the seat. And if the truck was locked, I could knock at the door. Her Mazda was here, so she was still at home.

But the truck wasn't locked. What's more, it wasn't even shut. I pulled it open and saw her.

Rosemary Robbins. On her right side across the vinyl seat, face turned up, empty eyes open, glassy, sightlessly staring. A neat, smooth, black hole under her left cheekbone, the seat under her head thick with dried blood, furry with flies. Dark blood, like red ink, spattered all over the passenger side of the cab, the dashboard, the windshield. Blood and bits of something. Bits of the inside of Rosemary's head.

I gagged and stepped back. The cicadas were a hundred buzzing rattlers, the heat a hard, sweaty hand pressing on my head. I grabbed the door to steady myself, then yanked my hand back, hoping I hadn't smudged whatever prints there were.

After a minute I forced myself to look again, but not at Rosemary. The keys were in the ignition, Rosemary's purse on the floor, the wallet visible. A plastic grocery sack beside the purse spilled bars of soap, a carton of milk, a head of cabbage, all polka-dotted with blood. A Handy Jack Dry Cleaners bag full of clothing hung from the hook over the passenger door, blood-spattered. In the back of the truck I could see a gray metal file cabinet and a chair. Groceries, the dry cleaning, used furniture. Ordinary artifacts of ordinary, everyday life.

But for Rosemary Robbins, there was no more ordinary life, no life at all. The brassy rattle of the cicadas was suddenly swallowed up in her stillness, and all I could hear was my heart pounding, my breath roaring like surf. A sour sickness curdled in my throat. I swallowed it down and leaned over her body—clad in expensive beige slacks, creamy silk blouse, paisley scarf—to feel for a pulse at her throat. Nothing. Her skin was cool, her stillness utter, complete, final.

I looked down, feeling her separateness, sensing the absolute distance between us. Who had she been, this woman I had admired but barely known? What had empowered her, wrought her pain, brought her peace? What had brought her to this terrible end? And I knew with sad certainty that it was only here, only now, in this last quiet moment, that Rosemary Robbins could be whatever woman she was. In a little while, she would be the coroner's corpse, the cops' homicide, the D.A.'s murder victim, the media's crime of the hour. Each of us, the living, would dissect her, construct her, imagine her, compose her as it suited our purposes, our needs. It was only in this moment, her death just discovered and not yet acknowledged, that she could be simply and purely herself, whoever she had been. Here, on the sly verge of death, I wished I had known her better.

I stepped back and took a deep breath. Then I turned away and left the body in peace for the time it took to find a neighbor at home and call 911. When the PSPD showed up, I was beside the truck again, waiting, pacing, collecting observations: the door had been unlatched, the window was rolled up, unbroken, her wallet was still in her purse, there was no sign of a weapon. Unless the gun was out of sight beneath her, she hadn't committed suicide. If she'd been murdered, the killer must have shot her through the open door while she was sitting behind the wheel—last night, probably, just as she got home with her furniture, the groceries, the dry cleaning. I wondered whether she'd known what was about to happen. And wondered *why,* in God's name. Why Rosemary? My eyes, of their own accord, went to the spattered blood, the bits of flesh. Why, why?